To London society, they were nothing more than a group of well-bred ladies gathering to gossip about the bachelors of the ton. But the women of Lavender House share an uncommon gift that will lead them to days filled with danger—and nights of desire.

She is the most ravishing creature in all of London, known for her demure smile and angelic demeanor. But Madeline Fallon, Lady Redcomb, is no mere blushing beauty. Blessed with a remarkable and mysterious talent, she is determined to discover the truth behind the recent kidnapping of a young girl. Though it means risking her own life, she will not be stopped by any man—even the haunted, handsome Jasper Reeves.

Sworn to keep the secrets of Lavender House, Jasper joins Maddie on her investigation, claiming his only concern is her safety. But his motives are not pure. Engulfed by desire, praying for passion's sweet release, he would do anything to be near the enchanting Lady Redcomb. He has been bewitched—seduced by her powerful, perfect spell.

Romances by Lois Greiman

SEDUCED
BY YOUR
SPELL

Lois Greiman

AVON

An Imprint of HarperCollinsPublishers

This is a work of fiction. Names, characters, places, and incidents are drawn from the author's imagination or are used fictitiously and are not to be construed as real. Any resemblance to actual events, locales, organizations, or persons, living or dead, is entirely coincidental.

AVON BOOKS
An Imprint of HarperCollins*Publishers*
10 East 53rd Street
New York, New York 10022-5299

Copyright © 2009 by Lois Greiman
ISBN 978-0-06-119201-2
www.avonromance.com

First Avon Books paperback printing: March 2009

Avon Trademark Reg. U.S. Pat. Off. and in Other Countries, Marca Registrada, Hecho en U.S.A.
HarperCollins® is a registered trademark of HarperCollins Publishers.

Printed in the U.S.A.

10 9 8 7 6 5 4 3 2 1

To Colleen Anderson, my show ring companion and one of the few people I know who is brave enough (aka foolish enough) to deliberately stand in front of a galloping horse. Thanks for sharing your time with me. May all good things be yours soon.

SEDUCED
BY YOUR
SPELL

Chapter 1

"Lady Redcomb." Lord Weatherby greeted Madeline with an affable smile, both hands extended, palms up.

Madeline Fallon smiled back and refrained from doing anything nasty. After all, she was only a witch in the most technical sense of the word. In actuality, she had always been quite a nice person. Soft-spoken, gentle, and well-mannered. But what had that foolish tolerance gained her?

"You look most ravishing tonight," Weatherby said, and lifting her hands, brushed his lips across her knuckles.

Madeline smiled with demure femininity. Truthfully though, she was fully aware that she looked ravishing. She had looked ravishing since the day she had popped from the womb, perfectly coifed and immaculately groomed. Or so her sister was wont to say.

It was simply that Madeline failed to care.

Delicately waving her fan, she gazed, limpid-eyed, over its lacy top at her admirer. He was probably not an unattractive fellow. Tall, wealthy, and confident, Lord Weatherby was a man to draw a woman's attention. Unfortunately, she was *not* drawn. Indeed, she wished quite desperately that he would go away. Wished, in fact, that she could skim her gaze across the cavernous ballroom in a foolhardy attempt to find the one man she must ignore.

"Lord Weatherby . . ." Madeline fluttered her fan and gave him her most beguiling smile. "You flatter me."

"Not at all." He preened a smile and leaned half an inch closer. "You are, very possibly, the most ravishing woman in this room."

Madeline blushed modestly and allowed herself a fleeting glance to the left, but Jasper Reeves had not yet arrived at Lady Sedum's annual ball. Indeed, he was probably doing what he did best: scheming like a mad Frenchman, and all the while planning to give the most harrowing missions to other members of the coven. Faye perhaps. Or Shaleena.

Madeline stifled a snarl of frustration. Snarling was, presumably, considered somewhat uncouth at posh soirees.

"And therefore the most sought after," added Weatherby.

"Hardly that, my lord," Madeline demurred, remembering her companion's presence and raising the frilly fan to cover her peaked chin. Just the carefully pigmented bow of her full upper lip would show. Which made her wonder who the genius was who decided women should carry fans. The lacy accessories were quite indispensable, able to hide a hundred emotions while conveying just as many. Or, in a pinch, they made decent weapons if delivered with panache and a reasonable amount of force to a man's exposed trachea. Then again, if handled properly—

Weatherby moved a little closer, brushing her knuckles with his. "Indeed, when I am near you I can think of little else but how you would look . . ." His eyes gleamed. ". . . au naturel."

Madeline caught her breath audibly and opened her eyes wide as if embarrassed. But annoyance would more adequately describe her feelings. Dammit. Had the conversation slithered so far in that lascivious direction? If she wished to avoid his attentions, which she most certainly did, despite the fact that she fully intended to become quite scandalous, she was going to have to pay better attention . . . or employ the fan. The idea was irritatingly tempting, but she only fluttered her would-be weapon with ladylike precision.

"My lord, I am quite shocked!" she said, and

glanced to the right, looking for someone more suitable with which to become outrageous. She hated to delay any longer; she had already wasted too much time pining over someone she would never have, someone who would never return her affections. But surely she could find someone more appealing than Weatherby to begin her life as an easy lady-bird.

Her companion laughed. The sound rumbled through the vast, buzzing chamber. "Are you indeed? Tell me, my lady, how long were you wed?"

It was time to move on, Madeline realized, before the conversation became any more involved, before he inquired about other issues she had no intention of addressing. Lowering her eyes, she made certain she looked soft and feminine and mournful. It was a fair performance, considering her dearly departed husband had never actually existed.

"I fear my sweet William succumbed to consumption well before his time," she murmured.

Weatherby shifted his hand up her arm. It was bare. Madeline didn't favor the long kid gloves oft worn by the ladies of the *ton*, for she was a tactile creature, able to "feel" as much as she could see.

Lord Weatherby, she mused, "felt" irritating.

"It is rumored . . ." He gave her a smoldering look, designed, she assumed, to make her smolder.

". . . that your bridegroom died before the two of you were truly . . ." He twirled a finger into a ringlet that had been designed to look as if it had somehow accidentally escaped the confinement that so artfully captured the others. ". . . joined."

Madeline managed another modest blush, letting it pinken her cheeks but not her ears. She had heard the rumors, of course. Indeed, she had initiated most of them herself. Few things were, after all, what they seemed. The idea that she was British, for instance. Or the ridiculous notion that she was normal . . . or wished to be.

Indeed, she would give much to possess her sister's dynamic powers. But while Ella had been gifted with seemingly infinite abilities, Madeline had been granted little more than a visage that drew men like fruit flies. A parade of foolish dandies that must be brushed away at every turn.

And all the while she had worked like a conniving mule to achieve even a modicum of what Ella could do in her sleep. But perhaps that was changing.

"I've embarrassed you," Weatherby said, and raised his hand to her inflamed face. "My apologies." His tone was raspy. "I had no wish to make you uncomfortable. Indeed . . ." He stroked her cheek. "I've a desire to make you so much more than comfortable." He raised a manly brow. "Ecstatic even."

Madeline refrained from laughing. Why did men forever believe sex was what every woman secretly desired above all else? It was a ridiculous notion. True, she herself had never actually experienced connubial bliss. Or bliss of any other sort, come to that . . . unless one considered the relationship a woman could engender with a truly fine chocolate. Regardless, she tended to believe the male of the species was wont to overemphasize the act of copulation. It was, after all, only one of many bodily functions, several of which could be relatively enjoyable if—

But in that instant Madeline felt a too-familiar flash of electricity and knew in that place where she kept her powers that Jasper Reeves had arrived. Something stirred restlessly inside her. Something feral and impatient and sharp. Something she herself had awakened. But she controlled her erratic heartbeat and allowed herself a momentary glance toward the door.

Lord Gallo stood solemn and silent, dressed to perfection in white breeches and a charcoal tailcoat that hugged his tight waist like a lover's embrace. He was not a particularly tall man, but his careful, military bearing made one forget that fact. And though most were unaware that he possessed the hard thighs and muscled chest more oft found on a street fighter than a pampered peer of the realm, there was something about him that turned heads and caused feverish whispers. His aged-whisky eyes seemed older than his years demanded, and his hair, dark and curling, brushed lovingly across the dusky hue of his southern-clime skin.

Madeline felt a little breathless at the sight of him, but she eased her gaze away, pushing it smoothly back to Weatherby. "My lord, you are quite bold," she murmured, and felt Reeves's attention fall softly on her face. He was watching her, she realized, but knew far better than to think the coolheaded director of Les Chausettes would show interest. Still, she couldn't seem to put him out of her mind, her dreams. Why was that? she wondered. She could have her choice of men. Indeed, she intended to do just that, for Les Chausettes had made her not only wealthy, but titled and learned as well.

"*Too* bold?" Weatherby asked, and with his hand hidden between their bodies, swept his knuckles across her nipple. She stifled a dark flush of irritation. "Or not bold enough?"

"My lord!" she gasped, and stepped abruptly back. It was then that she felt the electricity again. A bright flash of something from Reeves. But she knew better than to mistake it for any sort of personal interest. One must not forget that he was the guardian of Les Chausettes, paid to keep the *sisters* productive and safe. After most of a decade with the coven, however, Madeline no longer wished for safety. Not from the world, and not from him. But he had made his disinterest abundantly clear, and since she was not totally without pride, she would not badger him, would not beg for his attentions like a fishwife hawking her wares.

No. She had finally learned her lesson; she would find another. *Many* others perhaps. Men who adored her, who showered her with attention, with gifts, with praise. Maybe even men who made her laugh.

After all these years she was finally over Reeves. Done with him. Through pining and dreaming and fantasizing.

So what would be the harm in toying with him, she wondered, and against her better judgment—indeed, against her own principles—she crafted a shadowy image and quietly slipped it into Reeves's mind. It was vague, misty. The faintest suggestion of Weatherby and her together. Unclothed and . . .

She sensed Reeves moving toward her and stifled a smile. Oh, it wasn't as if he wanted her for himself. Hardly that. But the idea of one of his carefully trained Chausettes *flaunting* herself made him all but—

"My lady! Thank heavens I've found you!"

Her thoughts were torn asunder as a man tugged at her sleeve.

She turned, startled to find Bertram Wendell at her elbow. He bobbed a greeting, but his florid face was not glowing with friendly bonhomie as it always did when he chided her for wearing her dancing slippers too thin. As it did when he bent over his workbench, plying his trade.

"Mr. Wendell," she said, shocked by the worry on his face, by the sweat that soaked his simple tunic. He crunched his tattered slouch hat fretfully in his hands, looking old and harried amid the foolish foppery of the *ton*.

"Who is this?" Weatherby demanded.

But Madeline didn't turn toward him, though the cobbler dashed a worried glance toward the other.

"Mr. Wendell . . ." She brought his attention back to her and reached for his hand. Feelings struck her like lightning: terror, dread, worry as sharp as a blade. "Whatever is amiss?"

His eyes, deep and dark, turned back to her. "It's my Marie!"

"Marie! No!" If asked, Maddy couldn't have explained exactly how she knew what had happened. But she felt the panic, sensed the horror. Or maybe . . . maybe she saw the story in the old man's eyes. "How long has she been gone?"

"She failed to return home last night," he rasped.

"Where—"

"Good heavens!" Weatherby's tone was rife with annoyance. "Why are you bothering the lady with your troubles, man?" he asked, but in that instant Jasper Reeves arrived at her side.

"Lady Redcomb," he said, and sketched a bow. His costume was immaculate, his expression impassive, but Madeline had no time to play at elegance.

"Mr. Wendell's daughter has gone missing," she said.

For one sparkling moment their gazes met, but Jasper shifted his smoothly away, settling on the cobbler. "Missing?" His tone was cadenced, just short of bored. "Surely not."

"Aye," Bertram said. "She drove the dogcart to Islington the morning past. I had no wish to send her alone, but she assured me all would be well. She laughed at my worries. Said . . ." He winced, remembering. "Said a well-turned ankle could do as much as a tankard to improve the tanner's—"

"How old is the chit?" Weatherby asked.

Bertram sent him a hunted glance. "Barely eight and ten. I knew better than to let her go alone, but when she smiles I cannot seem to—"

"A pretty miss, then?" Weatherby said.

Bertram crushed his hapless hat again. "She's got her mother's dimples." He said the words with a quiet reverence that seemed to steal the very breath from the room, but when Reeves spoke, his tone was unaffected.

"I assume you've notified the proper authorities."

The old man rushed his gaze from one face to another. "In truth, the news seemed of little interest to them."

"Which is as it should be," Weatherby said. "The girl probably spent the night in some . . ."

Madeline flashed her gaze to him and he caught himself.

". . . friend's home," he finished, but his tone suggested more.

Bertram shook his head vehemently. "She wouldn't allow me to worry so. She's headstrong, aye. But she knows I can't live . . ." He paused, his voice cracking, his eyes imploring Madeline again. "I thought perhaps you could help, my lady."

"Lady *Redcomb*?" Weatherby laughed. "Whatever made you think such a thing?"

"Surely the authorities will come to your assistance once they realize the seriousness of the situation," Jasper said, but Maddy turned her attention on him, letting her emotions storm through, letting him feel the truth.

"Bertram is a friend," she said.

Jasper held her gaze for an elongated instant, then gave her a carefully patronizing smile and turned smoothly toward Weatherby.

"Well, perhaps woman's intuition is just the thing that is needed here.

"Lord Weatherby, it is said you've a fair team of bays to carry your phaeton."

The baron raised his brow and his ire in gentlemanly unison. "Fair? To whom have you been speaking? Some inebriated houseboy who has never laid eyes on a horse in his life?"

Reeves gave him a jaded glance as he made his way toward the buffet table. "Sir Exter seems to believe your beasts capable of matching his sorrels if the former were well rested."

"Sir Exter wouldn't know a Thoroughbred from a thimble if he—" Weatherby began, but Madeline tugged Bertram away from the fray, urging him to a quiet corner of the room.

"Lord Gallo is correct. The authorities will surely—" she began, but Bertram held up a leathery hand.

"I am not a wealthy man, my lady," he said. His eyes were a pale winter blue, set deep in a face seared by years and troubles. "But what I have I offer you."

She felt his pain in the pit of her being. Felt it like an ulcer, mirroring the agony she had felt not so many years before when Ella had been taken. Taken and tortured.

But even from this distance she could sense Jasper's disapproval. Les Chausettes did not choose their own missions. Their tasks were appointed by some unknown committee. Indeed, no one outside the secretive commission could know of their powers. It was their foremost rule, set in stone, cemented in tragedy.

Yet here was this man, a good man, an honest man. A man who had known more than his share of sorrows. He stood before her, his soul as tattered as his hat, begging for help. But she dared not admit her gifts. Dared not compromise her coven.

"I fear I can do nothing for you," she said. "You must return home. Surely by morning she will have—"

"She's my life," he said. "The very air I breathe." His voice was quiet, almost drowned in the intensity of his feelings.

Madeline felt herself wince, but steeled her resolve. She couldn't take the risk. For her own sake as well as for the others. "I know she is, Bertram." Her tone sounded trite and worthless to her own ears, but she continued on, a wintry shadow of the woman she wished to be. "She will surely return though. I am certain of—"

"Something dreadful has happened." His voice was low and deep, shivering across her senses like an eerie note on a silent night.

And he was right. She knew it, *felt* it, but she laid

her hand on his arm, placating, lying. "All will be well. You'll see. But if she does not return by—"

"She has always admired you," he said, and straightened slightly so that he exceeded her height by a few scant inches. His hands looked large and red, bisected by a thousand dark, wayward lines as he squeezed his hat harder. His balding pate shone in the golden lamplight.

Madeline's chest hurt.

"Said you were not like the other fine ladies who stopped by our shop. Said you had a heart as lovely as your countenance."

"Mr. Wendell . . ." She felt breathless, lost. "I cannot—"

"You can," he said, and suddenly she realized the truth.

He knew what she was. Knew, and asked anyway.

Chapter 2

Lavender House was all but dark. It had been fitted with gas lighting some months before, but Jasper Reeves preferred the candlelight. It felt right. As did the patient darkness that hovered above his shoulders. Ignoring the new steel dip pen residing in his desk, he dipped his quill in ink and gathered his strength for the confrontation to come.

Her steps were soundless. And yet he heard her. Or perhaps he smelled her. Who was to say what uncharted senses such a woman incited? In his mind he called her Esperanza, for she was hope. But to her face he would forever refer to her as Lady Redcomb, for there was something about a formal title that held him more accountable, that reminded him each day that she was well out of the reach of a street urchin from Caceres.

She would still be wearing the wintergreen gown she had donned for the ball, the one with the tiny bow at the cleft of each shoulder. The one that made her appear as bright and lively as a faerie, as ethereal as an ascending angel.

"It is not our affair," he said, and without turning, touched quill to paper.

She didn't pause an instant. He had known she wouldn't, for in the past few months she had become bolder, more assured. A natural progression of her powers, he wondered, or something else? She often brewed potions in the privacy of her chambers, but she never spoke of them.

"She's not the sort to remain gone without informing her father." Her voice was soft but firm.

"Perhaps that is so," he said. "But as you well know, I do not choose our missions."

"She's *not* a mission." There was passion in her voice. Passion and anger, though she had learned to control her emotions long before they met, "She's a child."

As Madeline had been when she had first come to him for help. But still he had seen the difference in her. The power, yes. But more. So infinitely much more. "Eight and ten, I believe her father said." He kept his tone emotionless. Bored even. He was a bloody master at bored. "Old enough to make her own decisions, surely."

"She has not yet returned."

"Certainly old enough for a tryst," he said, and

steeling himself, turned toward her. Still, despite his well-honed defenses, her beauty struck him like a blast of flame, searing his senses, trampling his calm. But it was neither her willowy figure nor her stunning face that left him breathless and stupid. It was her soul. It shone in her evergreen eyes like sunlight on emeralds, gleamed in the very glow of her butternut skin. But he didn't care. *Couldn't* care. She wasn't for him. Good God, no! The idea was laughable. If he ever laughed. Which he did not.

Still, she lifted her chin in that way she had. That way he saw when he closed his eyes at night. "Neither Milly nor Tipper have been seen since they were first reported missing," she said.

She remembered their names. Indeed, she remembered their *pet* names, and probably much more, though he hadn't intended for her to hear of them at all. He had no wish to deny her, no wish to make her angry; she had left Lavender House once already. God knew what had brought her back. But he didn't care. Only cared that she was there, under his protection, safe with the others. Still, this was not a cause the coven could rally behind. Les Chausettes had not been formed to save every wayward youth who happened to go missing. It had been formed to save worlds, to rally armies and topple governments. And trouble was afoot.

"Napoleon will soon—" he began.

"Damn Napoleon!" she rasped.

He raised one brow at her outburst. She had always been extremely sensible, always one who would do what she must. That he knew. Had learned seven years and eleven months earlier when he'd first seen her. Barely a hint of fear had shown on her dirt-streaked face then. Barely a hint of desperation.

"I am Colette," she had said, and lifted her chin just as she lifted it now. *"They hold my sister in the bowels of La Hopital. Take her from that hell and I swear to do whatever you desire."*

She had been beautiful even then, at the tender age of sixteen. Beautiful and brave. But she had not been magic wrapped in light and serenaded by angels. She had not consumed his thoughts every waking hour. Still, he had agreed to find the half-starved girl called Josette, for he knew the practices of the surgeons at La Hopital. Knew they delighted in experimenting on those who were gifted . . . or *cursed*, as they believed. Knew that in Josette he would find an invaluable thread to add to the growing coven. Within hours Jasper had sailed for Britain with the sisters in his care. Even then, in those first hours, he had marveled at their latent powers, though he had not yet guessed the depths of their potential. For many years he had believed Josette to be the more talented of the two. Only now was he beginning to understand all that Esperanza was. All that she could be. Light in the darkness. Hope in—

Gritting his teeth, Jasper yanked his thoughts to a halt. "Indeed," he said, and held her gaze with his own. He would look bored. Maybe a little sleepy if he could manage it. "We are trying quite diligently to do just that."

She scowled the smallest degree, just enough to implant one tiny crease in her perfect brow.

"Damn him," he explained.

A hint of irritation crossed her Gypsy-dark features. "You helped *me*," she said, and her voice had gone soft.

He struggled out of the web of emotions her misty tone evoked. She herself had admitted that she was not as powerful as her sister, but she had her own mercurial gifts, and they were growing stronger. He would be a fool to deny that. And he was not a fool. Sometimes.

"You helped Ella," she said, face solemn, eyes bright.

"Is this Marie gifted then?" he asked, and absently dipped his quill again. "As your sister is?"

"She is human."

"Most are," he admitted.

"*Most*," she agreed, and her voice had gone softer still.

He gave her a look, knowing she was separating him from that esteemed category. Knowing it was just as well. That, indeed, he had worked extremely hard to make her believe he was not so soft as to be human. "Let it go, Lady Redcomb," he said, and touched quill to paper.

He could feel her anger and wondered which evoked more emotion, the way he addressed her or his dismissive attitude. Lady Redcomb was not, after all, her true name. It was an invented title, an identity they had given her when they'd taken her old self. And in its place they had made a widow, young and guileless, but fully able to move among the calculating *ton* as if she were one of their own, the wealthy product of the doomed love match between a Sicilian poet and an idealistic Serbian countess. Her own marriage to the enamored Lord Redcomb had lasted no more than five months, for he had never been healthy . . . or real.

Madeline had not hated the lies immediately. Indeed, she'd been far too grateful that they had secreted her sister from the horrors of La Hopital to be so fussy. And Ella, well . . . she had been all but dead. They had tortured her there, after all. Had tried to determine what she could do. What she *was*. She would not have survived much longer had the committee not allowed him to intervene. But she had recovered miraculously. Had mended, had grown, had become Les Chausettes' most gifted member.

Still, it was the girl he secretly called Esperanza who bound the coven together. Esperanza who nurtured and loved and cared. It was entirely unfair of him to ask her not to care now. But it was not his place to be fair. It was his place to follow orders. To make sure his charges did the same.

"I'll not let it go, Jasper." Her words were little more than a whisper now, but he heard them. Heard them, knew the meaning, and felt his heart lurch drunkenly in his chest.

He knew better than to glance up. Knew that if he found her eyes he would falter. Still, he was able to speak, to spew weakness into the night air. "There is nothing we can do."

"If she doesn't return . . ." Her tone was mild but steady, and he could imagine her standing there, staunch and determined. "It will kill her father."

"Life is often difficult," he said, and forced himself to dip his quill again.

"Might you think I don't know that?" she asked. Memories stormed in, but he plowed them aside. He wouldn't allow himself to be drawn into the tarry past. Wouldn't remember how she'd cried when he'd reunited her with her sister. Wouldn't recall how she had looked at him as if he were her savior, her hero. Wouldn't care that that expression had changed over the years. From admiration to confusion to disappointment.

"I think, in fact, that you are forgetting," he said, but he knew better. She would never forget. "You can't protect everyone."

"But I can protect *her*."

Anger rushed through him on a wave of premonition. Girls were disappearing. Young, beautiful women with ties to high society were slipping out of sight. And although Esperanza appeared wise and polished, she was little more than a child herself. Surely too young to . . . But he tamped down the foolish worry, doused the flaring rage. "How?" he asked, tone smooth. "Might you have a clue to her whereabouts?"

Her dark brows dipped a little. "Not as of yet."

"And what of the others?" he asked. "This Tipper and Milly you spoke of. Any idea to where they might have disappeared?"

"I don't know—"

"Nor shall you." He rose to his feet, a little too jerkily. Calming his motions, he soothed his tone. God help him, he was acting more like a hounded street thief than he had when he was one. "Not without the support of the committee."

"I—"

"Not without someone to fund your travels, to do the research, to warn of the dangers."

"She's afraid," Maddy whispered, and the soft certainty of her words slipped through him like phantom emotions, tearing at his heart. He refrained from closing his eyes, from taking her into his arms, from stroking her hair and assuring her all would be well; he would right the wrongs, keep her safe. "This is not your task, Lady Redcomb."

"Why? Because you say it is not?"

Because she was everything that was good. Everything he had never been. Would never be. "Yes," he said.

She pursed her lips, as full and red as ripened berries. "Perhaps you underestimate me."

No. That he did not. "I believe I know your talents fair well, Lady Redcomb." Maybe he used the title to remind her who she had been . . . a tattered girl alone in the world, without family, without hope. Maybe he used it for other reasons. It was bloody impossible to be sure these days.

Her chin tipped up another notch. "As you have always underestimated me," she said.

"It is time to retire." He lifted the candle from his desk, hand marvelously steady. "Tomorrow will come soon enough," he said, but she shook her head, holding her ground, watching him with haunting eyes.

"Not here," she said, and her voice was little more than a wispy thought in his head.

Dread swamped him, roiling him under, but he fought it back, struggling to believe he was misreading her meaning as he honed a bored expression. "If I'm not mistaken, tomorrow arrives most everywhere at one time or another."

She drew a careful breath, unflinching. "I won't be here in the morning."

Their gazes met. He forced himself to breathe, to keep his expression bland. Life would not end without her here. Would not come crashing down about his ears like plaster from a faulty ceiling. Only the reason for life. "Are you threatening to leave again?" he asked.

"No."

He allowed himself a glimmer of hope, one sweet breath of redemption. "That is just as well," he said, "for I am not a man to beg."

She stared at him.

Panic brewed in his clenching chest. "Not one for flowery prose and sentimental songs." He was blathering like a lunatic, but he couldn't seem to stop himself. Without her, he might well *be* crazed. "I'm sorry if that—"

"I *am* leaving."

He paused, hearing his heart beat emptily in the cavity of his chest thrice before he allowed himself to speak. "The committee will not look favorably on this."

She smiled serenely, spoke quietly, though in the depths of her eyes he saw pain. "Damn the committee," she said.

"Lady—"

"Perhaps Ella was right."

He refrained, yet again, from pulling her into his arms, from begging her to stay, though every instinct in him insisted that he do so. "In what regard?"

"She said you care only for power." She tilted her chin up. "I told her she was wrong."

"You were correct," he said, and took a cheroot from the pocket of his best cutaway coat. His hand shook only a little. Lord Moore should be proud of what he had made from a shattered street waif. "I also have a fondness for money and fine claret."

She watched him. "In truth, I don't actually know if you care about anything at all."

He inhaled. The tobacco smelled sweet. He felt like vomiting. "Get some sleep, Lady Redcomb. It is quite likely that Wendell's daughter will have returned before dawn."

Her expression was impossible to read.

"By dawn I shall be well out of your life," she said, and Jasper's world silently crumbled.

Chapter 3

Elegance opened the door before Madeline ever reached the cobblestone walkway. For a moment she stood limned in the mellow light of the doorway, but then she stepped onto the stones, feet bare as she ran forward.

"Maddy!" she said, and folded her sister in her arms. Warmth flowed between them, around them. Acceptance, caring, comfort. "What is it? What's amiss?"

"Nothing." Madeline felt lost, shaken to the core. She had left. Had abandoned them all, the sisters of her heart. Darla, quiet and motherly. Shaleena, brassy and talented. Perceptive Francine. Gentle Faye. Rosamond and Beatrice and Heddy and Ivy. What would they do without her? What would she do without them? "Nothing. I just—"

"Save the lies. You'll need them later," Ella said, and tucking Madeline against her side, hurried back toward the house.

Inside Berryhill's arched entry it was little brighter than outside. A light flickered from the interior. A shadow swept, tall and broad, across the vestibule. Drake, Ella's bridegroom of only a few short months, stood there, his voice deep and strong. "Is aught awry?" he asked.

"It's Madeline," Ella said, tone taut. "She's left Lavender House."

"I didn't say—" Maddy began.

"She needs a place to stay," Ella interrupted. "Please have Amherst see that her mount is—"

"I already put Sultan up in your empty box with a bit of Dancer's barley," Maddy admitted.

"Good," Ella said, "then we've only to have Cecelia ready a room and you'll be able to stay forever."

Despite her vow to be strong, Madeline felt limp and weepy in the quiet harbor of her sister's arms, but she parried against the tears. "Oh please." She tried to imbue her tone with humor, but her voice sounded brittle, like twigs too dry to withstand the winter cold. "Mrs. Nealon is five hundred years old. I'm perfectly capable of fending for myself."

"Don't be silly," Ella scoffed. "She's barely a hundred. Drake, please—"

"She's right, lass," he said, his rumbling brogue soft in the quiet. "The woman's five hundred if she's a day. I'll ready the room meself." He turned away, barely limping as he left them.

"I don't mean to impose," Madeline said, but Ella ignored her as they walked side-by-side into a dark-paneled sitting room. The fire flared a greeting.

"What happened?" Ella asked.

"Nothing," Madeline repeated. She tried to sound dismissive but tears choked her best intentions. "It's simply . . . It was time to leave," she said.

Worry chased caution across Ella's fair features. "Forever?"

Maddy glanced away, trying to imagine life beyond the scope of Lavender House. Without the caring, the magic, the drama. Without Jasper. "Yes."

"What did he do?" Ella asked, and urged Madeline into a well-loved chair near the hearth.

"Who?" Maddy asked, but she had never been capable of fooling her sister. She might just as well try to fool herself. Indeed, perhaps she was doing just that.

Ella's eyes, just an emerald shade lighter than Maddy's, narrowed, though her voice was steady, her hands the same. "He didn't hurt you, did he?"

"Hurt me?" Madeline felt breathless suddenly.

Stunned. "No. How could you even suggest such a thing?"

"I just . . ." Ella knelt to undo her sister's shoes. "He's been acting strangely lately."

"Strangely. How do you mean?"

Ella shrugged. She was tall, slim as a reed even at four months into her first pregnancy, and plain. Unless she wished to be otherwise. "Almost as if he has emotions. Feelings. It's . . ." She shuddered. "Unnerving."

"He *is* human you know," Maddy said, though she had implied the opposite not a full hour before.

"Are you certain? Because I don't know . . ." Ella set one shoe aside, then gazed into middle space as if thinking. "It seems sometimes that he might be a machine, something created by the mad committee for the overthrow of the world as we know it," she said, and widening her eyes dramatically, swept her arm wildly sideways as if wiping out the universe.

Madeline laughed despite herself. "You're the one who's mad."

Ella smiled and undid Madeline's left shoe. "Honestly, Maddy, what happened?"

"Nothing." The denial was already beginning to sound worn. Maddy dropped her head against the chair cushion and stared at the ceiling. Light waltzed with shadows across the smooth plaster.

"I'm just feeling . . ." She shrugged. Her throat felt tight. ". . . frustrated."

"Did Shaleena do something untoward?"

Maddy gave her sister a sidewise glance. "Other than insisting on going about sky-clad?"

"Besides that."

"And dancing sky-clad?"

"In addition."

"And driving me out of my mind with her big . . ." She fluttered her hands erratically in front of her chest, feeling breathless for reasons she didn't understand and didn't care to decipher.

Ella watched her. "Her bosoms *are* unattractively large."

"Thank you!"

"Men don't like that," Ella assured her, then: "Do they, darling?"

Her husband stepped from the shadows. War had wounded him, but perhaps they were all scarred one way or another. "Certainly not," he said, managing his smile with gallant aplomb. "We find it quite revolting.

"Is there anything I can fetch for you, Madeline? A sherry?"

"No, thank you. I'm fine."

"A peach cobbler perhaps? I believe one survived my dinnertime assault."

Madeline straightened. Sir Drake was a handsome man, a military man, strong, composed, commanding. And yet here, in the toasty comfort of Berryhill, he seemed naught but gentle and caring. "No. Thank you. I didn't mean to impose."

"Your presence is never an imposition," he said. "Especially when it brings such stimulating conversation." He settled slowly into the chair on her right and stretched out his endless legs. He had nearly lost one of those legs, but Ella's potion had saved him, inadvertent though her intervention had been at the time. "How *is* Shaleena?"

"Besides naked?" Ella asked, and gave him an arch glance.

He stared at her, mouth quirked the slightest degree. "Well, no," he admitted. "That was, in fact, all that piqued my interest."

Ella swatted at his leg, but he caught her hand and kissed it. Their gazes met, and for a moment Maddy was trapped in the stirring emotion of the warm exchange. So this was love. This was contentment, she thought, and felt a sharp tug at the tattered core of her heart. It wasn't that she envied Ella . . . exactly. Her sister deserved happiness, after all. Deserved a man who cherished her more than life.

"And what of Jasper?" Drake asked, tearing his gaze from his bride's glowing face "How is he faring?"

Madeline forced herself to relax. "He is well," she said, and taking a careful breath, shifted the conversation. "Another girl has disappeared."

"What? When?" Ella asked, tone sharpening, already dangerous, already poised.

"Another?" Drake's voice was deep, edgy. Had Madeline not witnessed the tenderness he showed her sister, he would indeed seem formidable.

"I told you of them," Ella said. "Two girls had disappeared already. One from Camden. One from Westminster."

"But there was no reason to think their circumstances were intertwined."

"With this third disappearance, it is too big a coincidence to be believed," Maddy said. "All within three years of age. All unusually comely. They're not just wandering off. I'm certain of it."

"What else combines them?" Ella asked.

Madeline shook her head. "The committee isn't investigating."

Ella cursed under her breath.

Drake raised a dark brow. "Why not?" he asked.

"Because the girls aren't well-connected," Ella said, and rose hastily to her feet, devoid, for once, of her usual grace.

"What?" Drake asked.

"The damned committee," Ella said. "They only care if the person involved bears a title."

"That's not entirely fair," Maddy said, uncomfortable with the fact that she had said the same. "Jasper—"

"Jasper!" Ella rasped and laughed, swinging back. "Jasper is the worst of the lot. He could change things if he so wished. But he doesn't. He follows where they lead. Dances whichever way—"

"Her name is Marie," Maddy said. "Marie Wendell."

"Marie?" Ella stopped her pacing. "The cobbler's daughter?"

"You know her?" Drake asked.

She gave a quick nod. "When his wife died two years ago it all but killed him. Losing his daughter . . ." She shook her head, expression troubled.

"How did you learn of her disappearance?" Drake asked.

Madeline scowled, remembering. "Bertram came to me."

"What?" Ella's tone teetered on the sharp edge of panic.

"He approached me at Lady Sedum's ball."

"Why you?" Drake asked. "Why not the constable or—?"

"Because he knows!" Ella breathed, hands clasped, expression taut as she stared wide-eyed and horrified into Madeline's unblinking gaze. "He knows you're gifted."

"I believe so." Maddy's throat felt raw.

"Who else is aware?"

"I don't—" Madeline began, but just then she realized her folly! After all the training, all the years of terrible caution, she had somehow loosed the secret, and now, when things had gone awry, she had scampered like a hunted hare into her sister's waiting arms. "I shouldn't have come here." She stood abruptly. Breathless. Foolish. Terrified. "I'm sorry."

"What?" Ella grasped her arm with both hands, eyes sharp as broken shards. "What are you talking about?"

"She believes she's compromised you," Drake said.

They glanced at him in unison. Perhaps Ella too had momentarily forgotten his presence, but she was already speaking, brow troubled, disbelieving. "You think I'm concerned you will draw them to *me*?"

Madeline felt herself shake, and suddenly the years disappeared. They were young again, alone, their father gone. Ella had married, but the man who was to cleave to her for life had turned against her. She had been committed to a place of such dark horrors that even now Maddy could not bring herself to remember. "I couldn't bear it if something happened to you again," she whispered.

"Maddy, no. I am well," Ella murmured. "Safe. But surely you see that you must be cautious for your own account. If the cobbler realizes your gift—"

"He'll not tell."

"You've no way of knowing what people will do in despair. You can't guess the depths to which they might drop. Believe me. Even the strongest can break. You must leave. Get out of Britain. At least for a while."

"Leave! Are you—"

"Wait." Drake rose slowly to his feet. "'Twould be foolish to be hasty." Taking the few steps between them, he tugged Ella into his arms and stroked her hair. "All is well, lass."

She arched her back, searching his eyes. "You don't know—"

"Hush now," he said. "Hush. You are safe. Wee Maddy is safe." He swept a thumb with slow caring across her cheek and smiled into her eyes. "No one leaves. Not tonight at the least. Not after I went to the trouble of making your sister's bed." He reached for Madeline's hand, squeezed her fingers. "Sleep. You too, luv," he said, caressing Ella with his eyes. "Indeed, perhaps you should keep your sister company this night."

"That's entirely unnecessary," Maddy said, and found she could not look away, was held fast by the adoration that shone in his eyes. "I will be perfectly safe alone," she vowed, but when Ella finally pulled herself from Drake's gaze and reached for Maddy's free hand, she couldn't deny the draft of warmth that washed through her. They turned in tandem toward the hall. "But what of you?" Maddy asked, glancing over her shoulder at the lone figure draped in shadows.

"I believe I shall stay up for a bit, lass" he said, and though his voice was a low, sweet burr, his expression was dark and solemn.

One would have to be very brave or very foolish to challenge him.

Chapter 4

"**M**erry May, it has been far too long," Madeline said.

Jasper watched Lord Gershwin's mistress lean toward Maddy to murmur some unheard remark. Though she was not the baron's wife, she kept this fine house on Park Lane and entertained with style and charm in his name. While she was not particularly attractive, it was well accepted that she had an appeal few men could deny. Still, Jasper barely noticed her, for it had been two days since Madeline had left Lavender House. Two days, one hour, and fourteen minutes. He clenched his jaw as the women's laughter floated toward him.

Merry May moved on to her other guests, leaving Maddy alone for a moment, framed by an arched doorway behind her, frozen in time like a perfect miniature. But then she turned toward the entry and found him. Their gazes brushed like a spark of static. He felt her attention in the soles of his feet, the very air that he breathed. But what of her? Did she feel nothing? Did she see him as a guardian? An adversary? A pest? He tried to assess her reactions, a task for which he was not only trained, but innately well suited. For as long as he could remember he had found it necessary to judge people's emotions, to guess their reactions. But he learned little from examining her. Little besides the fact that she was magic come to life.

Oh, perhaps her body stiffened the slightest degree when she spotted him. Perhaps her emerald eyes widened. But in an instant all semblance of discomfort disappeared. She smiled, but remotely, as if they were the most distant of friends. As if, perhaps, she had known him in some former life.

Nevertheless, he was drawn across the floor toward her, pulled as if by an invisible wire.

"Lord Gallo," she said, and nodded a prim greeting. Any previous discomfort she may have felt had disappeared completely from her manner.

"Lady Redcomb." He returned her nod and clasped his hands behind his back.

"Lady Redcomb," echoed another. Fanny Epping floated past on her current lover's arm. It was said that she changed partners as often as she did her slippers, but high society didn't seem to resent her mercurial ways. "What a lovely gown."

"Not half so charming as your headdress,"

Madeline said, and as the demirep glided away, feathered hairpiece bobbing, turned seamlessly back toward Jasper. "A lovely evening, isn't it, my lord."

He answered, though in truth, he was not sure what inane words he spewed. For *he* had taught her that charm. *He* had given her the skills to survive, no, to *thrive* in this venue.

"It was good to see the sun, was it not? Autumn has been far too gloomy thus far." She smiled, the expression perfectly serene, wonderfully kind. "I suspect the roses are still abloom at Lavender House. How is everyone there?" She took a tiny sip of blackberry cordial, long neck bending, coral lips parting before she straightened, serene as an angel. "Well, I hope."

Behind his back, Jasper strangled his knuckles. How could she speak so casually of Lavender House? It had been her home. *Their* home. But there was no reason she should *not* mention it, of course. To London society, it was known as a high-shelf boarding establishment, one that attracted well-versed bluestockings, ready, at the drop of a veiled bonnet, to discuss politics ad nauseam. But the fact that she could mention it with such nonchalant disregard made Jasper's skin feel suddenly too small.

"Quite well," he said.

"Mrs. Nettles has found relief from her headaches, I hope."

Mrs. Nettles, better known as Faye by those who loved her, had come to Lavender House even more damaged than most. The headaches that sometimes accompanied her "visions" were often debilitating. "She is well."

"That is excellent news," she said, and took another genteel sip.

"Lady Redcomb," greeted a side-whiskered gentleman, striding up. "There's a rumor you are looking for a house to lease."

"The rumor is true," she said, and smiled.

Jasper's stomach clenched. But his expression, he was certain, remained unchanged. He had none of the powers possessed by the ladies of Les Chausettes. Few men did. But he could hide his thoughts behind bland expressions as well as any. Had learned that skill from Rae long before she had been hanged for a crime she had surely committed.

"I may have a possibility for you," continued the gentleman. "But for now the puddings call. We must talk later."

"Certainly, my lord," Madeline said, and curtsied as he made a beeline for the dessert table.

Jasper watched the movement. It was perfect, graceful, confident. She was a true creature of the *ton*. Only *he* knew how many times she had awakened with nightmares. Only *he* had paced the length of his bedchamber, waiting for the agonizing sound of her sobs to subside, not allowing himself to enter her room lest he—

He stopped the thought. After all, it mattered little that she had removed her belongings from Lavender House. He was not the least disturbed that the building echoed with emptiness, despite the others who lived there. Was not even remotely disturbed that she shone like a shooting star among her stodgy contemporaries.

"And what of you, Lady Redcomb?" he asked, tone commendably bored. "Are you well?"

"Quite." She smiled, serene, and so beautiful it made the back of his head throb dully. "Sir Drake and his lovely bride were kind enough to take me in until I secure my own home. I hope to find something soon. Though certainly I'll be unable to afford anything as lavish as this," she said, and swept a graceful hand sideways.

He had taught her that grace. He had taught her *everything*, except how to have a soul. He had never quite got the knack of that.

She laughed a little. The sound was like springtime. Perhaps he had not taught her that either.

"The drawing room alone is large enough to—" she began, but at that moment his control snapped.

"What are you doing here?" he asked, and immediately reprimanded himself for such a foolish outpouring of emotion. He had come here to reason with her. Not to make her angry. Not to make himself a fool.

"I thought that much was obvious," she said, and laughed again. "I'm here for the dancing," she said, and nodded toward the doorway. The floating strains of a waltz were just wafting up on the scented air. "So if you'll excuse me . . ."

Jasper tried to stifle his burning frustration, tried to control his idiotic urges, but somehow he reached out. Without knowing, without meaning to, he caught her hand.

She glanced down at their fingers, surprised, then looked up, expression questioning.

A young couple moved past. But Jasper had been snared by Madeline's eyes and failed to identify them. "Perhaps . . ." His voice sounded strange, guttural, unused. Not at all like the posh lord he claimed to be. He cleared his throat and wondered why he had been saved. Why *he* had escaped the gallows. "Perhaps you would do me the honor of a dance," he said.

Seconds ticked breathlessly away, and for a moment he thought she would refuse, but eventually she gave him the faintest sketch of a smile and nodded graciously. He lifted her hand. Her fingers felt warm, as fragile as a swallow's wing, as soft as a dream. He guided her onto the dance floor. The melody was smooth and lovely. She was the epitome of reserved elegance as he settled his hand on the firm curve of her waist, and yet he could think of nothing but how it would feel to kiss her. How she would feel beneath him. Atop him. Around . . .

Good God! What was he thinking? He was beginning to sweat, while half the people in that very room would refuse to believe he possessed the ability.

"The orchestra is quite good," he said, forcing himself to act as if all was well. All was normal.

"Near as accomplished as the one hired by Mrs. Bentwood," she said, and though her voice was prim, he recognized the wry humor that so often hummed below the surface of her conversations.

It had been three months since they had attended the ball at Bentwood Manor. They had arrived separately, of course, but they had been united in their mission to garner information. Indeed, Mrs. Nettles had accompanied Madeline, for only the pixielike Faye could identify the man they sought.

"They were quite extraordinary," Madeline said.

Jasper let the memory soothe him. There were many such recollections. Simple, aging memories of days past, for they worked well together. Always had. "Until Mrs. Nettles attacked the oboist."

Her sweet-tart lips curved up the slightest degree. "I don't believe it was so much an attack as a retreat."

Little pixie had an inexplicable fear of men. All men. Sometimes she was more successful at controlling her phobia than at others. On that particular evening, she had inadvertently stumbled into the orchestra when Lord Hapley asked her to dance. Hapley, as it happened, was not known for his gentlemanly manners with the ladies.

The oboist had toppled into the cymbalist, who had collided with a trio of unhappy violists. The cacophony that followed still made Jasper's ears hurt.

"I don't believe she has attended a ball since," Maddy said.

"Or spoken to a man," Jasper added.

"Including you?" she asked, and found his eyes with hers.

He reminded himself to breathe. "Especially me."

Her hand was like silken magic against his shoulder. "Perhaps you should not be so intimidating, then."

It was becoming increasingly difficult to function in her presence. How the hell had it come to this? "Tell me, Lady Redcomb . . ." When had she become beauty itself? "Are you intimidated?"

"Always."

He nearly laughed, for if the truth be told, *he* was the one who was unsettled when she was near. Though he would rather be hexed than admit the truth. "Then perhaps you should do as I suggest," he said. His tone was marvelously level.

"Did you make a suggestion, Lord Gallo?" she asked.

"I believe I did."

"Maybe I mistook it for an order."

He sensed the swirling couples around them without turning and took a fortifying breath. "Perhaps when our current assignments are resolved, you can look into the problem of the missing maids," he suggested, and prayed to God the girls would be found before such an eventuality took place; he had no intention of allowing such a risk, just as he had not allowed her to work on a dozen other cases where he sensed such an intimate undercurrent of danger. It was not that he worried for her safety . . . exactly. It was . . . Well, yes, perhaps he did worry about her, but it wasn't because she was beauty and goodness and hope. It was merely for the good of the coven. They needed her. She was their anchor, their light, and he couldn't risk seeing it extinguished. Thus he had always chosen her missions carefully and would continue to do so despite her passionate desires to right the wrongs that grieved her so. Marie Wendell's disappearance was not for her to decipher. Not today. Not ever. He would learn what he could, ferret out all possible information . . . but he would not see her involved, for there was death down that path. That much he knew, though he could not have said how. It was that kind of indefinable knowledge that had brought him the guardianship of Les Chausettes.

A shiver coursed over him, but he staved it off. She was safe. She was whole. "But you must be patient," he said, expression carefully insipid.

For a prolonged moment the music was drowned by her silence, then: "And lose how much time, Jasper?" she asked. Her smile was perfect, the very portrait of a lady's cool superiority. "A fortnight? A month?" If she was angry, even *he* couldn't tell, and there was none but her sister who knew her better than he. "It may well already be too late."

He refrained from gritting his teeth, from shaking her, from reminding her that he knew her every secret. Had, in fact, hidden them away himself. "Surely you are not so deluded as to think you can solve this problem on your own."

She raised one perfectly arched brow. But humor still shone on her honey-toned features. "Are you saying I am deluded, my lord?"

He whirled her, making her tangerine gown billow like a sail at sunset. She was as a feather in the wind, as delicate and light as a sparrow beneath his hands. But she was strong too. Trained. Intelligent. Yet that hardly made her invincible. Indeed, those most talented were often those who were lost. Who took too great a risk. Who overstepped their abilities. Rae had been a magician at sleight of hand. A maestro. And she was long dead. Sacrificed for some pompous duke's silver-plated snuffbox. "I am saying you could achieve far more with the assistance of the committee."

"Not if the committee refuses to help." She smiled at a couple who glided past. "Or to care." Perhaps her hand tightened the slightest degree in his, but her expression was still angelically serene.

"It does little good to care if you get yourself . . ." He paused, fought down the foolish tension, the strangling terror. He was no longer a child, for God's sake. No longer standing at the foot of the gallows, watching his mentor take her last gasping breaths. Still, the thought of Madeline in danger make his chest feel just as tight, just as tortured. "Your place is at Lavender House," he said.

"My *place*?" She tilted her head a fraction of an inch as if merely curious. Her hand was light against his shoulder, but it felt hot, as if it were burning a path straight to his heart.

Her *place*, he thought heatedly. Near him. Where he could watch her. Protect her. He didn't curse out loud. Ever. But perhaps it was time to begin. "You can do the most good there," he said.

"For whom?" she asked, tone congenial. "The committee?"

He wanted to pull her close. Kiss her until he could think clearly once again. "What are your plans, then, if not to use the advantages offered you?" he asked.

"I plan to find Marie." Her smile was beatific, as if she had just proclaimed nothing more difficult than hosting an ice cream social.

He felt his ire ignite like a cannon fuse. "And how exactly do you plan to do that?" he asked. "By dancing with every overfed lord who finds you comely?" He tried to hide his disdain, but they were a tepid lot. Tepid and insipid, and he was not one of them, though in some hidden place he wished to hell he was. Wished he was good enough for her in some small way. Any way.

"Yes," she said, and nodded serenely to a twirling couple.

"And may I ask how?" His voice was smooth again, but it came at great cost.

She shifted her gaze to his. A spark of light gleamed in her emerald-fire eyes, and her tone changed the smallest degree, becoming almost breathless. "The girls all had ties to society."

One had been a parlor maid. Another, an actress.

The third had sold tailor-made slippers to those particularly flush in the pockets. And they had all been beautiful. He knew that. Had garnered that much information while trying not to pace, trying not to wonder about her whereabouts. About her safety. About her sleeping arrangements.

Jasper steadied his breathing. He had never questioned her virtue in the past, but things were changing, shifting. She had left the shelter of Lavender House, questioned the wisdom of the committee that had saved her. Had saved her sister. What was next? Might she actually be contemplating Lord Weatherby's offer? Surely he had invited her to his bed. What sane man would not? The question was whether she was considering his suggestion. Jasper's gut clenched, twisting like aggravated serpents as he thought of her in another's arms, but he kept his voice steady.

"Many have ties to society," he said.

She continued as if he hadn't spoken. "Hence, we can suppose that someone in society knows what happened to them," she said.

Dread sliced him as he realized her intent. "So you plan to do what exactly? Feel your way through the crowd?" He could imagine her, touching them with her velvet hands, feeling what they felt, absorbing their thoughts until she found someone evil enough to have taken three innocents.

"If I must," she said.

Dear God. "Then you believe the culprit is here now?" he asked, tone carefully acerbic.

She glanced about, placid expression perfectly combating his snide manner. "Most probably not."

"Then how—"

"I will attend another soiree. And another. Until I find the ones responsible."

And touch them again. Open herself to their malevolence. Again. "The *ton* is easily bored," he offered, "but there is no reason to assume the villain will show up where you wish."

"Then I suspect I will need to think of some way to be extremely entertaining," she said, and smiled.

His heart lurched in his chest. What did she mean? Flirtations? Worse? God knew no man could resist her. No man in his right mind would even try. Unluckily for him, he had not been in that state for some time. "I hate to see you embarrass yourself," he said.

Their gazes met with a clash. Hers was glowing. The song came to a sweeping crescendo.

"Then don't watch," she suggested, and pulling from his grasp, swept away, gown furling like an angry orange tide in her wake.

The remainder of the evening was just as painful as the beginning. A hundred times Madeline thought she felt Jasper's gaze on her, but when she turned, he was with another, involved in some conversation beyond her hearing.

Damn him. She had more important things to worry about. More pressing issues with which to concern herself. She had not come to May's gathering to flirt and fawn, but to find the girls, to interpret the truth in others' faces.

Since residing at Berryhill she had redoubled her experiments with potions. She would never be as gifted as Ella, would never be capable of simply changing her appearance with a thought or building a flame from naught. But she was learning to mix powerful elixirs. Learning how wolfsbane reacted with vervain. How long to expose mandrake to a waning moon for maximum effectiveness. True, after sampling the potions, she was sometimes barely able to know her *own* mind much less read others' as she hoped, but she was making progress. She was sure of it.

She wished she could say the same about finding the girls. Even though she had been given the opportunity to touch men during the dances, the exchange was oft too brief to get a true feeling of the dancers' emotions. And despite her implications, she was unwilling to carry on liaisons in her efforts to gain information. Even if she took every man in London to bed, that left the women unquestioned.

She could speak to them, of course, could touch their hands, but they often wore gloves, which hindered her perceptions.

"Lady Redcomb."

She turned at the sound of a man's voice. "Mr. Menton," she said, and smiled. Henry Menton was tall and bent, with sad, ancient eyes that only looked sadder since the loss of his wife. He had narrow hands and long sensitive fingers. He reached one of those hands toward her now. She gripped it in her own.

"I hear you are hoping to rent an estate."

"Well, I have been considering—" she began, but suddenly she felt the painful probe of his emotions. Regret. Worry. Sorrow. "Mr. Menton," she said, leaning in a little and studying his eyes. "Are you quite well?"

"Yes. Yes of course," he said. "Just a bit of a headache."

An image flashed in his eyes. A woman's face. But it was not the wife she remembered. Not the wife he had lost just six months prior. Instead, it was a young maid. Beautiful, enigmatic, almost smiling. Could it be one of the girls who had disappeared? But wait . . . Maddy tightened her grip on his fingers. Perhaps it *was* his wife. Long ago, before time had touched her with its harsh hand.

She gazed deeper, felt his sorrow like the blow of a blunt object, and knew she had guessed correctly.

"You must miss her terribly," she said.

He looked startled for a second, then nodded, eyes welling with the need to share his pain.

"She was lovely," she said, and saw Mrs. Menton's face as clearly now as if the woman looked through a window at them. A round window. Small. Framed in gilt.

"Yes. Yes, I do," he said, but in that moment she realized the lady was not looking through a window at all. She was gazing at them from a picture frame. A tiny portrait that was tucked firmly away, hidden in the darkness. But why? If he cherished her so, why would he stow it out of sight?

"I had a miniature done of her. Years ago. It brought me comfort during the worst of the loneliness but . . ." He shook his head, pained by the thought. "I seem to have misplaced it."

She squeezed his hand between hers, felt the rough and the soft of it, the sharp bones and stringy tendons, but kept her gaze fixed on the story behind his eyes. Mrs. Menton gazed back from the darkness. The room was quiet where she resided. The light was dim, the leather soft against her cheek.

"The settee," Madeline murmured.

"What's that?" Menton asked, long face drawn in a scowl.

Madeline drew herself back to reality with a start. "The settee," she said, and brightened her tone, as though she were just guessing, as though she could not see the miniature tucked away between the calf-hide cushions. "People oft lose belongings in their furniture."

But he shook his head. "I've looked everywhere, I fear. The parlor was her favorite place. Each spring she would fill it with roses. I go there sometimes to sit and thought perhaps I had lost it there. But I searched to no avail."

In her mind, Madeline saw him tossing cushions aside, but the pastel colors were wrong, the lighting too bright. "Not the parlor," she said.

He scowled at her. She smiled.

"Have you a study, Mr. Menton? Or a library, perhaps?"

"Why do you ask?"

"Check the cushions," she suggested. "It might just be that you will find what you seek there."

"But I . . ." He paused. His eyes widened. "I wandered in there just last week to . . . I fell asleep, and . . ." His old eyes widened. "Thank you, my lady. Thank you. You're a wonder," he rasped, and hurried, bent but eager, from the house.

Chapter 5

"**L**ady Redcomb, I've lost my favorite ring and hoped you might assist me."

"Old man Menton said you were a marvel. And I—"

"My lady, please, I am most perplexed. Might you help me?"

Voices chimed at Maddy. In the few days since Mr. Menton had told the story of his meeting with her, things had changed dramatically. Overnight, the *ton* had begun treating her as if she were a traveling circus.

She stood in the middle of a lavish garden. Shrubbery reared and twisted in a hundred exotic shapes. Autumn flowers bloomed on every trellis, saturating the air with heady fragrance. Lady Bleacher's party was supposed to be a private affair, but half of London seemed to be present. And all appeared to be enamored of her. She didn't know what to make of it.

"I swear to you," she said, laughing at the mob that arced about her. " 'Twas naught but logic that helped poor Mr. Menton find his miniature."

"He said you gazed into his eyes," said Lady Sedum.

She forced another laugh. "Gazing has nothing to do with it. 'Tis simply that I lost my brooch in my own settee not two days before."

"Can you tell the future too?" asked a young man she had only just met two minutes before and had decided she didn't particularly like thirty seconds after.

"Oh for heaven's sake. I have been amongst you most of a decade. You know I cannot—"

"Of course she can," said Weatherby, and moving closer, lowered his voice. "For she is magic. Yet I would be content if she would but agree to hold my hand and gaze into my eyes. No fortunes necessary."

She laughed. "You are daft, the lot of you."

"Please, Lady Redcomb, I would ask a favor," said a voice. She turned. Thomas Echer reached for her hand, and suddenly she felt a flash of something from his skin to hers. A shade of regret. A shard of sharp guilt. She glanced up, surprised.

"Tell my future," he said, fair lank hair falling beside his solemn, narrow face, Adam's apple bobbing nervously in his scrawny neck.

Time ticked away. The tittering others seemed to recede for a moment.

"Very well," Madeline said finally.

The crowd murmured louder. She shook her head as if humoring them. "But I will need a quiet place. No one can work miracles in such pandemonium."

"Bleacher," someone yelled. "Lady Redcomb is telling fortunes. Where can she practice her tricks?"

In a matter of minutes she and Echer had been sequestered in the middle of a curving hedgerow. They sat with a small, round table between them, his hand in hers. She closed her eyes, wondering how she had come to this. The potion she had concocted on the previous night had made her feel strange, not at all herself, but it had done nothing to improve her ability to read minds.

"What do you see?" Echer asked, voice hushed with worry, with belief.

"Very little," she began, but in that instant he met her gaze and suddenly she *did* see something. A glimpse of sorrow and then the flash of naked skin.

She drew her breath and remained very still.

His eyes were worried, his expression pained, but past that mien, as if looking through a mirror, she saw a girl's face. "Tell me the truth," he rasped.

The fair-haired maid had surely not yet reached her seventeenth birthday. She was small and buxom and filled with sorrow. Tipper, one of the missing maids, was said to be blond and petite and—

"Will she ever forgive me?" he asked.

There were tears in the girl's eyes. A bruise darkened her eye.

Horror filled her. "What have you done?" she whispered.

His face contorted. "I am sorry."

"Where is she?"

"Where? I don't know." His expression was tortured. "I had no plans to lie with her. I simply . . . The wine . . . She looked so sad. Six shillings was all she asked. Six shillings and my soul."

"What are you talking about?"

"She was comely. Young. And my wife had been sharp with me." He winced.

Madeline drew a careful breath, steadied herself, and focused on what there was to feel, not what she *wished* to feel. Emotions and thoughts and something she could not quite put a name to, flowed through her. "Are you saying you . . ." The world was a strange and unlikely place. "Did you cheat on your wife, Mr. Echer?" she said.

His mouth twitched miserably. "I didn't plan to do it. Tell me. Please. Will she ever find it in her heart to forgive me?"

Madeline closed her eyes to the lunacy of the situation. "Do you cherish her?" she asked.

He glanced out the window, Adam's apple bobbling. "I know it is gauche to say so. But yes. I do. More than life itself."

"Have you told her this?"

"Not . . ." There were tears in his eyes. "Not in so many words."

"Then I suggest you do," she said.

He tightened his grip on her hand. "And she will forgive me?"

Worry and regret twisted his face. But there was hope too and earnestness, and in that place that held her burgeoning powers, Madeline saw him with his wife, laughing as they swung a child between them. The boy's brown, tousled curls bounced as he giggled, eyes gleaming.

"I hope you favor dark-headed children," she said.

He sat very still, expression momentarily frozen. "We will have a child?"

She didn't answer immediately.

"Dark, like her lovely mother?"

"A boy," Maddy corrected.

For a moment she thought he might actually swoon, his face went so pale. "We'll have a son?"

Madeline drew a careful breath. Did she have the right to interfere so in people's lives? Did she have a *duty?* "Life does not often offer second chances, Mr. Echer," she said, feeling the uncomfortable weight of responsibility across her shoulders. "Use it wisely."

He rose to his feet, stumbling slightly over the leg of his chair. "My Lorraine has hair as dark as a moonless night," he said.

Madeline smiled as the little family laughed in his eyes. "I would also suggest that you drink no more wine," she said.

"Ever?" He looked dismayed for an instant and a little shocked.

"For so long as you care for the good opinion of your wife," she said.

He stared at her for one long moment, then nodded solemnly. "I will do as you say," he said, and taking her hand, bowed somberly over it. "I will do it. Thank you, Lady Redcomb. Thank you ever so much."

She rose too. "I fear I did nothing that—" she began, but he had already disappeared behind the carefully pruned hedge.

Voices murmured around him.

"Miraculous. Absolutely miraculous," Echer said, and hurried away.

On the following day Madeline received three offers. One was a marriage proposal from an octogenarian duke. Another was an invitation to become the fortune teller for a Russian prince, and the last was a sprawled note on expensive stationery inviting Madeline to stay at the quiet, little-used estate of an eccentric peeress called nothing more than Lady Linn. Madeline discounted the first two out of hand, but considered the estate.

News traveled quickly among the twittering *ton*, and the eccentric peeress, who spent her time between several properties, had heard of Madeline's need for a home. Upon seeing it from Sultan's glossy back, Madeline couldn't help but think the lovely brownstone perfect for a witch. The creeping ivy, the narrow windows, the rambling garden with its tilted arbor all spoke of clandestine meetings and lingering spells. The house was tall and narrow, set regally on a close-cropped hill and ringed by chestnut trees older than time.

Not wishing to risk Ella with her own burgeoning notoriety, Madeline moved her possessions to Cinderknoll the very next day, but despite her fear that her inherited staff might be leery of her growing reputation, all went well.

Though there were no male servants employed and only three maids, the women seemed happy enough to have her about and treated her more like a visiting cousin than an employer. Daphne, a round-faced, round-bodied woman well into her fifties, called everyone "sweetums," except herself, of course, whom she referred to in the third person.

On the following morning, Madeline left the lofty estate in her employees' casual care and rode Sultan alone to investigate the girls who had been lost.

Despite the hours spent with their friends and families, however, she learned little more than a physical description and tiny inconsequential details of the maids.

She returned to her new home weary and spent, wanting nothing more than to soak in a hot tub and forget all.

"Good evening, sweetums." Daphne met her at the door, bobbing an abbreviated curtsy. "Oh, but you look tired."

"Well, it was—" Maddy began, but the older woman was not one to wait for answers.

"A nice bath is what you'll be needin'. Daphne will draw it herself," she said, and turned, only to pivot back in a moment. "Will you be wantin' to see your cards here or in your chambers?"

"Cards?" Maddy asked.

"From your visitors," Daphne said, and scurrying to the nearby table, retrieved a silver tray littered with a dozen scattered calling cards.

Madeline eyed them warily. "They all stopped by today?"

"Seems you have a host of admirers."

"What did they want?"

Daphne canted her head for a moment, then: "They're wantin' what everyone wants, sweetums. Magic," she said, and turning, shuffled quickly away.

Fifteen minutes later Madeline leaned back in the cast-iron tub and closed her eyes. Terror swam behind them. How many times had she been warned not to expose herself, to let others know of her gifts? Scores surely. Perhaps hundreds. She steadied her breathing and reminded herself that that life was behind her now. She was no longer associated with Les Chausettes. They were safe from her. As was Ella.

But Bertram's daughter was not safe. Neither was Tipper with the musical laugh. Or Milly with the summer blond tresses. They were gone. Lost to those who loved them. Lost. Just as Ella had been.

And perhaps there were more. Additional girls whose disappearance had not yet been reported. Girls who were afraid and alone, shivering in isolation. Just as Ella had been . . . and might be again if she was not careful.

Dark thoughts roiled through Maddy's mind.

But she pushed them back, out of her range, out of her head. No one was accusing her of witchcraft. No one was knocking down her door. Indeed, the *ton* had been more than thrilled to believe she had some kind of unusual skill. And why would they not be? They were a whimsical and mercurial lot, the same people who celebrated the coming of the Cossacks. Who dressed as milkmaids and welcomed life in the dairy as if they were born to it.

So what if they believed she had some kind of drawing room magic? Why not use that? Perhaps in that manner she could ferret out whoever was responsible for Marie's disappearance.

Stepping out of the tub, Madeline toweled dry and slipped into a black satin robe.

"Daphne," she called.

The woman hobbled into view in a few moments. "Yes, sweetums, what might you be needin'?"

"A party," Madeline said, and Daphne widened her round eyes in her round face and clapped her hands, not missing a beat.

"A party! How lovely. When's it to be?"

"Will three days be enough time to locate additional staff and—"

"Well, it'll be a stretch and no mistake, but old Daphne keeps her ear to the ground, she does, and will be able to find you some good people. Och. I know the perfect butler," she said. "The perfect one. A party," she said again, and scurried away without further instructions.

Chapter 6

Cinderknoll was set apart from its neighbors by a copse of ancient horse chestnuts that towered over the manse like wizened wardens. Candlelight glowed gold and mellow in every window. Inside, servants bustled industriously about, bearing silver trays with crystal goblets and confections of every sort.

But it was neither the silver nor the confections that caught Jasper Reeves's eye. It was Madeline.

She held court in the center of the room. Her eyes were as bright as emeralds. Her hair, sable dark, was upswept, revealing her swan-slim neck. Catching the light of a hundred flames, it reflected the gleam back a thousandfold.

One of her admirers spoke. She replied and the crowd laughed.

Jasper gritted his teeth and wished to hell he was a drinking man. But he was not. Jasper Reeves was all about control. Alcohol tended to slow one's reflexes, impair—

"Champagne, my lord?"

Jasper turned toward the server. Tall and dark-skinned, he had a foreign cast to him. His accent was an indecipherable blend that suggested French ancestry but questioned other possibilities. Beneath the innocuous broadcloth of his fine livery, he appeared to be as broad-shouldered and hard-muscled as a smithy. But the bright gold piping of his uniform and agreeable expression defused the impression of strength, making him seem mundane to the untrained eye.

Jasper stifled a scowl and shook his head at the offering. The server nodded once and turned away, his neck corded with muscle.

"Tell me," Jasper said. "Are you Lady Linn's man?"

The waiter glanced back, black eyes steady. "No, my lord. I was hired for this event only."

Bile sloshed in Jasper's churning system. Why had Madeline hired a servant built like a draft horse?

"And your name?" Jasper asked.

"Joseph, sir."

Jasper nodded. "May I ask how you know the Lady Redcomb?"

Something sparked in the other man's eyes. "I

did not, my lord, until she asked me to service her."

Jasper's guts twisted into hard knots. "Service her?"

Their gazes held for one hard second, then, "My apologies, my lord. I meant *serve* her. My English is not what it should be."

Yet it sounded all but perfect. Jasper watched him, considered smiling, and decided even he could not quite pull off that much deception. "So you will be gone after this night?"

"Unless Her Ladyship asks me to service her . . . forgive me, *serve* her longer."

For one convoluted second Jasper considered whacking the edge of his hand against the other's trachea. The size of one's opponent made little difference when met with enough force to his throat, but he drew a careful breath and considerately refrained from killing Madeline's server. "You have no permanent position elsewhere, then?" he asked.

"None that would keep me from this house," he said, and bowing diffidently, turned away.

What the hell did that mean? Jasper wondered, but just then he saw Madeline take a man's hand and lead him into a private chamber.

He gritted his teeth and caught the curses behind them. The rumors couldn't be true. They couldn't.

Madeline was no idiot. She had been trained, had been educated. Had been warned a thousand times never to reveal her gifts. And yet, there she was, closeted away, alone with a man. She *must* be telling his fortune.

Good God. Jasper almost laughed at the thought that her powers would be wasted so. But the thought that she might be doing something entirely differently struck him suddenly. And just as suddenly he was across the floor, pulled in that direction by an instinct as primitive as time itself.

"Lord Gallo," said Weatherby, approaching from the left. "Is there a date yet for my contest with Lord Exter's flea-bitten bonesetters?"

"Not just yet," Jasper said, barely remembering the vow he had made to arrange a match.

"But soon?"

Reaching casually to the right, Jasper took a flute of champagne from a passing servant. Luckily the man wasn't built like a well-conditioned draft horse. "I've been rather busy."

"Oh?" Weatherby scanned the room "Whatever with?"

"The usual problems with button makers and cobblers. And—" Jasper began, but suddenly Madeline appeared, and all thoughts raced like scattered vermin from his head. She looked flushed. Why? Was she distressed? Was she fearful? And suddenly he could do nothing but step forward, push through to the edge of the mob that surrounded her.

"Me next, my lady," said a man with a lisp. "I must make a decision between a gray and a chestnut."

"Horses!" said another. "I must choose a *wife*."

Several people laughed. Jasper was not one of them. But neither did he deign to exterminate the man standing next to him.

"And what of you, Lord Gallo?" asked Weatherby who had followed him there. "What do you want of Her Ladyship?"

Everything. The answer slammed into Jasper's cranium. He battered it down. Yet he could not quite look away, even as he answered. "I fear I have little faith in enchantments and the like."

"Little faith." Weatherby smiled smugly. "Didn't you hear how Lady Redcomb divined the location of Mr. Menton's lost miniature?"

Dear God. "In fact, I did."

"It's quite miraculous," said an unknown bystander. "She told Barnes he would gain a great fortune and he won fifty pounds at whist just the next night. What say you to that?"

That she was out of her mind? "Luck," Jasper said.

"Luck!" rasped Weatherby and the bystander in unison.

"Lady Redcomb," Weatherby called, raising his voice above the hubbub of the mob, "did you hear that? Lord Gallo believes your abilities to be naught but luck."

She laughed. And though Jasper tried to remain unmoved, he could not help but look at her. For she was sunlight to his darkness. Hope to his despair. She stood not six feet away now, dressed in a lavender gown that made her faerie-bright features seem to shine with magic.

"Is that not what I have been telling you all along?" she said. "It is a parlor trick, nothing more."

"A parlor trick," said Mr. Haviard. "Then tell us how it is done."

She laughed again. "The trick would not be of much worth if I did so, now would it?"

"So modest," someone murmured.

"A wonder," said another.

"Share with the doubting Lord Gallo his fortune," someone called.

She didn't turn toward Jasper, but remained as she was, smiling as if mildly amused. "I do not think he wishes to be privy to it," she said.

"On the contrary," Jasper said, and watched as she turned toward him, watched as the light of her spilled across his face, across his being. "I am quite interested in what you have to say."

Her gaze caught his. "But I thought you did not believe in enchantments and the like, Lord Gallo."

So she had heard him. But of course she would. She was a witch, and her powers were growing. That knowledge caused consternation and pride to bloom in equal measures somewhere in his gut. "Perhaps you will make me a believer after all," he said.

"Take him and learn his secrets," someone called.

"Take him," said another.

"Take him," they urged, and somehow Jasper found himself stepping into the room behind her, pulling the door shut as one in a trance, or a dream.

She turned toward him, hands clasped. "You have no right to come uninvited into my home, Lord Gallo."

He watched her for an instant, knowing he should reprimand her for her foolishness, but wanting nothing more than to drink her in, to make certain she was well.

Instead, he said, "I hear you are an expert at divinations."

She ignored that. "Marie has not yet been found."

"Nor is she likely to be," he said.

Her eyes widened. Her breath stopped. "What do you mean? What do you know?"

Frustration burned through him like acid, but he

kept his tone placid. "I know you cannot expect to help her without the committee's strength behind you." Neither could she expect him to *ask* them to assist her, for he wanted nothing more than to keep her apart from this mission. There were other agencies that could find the girls, others who could risk their lives. Madeline was far better suited for other tasks. Tasks that could use her stealth, keep her hidden, keep her safe.

She drew a deep breath through her nose. It was perfectly straight and elegantly narrow. "So you continue to underestimate me."

He laughed. How the hell could she think he underestimated her? It would be impossible. For she was everything. "Tell me, Lady Redcomb, did you think this . . ." He motioned to their surroundings, wondering vaguely if he were about to lose his mind. ". . . demonstration would make me think more highly of your skills?" he asked.

She separated her hands, then placed them back together at a slightly altered angle. "I would like you to leave my house now."

Anger and regret and a dozen other emotions plowed through him. He ignored them all. "But I wish for a reading," he said, and put his hand on the back of a doweled wooden chair.

She stared at him, lips pursed. "I fear I am not in the mood."

"Is that what powers your gifts, then, my lady? Your mood?" He wanted to grab her. To shake her. To tell her he hadn't protected her for eight years only to allow her to endanger herself now. But he did none of those things. Instead, he remained stupidly immobile as he always did.

"Please remove yourself from these premises," she said. "Before I call Joseph."

Surprise and anger spewed through him in equal measures. "You would call your draft horse?"

She scowled. "My hired man."

"Did you read his future too?" Jasper asked. "Will he soon be pulling wagons?"

She narrowed her eyes, studying him. "Why have you come here?"

"Why?" He couldn't believe the question. She must know the truth. Must realize that life without her was no life at all, was worse than death. "We have invested a good deal in you, Lady Redcomb. Eight years. Countless pounds."

"I believe you got your money back for your investment," she said.

But he wanted *her* back. "That is not for you to decide."

"What is then?" she asked, tone clipped, brows raised slightly as she paced across the narrow space.

He stared at her, for he could do nothing else.

"Are any decisions mine, Jasper? Or is my entire life at the whim of the committee?"

"As I told you previously, it is your task to complete the mission assigned to you. The committee can find another to—"

"My mission!" She scoffed. "What was it again? To learn how many crumpets Lady Drexell has planned for her next soiree?"

"Perhaps your appointed task does not seem important to you at this juncture, but that is not for you to decide, for I believe you agreed, some years back, to follow the orders given you regardless of your own whimsical—"

"I have followed orders," she hissed. "You cannot say that I have not."

He watched her, beautiful and brave and angry. "No," he said, "you have been a fine addition to the organization. A good—"

"I've been a good girl. Following orders, listening to *wisdom*, waiting for you to . . ." She paused, lowered her voice. "They may already be dead," she said, voice steady again, but chin lifted in the expression that personified her.

"They are not."

Her mouth opened. Her breath stopped. "What do you know?"

Nothing. Or very little. Try as he might, he had

not learned a great deal. But he had his suspicions. And a little more. Rumors. Experience. Intellect.

"Where are they? Are they well?"

He shook his head. "I do not know."

"Then how do you know they yet live?"

"I cannot tell you that," he said.

Anger swept her face. "Because I no longer belong to your coven?"

She would always belong. Till the end of time. Nothing could change that. She was the heart of Les Chausettes. The tender, aching soul of it. "Because it is not your mission," he said.

"Tell me . . ." Her voice was sweet, but her hand, where it gripped the back of a chair, looked pale and sharp-boned. "Are you so hungry for power that you would allow innocents to die that you might keep it?"

He almost winced at her words, but he was not yet so foolish as to admit he was human. "As you well know, my lady, people die every day whether I would allow it or not."

She stared at him, eyes steady, mouth set. "There was a time I thought I knew you."

She could wound him with a glance, sear him with a thought, but he would not show the scar. "Truly."

"I see now that I was wrong."

"Were you?" He had meant to sound jeering, but there was a soft sadness to her words that was all but unbearable. That ripped at the very heart of him.

"I would ask that you leave now," she said.

But he couldn't. Couldn't walk out. Leave her here, alone in this mob. Unguarded, unloved. "Without my reading?"

"Yes."

He should go. He knew that much. He had lost her. Did not deserve her, but despite everything, he found himself unable to turn away. "But what if I am lying?"

Her eyes narrowed the slightest degree. "What are you saying?"

"What if I know all there is regarding the girls' disappearances, but refuse to tell you?"

For a moment emotion echoed in her eyes. "Why are you doing this?" she murmured.

He refrained from grinding his teeth like a rabid dog. From throwing things like a child, yet he knew he was acting childishly. What the hell was wrong with him? He used to be so controlled. So sure. "Certainly if you touched my hand you could ascertain if I am telling the truth," he said. "You are Lady Redcomb. The wonder of the *ton*."

She said nothing.

"Surely you are not risking your life . . . risking the lives of your sisters simply to garner a bit of attention from your preening contemporaries."

She stared at him, and for a moment he thought his ploy would fail, but finally she raised a hand to indicate the chair near which he stood. "Sit," she said.

He was almost able to force himself to turn, to leave, but in the end he could not. He was weak. Lost. Willing to endure all for the slightest touch of her hand on his.

Stepping past him, she took a seat on the far side of the tiny wooden table. Solemnly, she reached out. He did the same. They touched. Skin against skin.

Her fingertips brushed his palm, and suddenly an image crackled like lightning in his mind.

Madeline! Naked. In his arms. In his bed. And then . . . though he couldn't say why, though he couldn't have explained it in a thousand years, he jerked to his feet. The tiny table crashed sideways, and suddenly she was crushed against him. Their mouths met in a clash. He was yanking up her gown. And she . . . God help him . . . she was tearing at his belt.

He felt her hand against his flesh. Felt his desire roar to life like a wild beast. There was nothing but her. Her skin. Her scent. Her—

A noise sounded on the door behind him, but it hardly mattered.

Her skin smelled of sex and her thoughts were just as—

"Is everything quite all right in there?"

Her breathing was a siren song against his ear, begging him to—

"Lady Redcomb?"

She jerked from his grip, hair tousled, lips swollen. He growled and stepped toward her.

"Lady Redcomb!"

And suddenly his senses came flooding back. Her gown was askew. His chair was upset. The table was tilted against the wall. Above the lacy edge of her gown, her breasts were leaping from bondage. Her lips looked bruised. Her eyes ablaze.

He ground his hands to fists, breathing hard. "What did you do?" he growled.

"Me!" Her voice was raspy, deep.

He shook his head, trying to clear it. "You can . . . I didn't know . . ." God, he felt as if his brain was in a vise. Not to mention other throbbing regions. "But it changes nothing. Regardless of your powers. You cannot do this."

"Do—"

"This!" he said, crazed. Out of his shattered mind. "You're not ready to be on your own." Or was it *he* who was not ready? "You are skilled." His skin was still vibrating from her touch, brain humming from the image of her naked. "That I admit, but there is much you don't know. Much—"

But suddenly the door burst open. Lord Weatherby stood in the opening. "We heard noises and feared something had gone amiss." He eyed them, first Madeline, then Jasper, expression concerned, then curious. "Is everything quite all right?"

"Yes, of course," she said, and smoothed her gown. "It is simply that my findings . . ." She drew a steadying breath. "They were quite surprising."

"Ahh, how interesting." Weatherby eyed Jasper for a moment, then turned away, rubbing his hands together. "Well, my lady, I hope you are ready for your next reading."

"Yes. Certainly." She drew a careful breath, nodded. "Lord Gallo was just leaving."

"My turn then," said Lord Weatherby, striding the short distance to the table.

"You're out of your depth," Jasper said, able, at least, to keep his voice quiet.

"Well . . ." Weatherby smiled. "'Tis a good thing I am here to make certain she doesn't drown then."

Anger flared like a wildfire inside Jasper's head, and for an instant he was tempted almost beyond control to slam the smirk off Weatherby's face. But he held himself at bay.

"Don't do anything foolish," he murmured.

Madeline raised her chin, caught his eye, and in that second an image flared in Jasper's mind . . . a picture of her in Weatherby's arms, her breasts crushed to his chest, her eyes ablaze with desire.

The picture was so clear, so bright and intense that he all but staggered beneath the pounding weight of it. And indeed, in that instant, he curled his hands to fists and took one taut step forward.

"Is all well, my lady?" Joseph asked. He stood in the doorway suddenly, filling the space, his gaze steady on Jasper.

Bending, Madeline righted the fallen chair, and when she straightened, her expression was serene, her hands steady. "Make certain Lord Gallo arrives home safely if you please." Her voice was cool, her eyes frosty. "I fear he's not feeling quite himself."

Chapter 7

Dammit!

Crumpling the sheaf of paper in his fist, Jasper hurled the offending wad across the room, then followed it, prowling the parameters of his office. He couldn't scrape the burning image of Madeline from his mind, couldn't forget how she had looked as she gazed, limpid-eyed and yearning, into Weatherly's idiotic face.

She had conjured up the image. Had placed it in his psyche. It wasn't real. He was aware of that. Knew it! And yet . . . Only moments had passed between the time he had . . . they had . . . He shook his head and paced again. Only moments had passed between the time of his startling insanity and the time she cast the image of herself in another's arms.

How could that be? He was no witch. Not even a warlock, but he knew something of spells. Knew it took concentration to craft them, focus to cast them. But she had been able to implant the picture in his mind with perfect clarity. How could she have been so unaffected by his touch that she could do such a thing?

He growled something even he couldn't understand and paced again.

How the hell could he be so stupid? He couldn't kiss her! Couldn't even think about her in that manner. He knew that too. Had known it since the first moment he saw her years before. Had made it a strict rule. He lived by rules, survived by rules, but when she had touched his hand . . .

The feelings struck him again, softer now, muted. But still they felt like lightning. Like thunder crackling through his tinder-dry system. And yet she had acted as if the feelings were nothing. Had turned aside. Had had the capacity to implant the image of herself with another in his mind. Image conjuring took time. Took focus. In that moment, he himself would have been unable to do so much as muster his own name, much less create a spell that affected a man familiar with her gifts. Familiar with her scent. Her . . .

He slammed his fist into the wall and squeezed his eyes closed.

Uncertainty haunted him. Had she felt nothing? She was angry. That he knew. But so was he. How could she so callously disregard her own safety?

She was skilled. She was trained; surely she had gained a sense of the danger that lay in that direction. But maybe she didn't care. Maybe she was willing to take the risk. In which case his own caution was all the more reasonable. She was too close to this mission. Too involved. She considered Bertram Wendell a friend and she was faithful to a fault. There was not a soul at Lavender House who hadn't felt the soothing caress of her caring. When Faye's headaches became debilitating, Madeline would stroke the girl's brow, sharing the pain. When Rosamond shivered from a heavy sense of evil, Madeline would lean close, whisper encouragement, remind her that there was good amid the bad. When others mourned, Maddy cried. When they rejoiced, her laughter tickled the ear, making the very air vibrate with gladness.

No. He was right to rein her in, for she would risk too much. Forget her own vulnerability. He couldn't allow it. It was his job to prevent Les Chausettes from making foolish mistakes.

He couldn't help it if she was angry. They were often angry with him. But had her anger provoked the kiss? Had she merely meant to torment him? That's what he wished to know. As for himself, he had had no choice in the matter. Control had been out of the question. He had slammed into her as if thrust forth by a gale-force wind. But what of her?

Had she *wished* to kiss him? Had she been hopeless against the desire or had she *caused* it? Had she purposefully made him lose control?

No! He shook his head as if the question had been voiced aloud. She wasn't powerful enough to overtake his will. Not when he was aware of her gifts. Not when he was the one who had helped her hone—

But wait. What the hell was he thinking? She had implanted the image of her and Weatherby in his mind. He knew that. It was too clear, too absolutely sparklingly vivid to be nothing more than his imagination. Even now he could see her dusky nipples straining against the bastard's chest. Could all but hear her rapturous sigh as she—

He slammed his fist into the wall again and ground his teeth against the consuming frustration, and in that moment the door swung open.

He jerked toward it, rage and frustration melding like a toxic brew. Shaleena stood in the doorway, her brows raised, her generous mouth quirking.

"Is there a problem?" she asked. Her voice was husky, her eyes dark, her skin as pale as a peach against the living flame of her wayward hair.

Jasper cursed long and viciously in his head, but wasn't quite foolish enough to let the profanity escape his lips. "No. All is well." He smoothed his jacket, adjusted his cravat. He habitually wore a cravat. Would wear it to bed if doing so would make others think him more controlled. "I did not mean to disturb you."

Shaleena watched him, eerie eyes steady as she stepped into the room. "I thought I heard something fall."

He thought of the worst swearwords he could imagine and ran them around in his head like well-rested racehorses. It failed to improve his mood. "You must have been mistaken," he said, struggling to keep from ripping his hair out in handfuls.

Smiling, she closed the door behind her. "So all is well?"

"Yes." He stood very straight. He was not a tall man. Heredity perhaps. Or lack of nutrition during his formative years. Who could say? He had never met his parents. But it hardly mattered; creating one's own past was so much simpler. No messy ties to worry about. Rae would have agreed with that . . . had she been sober. Had she been thinking clearly enough to escape the gallows. But she had not. Had failed even though she was gifted. Even though she knew the tricks of street survival. Had taught them to him. Had . . . Rage surged through him, blending with emotions he would not claim. Had not claimed for years. Control. Control was everything. "All is well," he said, tone just short of steady, hands the same.

"What was the noise then?" Shaleena asked.

God help him, he despised witches. They were so irritatingly nosy. Not to mention their propensity for turning folk into nonhuman entities. Or worse still, making them crazy with desire, driving them past the point of ever-important control.

But who the hell did he think he was fooling? He'd never had trouble controlling himself with the others. The case in point standing in front of him right now. He rubbed his eyes and stifled a sigh. "Would it be too much to ask that you remain clothed?" he asked. Weary. He was bone weary. Maybe it was time he quit. Maybe it was time to turn Les Chausettes over to another.

She didn't answer. He glanced at her. The suggestion of a smile twisted her lips. Beneath the long, undulated sweep of her hair, her body was absolutely naked. "True witches prefer to be sky-clad," she said.

He refrained from groaning. Lord Gallo did not groan. "You are not *under* the sky," he reminded her.

"Would you prefer it if I went out of doors then?"

He didn't roll his eyes. Lord Gallo didn't do that either. Didn't curse or rage, or *feel*. "Do you have need of something?" he asked.

"I was wondering the same of you," she said, and stepped toward him, hips dancing.

He was actually stunned into silence by her actions.

Seduction? Really? That was what was on her mind? Good Lord, this had been one hell of a day.

"No," he said, tone steady as a rock suddenly, control back full force. "I need nothing." Lord Gallo simply didn't need things. Hadn't since Lord Moore had found him shaky and starving in the dark hell of Newgate. Hadn't since the ageless earl had seen something in him that was worth saving. Perhaps Moore had somehow realized Jasper was one of only a few who could recognize those who wielded unusual powers. One of only a handful who were unaffected by those powers. Or perhaps it was the seething control Jasper had already learned to exert, for Les Chausettes' director would need to remain coolheaded under rather unorthodox circumstances.

Jasper Reeves had been the man for the job. For if one did not touch, one was unlikely to feel. And he had made it a strict rule never to touch.

Until now.

The bright image of Madeline flared in his mind, shocking in its clarity.

"Ever?" Shaleena asked.

Jasper scowled, trying to draw himself back to the present. "What?"

"You must have needs . . . sometimes." She turned her head, tossing her hair over her shoulder.

It was generally accepted that she was an extremely attractive woman, he realized, and wondered vaguely if a yawn would be poorly accepted. "Surely you know me better than that, Shaleena," he said. Good Lord, he was tired.

She tilted her head. "I am not sure I know you at all . . . Jasper."

Jasper! The name still seemed strangely unfamiliar, for his name wasn't Jasper. Nor was it Gallo, but that was neither here nor there. He lowered himself into his chair. Looking up at her wasn't any more comfortable, but at least it was less tiring. When was the last time he'd had a full night's sleep?

"I could help you with that problem too," she offered.

He glanced up. "What problem is that?"

Sauntering toward him, she perched on the corner of his desk. The hair between her legs was as red as an autumn apple. "You are exhausted," she said.

"Reading others has never been your forte, Shaleena."

"Are you saying you are not weary?"

He was too tired to guess her exact intentions. "Yes."

She watched him. "And you are not randy."

"No." How the hell had he gotten himself into such a ridiculous conversation? "No."

She smiled, rose from his desk, and turned. Her rump was as round as a plum. Turning at the extra chair, she plopped down in it.

"Tell me the truth," she said.

He glanced up. True, he wasn't attracted to her. In fact, he found her as irritating as a damned burr, but it was still harder than hell to draw his attention all the way up to her eyes. "Very well."

"Is it men that move you?"

Had he been another man . . . a *normal* man, he might have laughed at her question. After all, just hours before he had felt as if he might very well burst into spontaneous flame at the mere *sight* of a woman. Now he was simply worn and frayed and so damned edgy he felt a little like tossing *this* woman out of the room by the hair. "No," he said.

"You can tell me the truth. I have nothing against womanly men."

God help him. "How very refreshing."

"Indeed . . ." Twisting slightly, she rested an elbow on the chair's arm and propped her chin on her knuckles. "I would not be adverse to . . . participating."

He stared at her, doing his best to keep his face impassive. "I shall surely keep that in mind should I decide to become interested in my own sex."

She laughed a little, then stared at him again. "Is it because of the newly departed?"

He stared back. "I fear I have no idea what you're talking about."

She scowled, canting her head a little and lowering her arm to her lap, where it rested against things he refused to consider. "Surely you are not hard for Madeline."

Hearing her name did something primitive to the deepest part of him. He rose to his feet, careful to keep his movements smooth despite the renewed discomfort in his breeches. "As ever, conversation with you has been . . . unusual," he said, and casually lifted a book from his desk. "But I am for bed."

"Mine or yours?"

Was there something fundamentally wrong with her? "Mine, Shaleena. Mine. As always," he said, and raising the candle, turned toward the door.

"It's not my fault, you know."

He ground his teeth now that she could not see. "Just where are you blameless?"

"I cannot help it that she harbors jealousy toward me."

"Ahh."

"She will never be as powerful as I."

Five hours ago he would have agreed with her. But after the kiss he was less certain. About almost everything.

"Or as beautiful," she added.

There he would have to disagree. But he didn't. "Go to bed, Shaleena," he said, but suddenly she was standing in front of him. Her legs were spread and her arms akimbo, showing every inch of her womanly charms.

"I know you desire me," she said.

He stifled an irritated sigh. "You are, sadly, quite mistaken."

"Do you fear me? Is that it?"

He chuckled now, actually laughed, though it was against his policy. "I would be a fool not to."

"Yes," she agreed. "You would. But I will not kill you. That is my vow."

He glanced at her askance as he shoved the book back among its mates. "I am not certain if I should thank you or—"

"When we couple," she said, "I will not kill you."

"Ahh."

"You may scream."

Holy mother of God. "Scream?"

"Many men do."

He wondered if he should be tempted to ask why. Or how many. He wasn't. "I fear I would be a disappointment to you, Shaleena. I am not the screaming sort."

"No." She was watching him as a peregrine might eye a juicy hare. "It would take a good deal."

He nodded, skirted her, and headed for the stairs. "Good night, Shaleena."

"Some other time then," she said.

"Wear clothes, Shaleena," he said, but just then he felt something strange. Something foreign. He was not gifted, but long ago he had been taught to listen. And he listened well.

Glancing behind him, he saw that Shaleena was already out of sight. Setting the candle on the balustrade, he closed his eyes and concentrated. Someone was out there. Pacing silently across the vestibule, he opened the door and stepped into the night. On his right, an unidentified being blended with the shadows of gnarled oaks and stunted topiary.

"What is it?" Jasper asked.

"I have come with a message," murmured a disembodied voice.

Jasper peered into the shadows, but there was nothing to see, no movement, no face showing pale in the moonlight. "Then leave it and be gone."

"I am to remind you to do that for which you are paid."

Jasper's gut tightened in premonition. "What do you mean?"

"They are just women. Frail, delicate . . ." The voice was almost singsong. "Not so very difficult to control."

"Who are you?" Jasper snarled.

"Keep her quiet or someone else will be forced to do so," rasped the voice.

Dread washed through Jasper like a flood as Madeline's image flashed into his mind. "You'll not touch her," he growled, and leaped toward the shrubbery, but the shadows were already empty, the raspy voice silent.

Chapter 8

Lady Tillian, baroness of Newtonshire, was an unmitigated ass, but she had also been Milly Blanchard's employer, and Madeline had so few leads. While "reading palms" a few nights past, she had felt something odd when she'd touched the hand of a man named Frederic Lambert. A spark of guilt, a flare of excitement, and a few scattered images, but she had not yet deciphered whether his jumble of emotions had anything to do with the missing girls. Thus she was here, seeking clues from the ass.

Madeline smiled across the table at her. "Sugar, my lady?"

"Oh no. I never indulge. 'Tis ever ruinful of your complexion, you know."

"How I admire your discipline," Maddy lied, and dropped two lumps into her cup.

The baroness smiled tolerantly at Madeline's obvious shortcomings. "Cinderknoll is quite lovely."

Lady Tillian glanced about. Her bonnet was the newest shade of blue, and despite Britain's troubles with Napoleon, her gown had been designed in Paris, for while men's fashion was dominated by England, France still held sway over feminine styles. And Lady Tillian was all about appearances. She held her teacup just so, pronounced each syllable with clipped precision. "But the house shows a bit of wear, does it not?"

Madeline smiled. "I imagine your lovely home is as perfectly kept as your figure," she said.

"Well . . ." The other smiled primly. She was as narrow as an icicle. "We do our best."

Maddy sipped her tea, plotting patiently. "It must take an entire troop of servants for the upkeep."

"Oh my heavens," said the other, and pursed her lips. "You've no idea. Hours are required just to keep them in line. The working class has no scruples whatsoever."

"Might there be something more I can get for you?" Joseph asked, approaching from the left. After the soiree, Madeline had surprised herself by asking him to stay on. She had been even more surprised when he had agreed. Surely a man like him had better places to be. Yet here he was. As silent as a wraith and just as mysterious. How had Daphne located him on such short notice?

Madeline gave Joseph a smile, adding a hint of

apology for her guest's rudeness. "My thanks," she said, "but everything is just—"

"The sandwiches are unacceptable," said the baroness.

Joseph shifted his gaze to her. Something shone in his eyes.

"They are stale," snapped Lady Tillian.

"A fine match for your esteemed company, then," Joseph said solemnly, and nodding, walked away.

Maddy watched him go with raised brows.

Lady Tillian huffed a response. "I would not tolerate such rude behavior in my home if I lived to be a thousand."

So she hadn't yet reached that venerable age. 'Twas good to know. "You're right, of course," Maddy said. "I shall have to have a word with him immediately upon your exodus. I'm certain your staff is much better mannered."

The baroness dropped her sandwich contemptuously onto the hand-painted crockery. "It is never easy with these people."

"Oh, I am so sorry," Madeline said, letting her eyes go round with feigned sincerity. "I had forgotten that one of your girls has disappeared."

"Milly," Lady Tillian said, tight-mouthed again. "We treated her like a guest in our home. Like a daughter. But one morning she was gone. Simply vanished."

"How awful," Maddy gasped, hand frozen in horror halfway to her mouth. What would happen if a servant went awry? One might have to pick up her own hairbrush. Or . . . She stifled her uncharitable thoughts and scurried back on track. "Whatever do you think might have happened to her?"

"I don't have to think," said the baroness. "I know."

How lucky for her. Maddy remained still, barely breathing, hoping the other's company was worth the information she was about to receive.

"She is bearing the consequences of her decisions."

"The consequences?"

"She was a . . ." Lady Tillian paused, pursed her skinny lips. "She thought herself quite comely. Indeed, some men seemed to agree, but you know how men are."

Actually, she wasn't at all certain she did.

"Are you saying she was . . . promiscuous?"

Lady Tillian gave her a look. "I am saying she was carrying her penance in her womb."

"Was she seeing someone specific?"

"I can assure you I don't listen to the gossip."

"I'm sure you're wise, my lady," Maddy said, "but does it not seem that if she were with child she would return to you? Certainly she would need funds more than ever."

"Perhaps she went to be rid of the thing."

Maddy stifled a scowl. "Surely not."

"I wouldn't be a bit surprised."

"Did she give any indication that she was about to leave? That is to say, she must have had plans. A girl doesn't simply—"

"Why such interest?" Lady Tillian asked, eyes narrowed irritably.

Madeline's mind churned. "It is simply that Lady Linn has been so kind to lend me her estate. And I worry so. How horrid I should feel if something untoward happened to her staff." Although Daphne and Joseph seemed more than capable of caring for themselves and the others.

The baroness sniffled and sipped her tea. "They are an unpredictable lot."

"So Milly was known to be flighty?"

Lady Tillian set her cup primly onto its fragile saucer. "No more than most."

"She didn't steal anything, I hope."

"Not that we've noticed thus far. But we are still looking into the matter."

"She took all her own possessions though, I assume."

"In truth, she did not," Lady Tillian said. "That is how I realized she was in the family way. She left without her clothing."

Maddy waited for some semblance of sense.

"Do you not see? The chit must have realized she would soon be too big-bellied to wear her own garments and thus left them behind."

Madeline refrained from gaping at that leap in logic and kept her tone steady. "But if, as you suggest, she planned to be rid of the child, surely she would want her clothes."

The baroness scowled as if thinking against her will, then gave a dismissive flip of her bony hand. "Honestly, Lady Redcomb, I cannot guess what goes through an underling's head. And truly, I find it a waste of my time to try."

"Of course," Maddy said. "A busy lady such as yourself." There were probably a score of servants to abuse.

"I treated her exceptionally well," Lady Tillian said, as if reading Maddy's thoughts.

"And she had no trouble with anyone else in the household?"

"Why ever would she?" She looked offended.

"You know how servants are," Maddy said, certain none was in the area to take offense. "Sometimes they squabble."

Lady Tillian snorted again, a ladylike puff of air. "You certainly don't need to tell me."

"Did she have trouble with the others then?"

Her face pinched. "Lord Tillian would never have stood for any of our people bothering her."

Maddy glanced innocently over the tilted edge of her teacup. "How kind of your husband to protect her."

Did she stiffen the slightest degree? "He is a godly man. Always looking after the young maids." The words were flat and cold. Tension here. Jealousy.

So old man Tillian had been interested in the girl for himself. What did that mean? Had he propositioned her? Had he scared her off? Or was it something more sinister?

"Was there anyone in particular from whom your good husband felt the need to protect her?" Maddy asked.

The baroness puffed again. "There were several young bucks making fools of themselves over her just the week prior. They were from quite good families, too."

Madeline felt her heartbeat escalate. "And this happened the week before her disappearance?"

"My husband insisted on having a party. I told him hazard is the devil's game."

Chapter 9

"Lady Redcomb." Lord Moore was still a handsome man though his hair had gone gray, his face craggy many years past. "I hear you are currently residing at Cinderknoll."

"Yes." Madeline smiled and reluctantly focused on the earl. She knew little of him, but he had always seemed a decent enough sort. Still, she had not come to socialize but to learn what she could of Tipper's disappearance, for it was said that the actress had a friend in the household, a parlor maid who was as plain as Tipper was lovely. But thus far she had seen none to match that description. "Lady Linn was kind enough to allow me to live there while she remains in Hungary."

"Well . . ." For the briefest moment Moore's gaze lit on her bosom, but she could hardly resent his attention. Her breasts were, after all, artfully displayed above her frilly décolletage, and there hardly seemed a reason to expose them if she had no wish for others to notice? And she did, for it was only to her advantage if men were put off their guard. She had not come to Byresdale to flirt, after all. "Who would not want a such a lovely young woman living in his home?" he asked.

"Why sir, you flatter me," Maddy said, and wished she had brought a fan. But she had none to match the beaded reticule she carried. And God knew it would be an unforgivable faux pas to have your accessories clash. Amid the *ton* it was tantamount to high treason. She might well be hanged.

"My lord, my lady." A quiet voice spoke diffidently from her left. "Might I interest you in a raisin tart?"

Maddy turned. A maid, plump and sallow-skinned, stood nearby with a tray propped upon her palm.

Moore glanced down, expression just short of dismissive. "Not just now."

"Lord Moore," called a flushed gentleman who hurried through the crowd toward them.

"If you'll excuse me," Moore said, and bowing, sauntered away.

Madeline smiled at the servant and reached for a tart. "They look quite delectable."

"Cook is a master."

Madeline took a bite and pretended to savor it, though raisins had never been her weakness.

The serving girl turned away, but Maddy spoke. "I believe we may have met before."

"What's that, my lady?" asked the maid, swiveling back, hand steady beneath her tray.

"Where was it? Somewhere out of the ordinary. The racetrack or . . . No. The theater," Maddy said, and smiled. "I never forget a face."

"How nice for you, my lady, but—"

"I believe it was Drury Lane." She was guessing wildly, hoping this was Tipper's friend. "Just after nine." The price dropped to a single shilling halfway through the night, making the latter part of the performances more accessible to the masses. "I saw *King Lear* there. It was quite good."

The girl looked uncertain. "I do enjoy a show now and again."

"Terrible about the actress who disappeared, though. What was her name? Topper? Tapper?"

The shadow of a frown appeared between the girl's pale brows. "Tipper."

"Tipper, that was it. What do you suppose happened to her?"

"I wouldn't know, my lady."

" 'Tis rumored she was with child and decided to disappear for a time," Maddy said, borrowing a page from Lady Tillian's unscrupulous book.

For a moment Madeline thought the girl would say nothing, but finally she spoke. "She wasn't expecting no child."

Madeline practiced her surprised expression. "You knew her?"

"Since we was girls together, a stone's toss from the Crown and Thistle."

"Tell me then," Madeline said, opening her eyes wide, "was she having some lurid romance? Perhaps with that good-looking gentleman who played Aladdin. I thought him extremely talented and quite—"

"Tipper wouldn't have no truck with Gregor Keets. He's got himself a wife and a half a dozen young ones."

"Who then?"

The girl shook her head, lips pursed. "Tipper ain't like that."

"Oh come now, you know these theater types," Madeline said. "She probably took a shine to one of the stagehands and headed for Gretna Green before—"

"Tipper was serious about the stage. And she was my friend. She didn't run off with no married man. Or no single man neither, come to that.

"Now, if you'll excuse me, me *lady*, I have things what need doing," she said, and shifting her gaze past Maddy's shoulder, stalked away.

Madeline turned with a scowl, only to find Jasper watching her from inches away.

She raised her chin, startled and embarrassed, and determined to hide both feelings. "Did you tell her not to speak to me?" she asked.

His eyes were deadly steady, slightly curious. "I've not known you to be paranoid in the past."

She sighed, realizing she had taken the wrong tack and fumbled an opportunity. "If only that were true," she said.

He watched her for an instant, seeming to remember back. "Except with perfumers," he corrected, and his eyes smiled.

She was momentarily caught in his gaze, in his memory. But she could hardly blame herself. They had shared much together. The good, the bad. The ridiculous.

She had not ordered a scent from La Fief and Son since that horrible day. Indeed, she had not stepped foot into their Haymarket shop. Though they probably wouldn't have allowed it if she had tried. "It was supposed to be my own personal scent," she said, still chafing after all these years.

His expression rarely changed, but there was something about his eyes that could speak volumes if he wished them to. Just now, they spoke of humor, carefully hidden, but sharp and dry just the same. "And you didn't think your personal scent should be that of sardines?"

She laughed despite her frustration and glanced at the milling guests. "I simply didn't believe I should have to pay to smell like a fish."

"I am certain you were correct. It was quite rude of them to threaten to kill you."

She gave him a look. There were few people who knew her as well as he. None who prompted such jagged feelings. "You'd be surprised how much *bill* sounds like *kill* when you're mad."

"Mad as in angry? Or mad like insane?"

"Are you saying I was insane?"

"Only momentarily."

She opened her mouth to retaliate, but he spoke again.

"On the other hand, you rarely smell like fish."

Across the room, Lord Moore was speaking to a woman with extremely large breasts. They were displayed openly and generously above a powder-blue bodice. "That may be the nicest thing you've ever said to me."

"Surely I've told you how beautiful you are," Jasper said.

"What?" she asked, and snapped her gaze to him.

He almost looked startled. If she hadn't known better, she would have actually thought he jumped, though his expression was still bland.

They stared at each other in stunned silence. She hoped to God she wasn't holding her breath.

"What did you say?" she asked.

"The way you relate to the other Chausettes," he said. "It's quite brilliant."

"The other Chausettes?" Her heart felt a little heavy. But what did she expect? He was her employer. She was . . . She didn't know what the devil she was to him.

"They miss you."

"And I them."

"Then come back," he said. His tone sounded strange. Rusty and strained. She searched his eyes. Was there hope there? Was there emotion?

"Why?" she murmured.

"Because I need . . ." he began, then paused. "I need to know you are safe," he said. "It's my job."

"Well then you can rest easy," she said. "For I am perfectly safe. Indeed—"

"You cannot do this alone."

Frustration mixed with disappointment and settled somewhere in her churning gut. "What exactly is it that I can't do?" she asked. "Survive without your assistance? Or do you think I cannot even think—"

"You can't save them," he said.

"I believe you're wrong. I believe I will find them before it's too—"

"Then you're naïve!" he said, tone clipped.

Madeline raised her brows and laughed. Jasper Reeves hated to be laughed at. Perhaps she knew little of the man she had worked with, had *lived* with, for eight years. But that much she knew. "Are you truly calling me naïve, Jasper?"

He drew a careful breath through his nose. Was it to calm his emotions? Were there any to calm? Oh yes, he had lost control just two days past, but that was *her* doing. He'd had little choice in the matter, for somehow she'd found a way to slide a simple spell past his defenses. She wasn't certain how she had managed it, but she had a sneaking suspicion it was somehow attached to the sense of touch. True, she had been able to slip a shadowy image into his mind even before she had brushed his palm, but that was a small thing and done before he understood how her powers had grown. Once her skin had touched his, his defenses had crumbled like an ancient wall. Humans, it seemed, were not meant to deny themselves physical contact for as long as he had. Were not meant to keep themselves so aloof, so elevated. Still, she should not have done what she had simply to see him react. Especially since she herself had acted so hideously undisciplined. The memory was embarrassing . . . and disturbingly stimulating.

"I've no desire to fight with you, Lady Redcomb," he said.

"Fight!" She laughed again, the tone almost pitch-perfect as she pushed the memories from her mind. Damned if he hadn't deserved to lose his precious control. "You don't care enough to fight for anything," she said, and turned away, but he grabbed her arm.

Fire shot from her wrist to her head, bearing a flaming image of them, together, naked, sweaty, moaning.

She caught her breath and snapped her gaze to his.

But his expression was ever impassive. Nevertheless, he released her arm.

She backed away a step, ready to flee.

"I wish to speak to you," he said. His voice was rock solid, but were his pupils dilated? Were his nostrils slightly flared? Had he glimpsed the image too? Had he seen them together? Might he have caused the image? He was a powerful man. That she knew, but if the truth be told, she had no way of knowing what his gifts were exactly. He controlled Les Chausettes' circumstances through careful planning and clever maneuvering, never displaying overt powers. And certainly he never spoke of his abilities. Indeed, he barely spoke at all. She and Ella had been warned early on not to challenge him, and now, with these glaring images storming through her mind, she wished like hell that she had not.

"But I've no desire to speak to you," she said. The words sounded childish. She was well aware of the fact, but she failed to care. She felt broken, exposed, strangely vulnerable. *He*, on the other hand, looked entirely unmoved, while her breathing felt harsh and raspy. Her heart beat heavily in her chest. Her hands felt shaky. And she knew better. Had been taught better. Indeed, *he* had been the one to teach her.

"Lady Redcomb."

Madeline turned woodenly at the sound of a woman's voice. Merry May stood to her left.

"Is everything quite well?" Miss Anglican, better known to the *ton* as Merry May, was the belle of every ball. Had she wished, she could have any man in the room. But she had chosen Lord Gershwin. Not to wed. But perhaps to torment. "You look a bit flushed."

"Oh." Madeline refrained from touching her hand to her cheek, but the lurid image of herself in Jasper's arms was still there, as sharp as a needle in her mind. "No. I am well. It is simply a bit close in here."

"Some men make it seem so." May flitted her gaze to Jasper and away. "You're quite sure all is well?"

"Yes, certainly," Madeline said. "But 'tis kind of you to concern yourself."

"Very well then. Carry on with . . ." She eyed them curiously. "Whatever it is you were doing," she said, and floated away.

Their immediate area fell silent. Voices murmured in the background.

"It is unlike you to cause a scene," Jasper said.

She turned toward him in surprise. Had he seen the image? Did he think she had caused it? Or was he simply playing with her mind? God knew he was not above such a thing. "Has anyone ever told you that you're something of an ass?" she asked.

For the briefest moment, something shone in his eyes. It almost looked like humor but it was gone long before she could identify the emotion. If, indeed, he were capable of such a thing.

"Neither is it like you to act childish," he added.

"Childish!" Anger ripped through her like a windstorm. "Three maids have gone missing and you think—"

"Lady Redcomb," someone interrupted. She turned, bent on her anger, but Mr. Pendent continued, nonplussed, spurred on by copious amounts of gin and possible stupidity. "I fear I have misplaced my father's best watch, and it has cut up my peace no small whit. Might you be able to help me?"

She tightened her fist, forced a prim smile. "I would like to, sir. Truly I would. But I fear my powers are nothing more than parlor tricks." Still, she couldn't quite keep the muted image of his father's watch from her mind. It lay nestled against coarse-grained wood, half hidden in the shadows from above. "Your best bet is to check your pockets and pray for divine intervention."

He looked dismayed. A little unsteady. "But I have checked my pockets already."

"And have you spent time in church?"

"Yes, I . . ." he began, but suddenly his eyes widened. "Come to that, I do believe I had it not two Sundays past. I was a trifle disguised, you know, after sampling Lord Denton's mulberry wine. And when I knelt for the sacrament I thought I heard something fall from . . ." He smiled broadly, grabbed her hand. "Thank you, my lady. Thank you." He hurried off. Maddy watched him go.

"So tell me, my lady . . ." Jasper's tone was hard and dry. "Do you truly think these parlor tricks, as you call them, are worth getting yourself killed?"

She turned toward him with a start, heart slowing dramatically in her chest. "Are you threatening me?"

His lean jaw tightened the slightest degree, but in a moment he had that flagrant display of emotion under control. "I see you are also prone to jump to ridiculous conclusions since leaving—"

"Lady Redcomb?" asked a gentleman just arrived at Maddy's elbow. "Might I have this dance?"

"No!" Jasper snapped.

Shocked, Madeline yanked her attention from the newcomer to Jasper with a start.

Jasper remained motionless for one spare second, back ramrod straight, one gloved hand behind his back, but then he nodded. "My apologies, Mr. Grenville," he said. "But the lady has promised this dance to me."

"Oh, very well then." Grenville smiled. "Some other time."

"Certainly," Maddy said, and watched him shuffle through the crowd. "I've no wish to dance with you," she said, but Reeves was already reaching for her hand.

"Childishness does not become you," he chided.

She stared at him for one hard second, then steeling herself, placed her hand in his. She felt stiff and cold, but heat permeated from his fingers, and with it came desire. Not the roaring tide of yearning she had felt earlier, but a warm glimmer of sensuality that shimmered through her system like wine as he led her onto the dance floor.

"What do you want?" she asked. Her voice was as cool as river water. He should be proud, but he didn't answer immediately. Instead, he turned toward her, resting his hand on her waist. His touch was respectable, careful even. But in her mind, his fingers slipped lower, skimming her naked skin with reverent, breathtaking slowness.

She steadied her hands, raised her chin. "What is it you want, Lord Gallo?"

"What do I—" His jaw hardened again. His nostrils flared. "I want you to . . ." He paused. His fingers tightened the slightest degree on her waist.

And in the shadowy images of her mind, she arched against the ecstasy of his palm on her hip.

He dropped his lids a fraction of an inch and watched her. "I wish for you to cease your meddling," he said, but in another world, his breath was nothing but a sigh against her skin. His hand slipped around the curve of her buttock, skimming down the long, sloped crease there.

"Meddling!" She tried to control her breathing, her thoughts, her ridiculous imagination. What the hell was wrong with her? "Is that what you call trying to save lives these days?"

He turned her in a sweeping circle. Her gown flared behind them like a comet's fiery tail. His leg brushed hers.

Her shadowy image closed her eyes and slid her knee up his thigh. His legs were as solid as stone. His hand behind her knee was strong, sure, as hot as a black witch's potion.

"I call it . . ." He gritted his teeth for an instant. ". . . foolishness."

"Foolishness!" In the candlelit shadows of her mind, he pulled her closer. His thigh nestled between hers, planted against her core. She moaned at the contact, wanting more. *Needing* more.

Jasper scowled, still dancing as he watched her face.

Good God! Had she made the noise aloud? She clamped her jaw and raised her chin, challenging him to call her out. He couldn't see into her mind. He couldn't read her lurid thoughts. She was sure of it. But in her imagination, he touched her with velvet softness between her legs and she moved into him, seeking warmth, seeking him.

"I am not your puppet," she rasped.

Between them, in the shadow-filled room of her thoughts, his arousal reached for her. She arched against it, ready. Hell, eager.

"What the devil are you talking about?" he rasped.

"You."

His dark alter image kissed her neck.

She closed her eyes at the lush, sultry feel of his lips, but forced them open again with a snap. "I do not jump every time you tug a string."

"When have I ever asked you to jump?"

"Ask? You don't need to ask. The great Lord Gallo demands. Insists." In the darkness, his hands were becoming bolder. He jerked her closer and she welcomed the contact. Their gazes met and clashed. It was time.

"And I suppose you meekly follow?" Was his breathing escalated? Did his hand tremble?

No. He felt nothing. But in the darkened image of them she growled her intentions, tangled her fingers in his hair, took his cock in her hand and thrust him inside her already contracting core.

Ecstasy swamped her. Heaven . . .

"Maddy!"

Ella's hissed voice snapped Madeline back to real time. She jerked her gaze sideways. Her sister was standing inches away. Behind her, Sir Drake stared in speechless astonishment.

Madeline's breathing was harsh. Her heart was humping in her chest. Her lips felt burned.

"Release her!" Ella ordered, and Jasper jerked his hand away.

Maddy's head reeled. Had he been squeezing her bottom? Had they kissed?

"For God's sake, Maddy," Ella hissed. "Let him go."

"What?" She felt disoriented, lost.

Sir Drake cleared his throat, moved closer, blocking them from view. "Mayhap it would be best if ye took yer fingers out of Lord Gallo's hair now, lass," he rumbled.

"What . . ." she began again, then realized her

fingers were indeed tangled in Reeves's hair. And was her other hand gripping his lapel? She let her hands fall to her side.

"There's a lass," Drake said, and took her elbow in a careful clasp, as if she might break under his hand. "How aboot a bit of air now?" he asked, and drew her carefully toward the door.

"Jasper?" she murmured, glancing back, but Drake drew her steadily away.

"I'm thinking yer wee sister will be wanting a word with him," Drake said, and tugged her toward the balcony.

Jasper watched Madeline disappear from sight, body vibrating with desire, with need.

"Reeves!" Ella hissed, and he turned toward the sister, feeling like a hunted hare.

"Yes, my lady?"

"What the devil are you thinking?"

Thinking! Thinking? Good God, he hadn't been thinking. At least that much seemed clear. "Whatever do you mean, my lady?"

She glared at him, eyes burning, "She's your ward. And my sister!" she hissed.

He straightened his elegant jacket with regal aplomb and wished to hell he had been gifted with some means of disappearing into the woodwork. If given half a chance, he would gladly become part of the dance floor.

"Not some . . ." She waved a restive hand, seeming unaware of the couples who twirled some yards away. "Not some demirep who you can—" But her words stopped abruptly. Her brows rose. Her back straightened. "So that's why she's been acting so strangely." She breathed a rasp of surprise and cocked her head at him as if astounded. "She's in—" she began, but stopped herself again.

Jasper stared at her, wondering rather vaguely when he had quit breathing. "Where? Where is she exactly?" he asked.

But Ella leaned close, green eyes snapping with humor or fury or some other emotion he failed to comprehend but assumed might well be deadly. Still, he could not quite stop himself from speaking again, though he knew, *knew*, it was foolish.

"Tell me true," he murmured, the words slipping hopelessly from his lips. "Do you think she might care? Just a bit."

"Oh she cares," Ella said, and despite everything, Jasper felt his heart stop dead in his chest, waiting, hoping. "She cares about Faye and Beatrice and Rosamond. She cares about every lost soul who ever crossed her path. She cares too much. Too often. Too fiercely." Her teeth were gritted, her fists clenched. "And I swear by the stars, if you allow her to be hurt you will rue the day you were born."

She turned then and strode away, leaving him to do nothing but stare after, his mind murmuring one pathetic question.

But what about me? Might she care about me?

Chapter 10

"My lady." Joseph appeared in the door-way of Cinderknoll's parlor.

Madeline straightened, momentarily ignoring the missive she had been writing. Beside her nattily clad elbow, her tea cooled in its bone china cup, delicately painted with ivy and jasmine.

"Yes, Joseph." She glanced up, perfectly cool. Perfectly coifed. She was no fool. After last night's ridiculous debacle she was not about to let a chink show in her armor. Holy God. What was wrong with her? Ella had acted as if she was out of her mind. And maybe she was. Indeed, her sister had insisted on escorting her home. And perhaps that was just as well. Because even after she'd left Byresdale, and Jasper was well out of sight, the images still played havoc with reality. She still felt wet. She still felt vulnerable. She still felt stupid.

And she would never let it happen again.

"You have a caller, my lady."

"A caller?" She smiled a little, though she didn't want a caller. She wanted to be left alone. In fact, she rather fancied the idea of hiding under her bed and never coming out. She lifted her teacup, pinky carefully extended.

"Yes, my lady." Joseph, it appeared, had no intention of being forthcoming with any other information.

"And who might this early morning caller be?" she asked, and took a sip of tea. Chamomile. To calm her nerves. Maybe she should ask Ella for one of her "potions," she thought. Something to ward off fantasies. Or stupidity.

"Lord Gallo, my lady," Joseph said, and bowed.

For one hopeful second Maddy almost controlled the frantic spasm that ran through her body from stem to stern, but then she jerked, and suddenly her teacup went flying from her hand, spinning across the room like a cricket ball gone mad.

Joseph watched it soar through the room before landing like a wounded dove, tea splattering in every direction. He turned impassively back, hands linked behind him. "He is accompanied by . . ." He paused as if thinking how best to phrase his words. ". . . a young lady."

"A young lady?" She kept her tone level, her face impassive, but to herself she snarled a curse as the cup spun wildly near the sculpted leg of the spinet. "What young lady?"

"In truth, I am not quite certain I understood her name correctly."

She forced a genteel smile. "What do you think it might have been?"

"Miss . . . Shaleena perhaps."

"Shaleena!" Madeline popped to her feet. The teapot clattered dangerously on the desk. "Shaleena's here? With . . ." She took a breath, calmed her nerves, wished like hell she had not sent Ella away. Her sister had offered to stay. But there had seemed little purpose. The danger was past, after all. She was quite sure she could control any unwarranted flights of fancy from here on in. But suddenly the image of Shaleena with Jasper struck her mind like a blow. It wasn't magical. It wasn't sharp or clear or so precise she could feel every breath, every thought; could see every shift of mood in his mesmerizing eyes. But it still made her madder than hell.

She cleared her throat, smoothed her skirt. "To tell you truly, Joseph, I am feeling a bit unwell." And shaky. Good God, her hands were shaking like wind chimes. "Might you ask them to come another time?"

"Certainly my lady. But . . ." He paused, considered, then bowed. "Certainly," he said again and turned away.

She closed her eyes and stopped him. "But what?"

He turned smoothly back, his dark face troubled. "Lord Gallo declared it to be a matter of some consequence."

In her mind she saw them together. His hands were like summer magic against her skin. They were standing very close, her cheek pressed against his chest, against his heart.

But wait a moment . . . Jasper Reeves had no heart.

"Might he have said what it was regarding?" she asked.

"No, my lady, but I shall surely ask if that is your wish."

A sensation of Jasper thrusting inside her shattered her calm. She arched against him, taking him in to the hilt, moaning against the impact. The sound almost reached her lips, but not quite. "No!" She cleared her throat again. "No. Thank you, Joseph. I shall receive them in the drawing room." Where there wasn't tea spattered across the rug as if she were a child who could not control her rawest impulses.

She paced to the drawing room, heels clicking against the hardwood. The room was decorated in pastels. The Greek influence was strong here. She took a seat on a winged upholstered chair. A scalloped settee stood in the corner. In her mind, she saw Jasper there, arms thrown across the top, shirt undone. His chest was bare and broad, smooth with muscle, dark with Spanish heritage. His hands were strong, long-fingered, his smile entrancing, inviting, and between his legs . . .

Madeline slammed her thoughts to a halt, clasped her hands, and closed her eyes, remembering her training. Good God, she had learned scores of ways to best an enemy, hundreds of ways to control her own emotions. She drew a slow breath, then exhaled steadily. She was a blade, strong and sharp. Nothing could best her. Pain did not affect her. She was—

Footfalls echoed in the hall. Her eyes snapped open. She stared at the settee. It was empty, but in that moment she heard him enter the room, gritted her teeth momentarily, then stood with well-versed grace.

"Lord Gallo, what an unexpected . . ." She stood very straight, searching for the proper phrase. ". . . pleasure." At the word, a tingle of anticipation sizzled through her. She stifled a shiver, but he didn't seem to notice.

Instead, he bowed with courtly grace. He wore the costume of the *ton* with easy panache. His coat was perfectly tailored, his cravat snowy white and precisely tied, his hair recently brushed and lying in glossy, well-groomed waves. Jasper Reeves, forever unmoved. "Lady Redcomb," he said, and turning smoothly, closed the door behind him.

Her heart jerked erratically in her chest. She raised one carefully groomed brow at his attempt at privacy. Where the devil was Shaleena? "Please, sit," she said, and motioned elegantly toward the far end of the room. He delayed a moment, then moved toward the settee.

An image flashed in her mind. Tousled hair; dark, Spanish skin; long, smooth muscles, flexing as he—

"Not there!" she rasped.

He turned, almost-surprise showing on his face.

She cleared her throat and told herself he was probably a dreadful lover, his chest flat, his skin pasty. Hell, he probably wasn't even Spanish. What did she know of this man, really? "My apologies," she said, and clasped her hands. "My parlor maid only just cleaned the settee. I fear it might yet be a bit damp. Please . . ." She pried her hands apart and motioned toward a nearby chair.

He moved toward it. An image immediately sprang to her mind. She was facing the chair's back, hands on the cushion. He was behind her. Between them her gown was rucked up and . . .

Jasper murmured something, making her thoughts clatter to a halt.

"What was that, my lord?"

He turned toward her, expression all but bored. "I said nothing."

"I thought I heard you curse."

He raised one brow. "I do not curse."

She stared at him, but if there were clues to be found in his eyes, she did not see them. "Of course."

"It was kind of you to grant me an audience on such short notice," he said.

She shut the images away, concentrated on his face, impassive, unemotional. He felt nothing. She was sure of it. Indeed, as far as she could tell, he was incapable of feeling.

"Would you like a bit of tea?" Bare skin flashed in her mind but she covered it up, replaced it with the uninspired image of a teapot.

For a moment he gritted his teeth, but then he nodded. "Tea would be much appreciated."

Excellent. Tea was safe, the pots round and heavy, topped by a long, hard spout that reached up to spew out hot liquid. Delicious and—

"Dear God!" she rasped.

"What?"

"What!" Her hands were shaking, her heart beating overtime.

They stared at each other in the deafening silence.

"I thought you said something." His voice sounded strange, breathless maybe.

"No, I . . ." She cleared her throat. "I did not."

He scowled, took a step closer, then stopped. "Are you feeling quite well?"

"Yes. Of course." If *well* meant she was possessed by some inexplicable need to see him naked, to touch him, to feel him explode inside her while she— She cleared her throat and wished to God she could do the same with her mind. "Why wouldn't I be?"

He said nothing. They stared at each other. Seconds ticked away like hours until she jerked her gaze away.

"Joseph," she called, and yanked open the double doors.

He was there in an instant, bowing from the entrance, eyes intense. "Yes, my lady."

She touched his arm for support. He was human, real, with emotions and everything. Beneath his jacket, his arm felt as tight and strong as a pugilist's. If she could have gathered her thoughts . . . if she could have thought at *all*, she would have wondered about him. Who was he? Where had he come from? "Might you fetch us some—" she began, but suddenly Shaleena appeared. Something inside Maddy seemed to snarl, but the other failed to notice. She sauntered into the doorway, red hair flaming, violet eyes glowing.

Joseph turned toward the interloper. "Madam," he said, "if you would be so kind as to wait in the salon I shall see to your refreshments in a—"

"How are you faring, Maddy?" Shaleena asked. Her lips curled up like a red velvet bow.

Madeline hushed a snarled curse. "It is good to see you again, Lady Onyx."

"Is it?"

Madeline refrained from spitting. Neither did she narrow her eyes or cast the simplest of spells. "You look well."

Shaleena smiled. "I do, don't I?"

"Clothing suits you," Maddy said.

"Shaleena!" Jasper snapped, stepping into the gathering storm. "I'm sorry to keep you waiting, but—"

"As you well should be."

"But I need a moment with Lady Redcomb."

Shaleena shifted her gaze from Maddy to Jasper. "Perhaps I should remain."

"I will be out in a moment," he said, and stepping back, crowded Madeline inside the drawing room with him and closed the doors behind him, shutting the other two on the far side.

Maddy heard the doorknob rattle, then stop abruptly when Joseph spoke.

"If you'll retire to the salon I am certain they will be finished soon."

"And I am just as certain they're done now," Shaleena retorted.

"I fear you may be mistaken, madam," Joseph rumbled.

"You *should* fear, you overgrown—" Shaleena hissed but her words were fading as her unwilling footsteps echoed in the distance.

"Where did you find the watchdog?" Jasper asked.

Madeline turned toward him, stunned both by this odd turn of events and by Joseph's bravery in the line of fire. She could count the men on one hand who had been bold enough to face Shaleena's anger.

"The watchdog," he repeated. "Was he roaming the streets or is he pedigreed?"

She blinked. The voices on the other side of the door were hushed and hissing.

"Tell me, Jasper, has Shaleena become so problematic that you must spend every moment with her?"

"She has a mission," he said. "I thought it best to accompany her for a time. Two birds, as it were."

"Indeed?"

"Someone has to pull up the slack left in your wake."

Guilt swamped her. She drained it away as best she could. A decanter of sherry stood on a sideboard near the wall. It was ten o'clock in the morning. Far too early to drink. She poured a glass anyway. The liquid looked rich and bright and lovely. She took a sip.

"Did her mission involve squabbling with my manservant?" she asked.

"Is that what he is?"

Madeline glanced at him. Was there an odd note in his tone? "I realize he looks more like a warrior of old," she said, and smiled. "A brave knight set against the world, determined to defend the damsels of yore. But . . ." She sighed dramatically. "In actuality, he is really quite . . . refined."

"Is he?" Jasper said, and now he sounded his old self, maddeningly confident.

"Mmm." She took another sip.

"I am happy to hear it." He sounded bored now. The tone made her rather want to tear his hair out by the roots. She had left him, dammit! Had left Les Chausettes. Why couldn't he care?

"And very . . ." She felt crazed, slammed down the drink, closed her eyes a moment, and turned back toward him. "Manly."

Something ticked in his jaw. But he raised his hand to his mouth as if hiding a yawn. "How nice for him."

"Isn't it?" she asked, and poured herself another drink.

"I don't believe there is any need for bitterness," he said.

Voices flared from the distant hallway and dimmed.

"Why did you bring—" she began, and stopped herself by sheerest will. "Why have you come, Jasper?"

His jaw tightened the slightest degree again, almost as if in irritation. Almost as if he had been sidetracked from his purpose. "There is something I have been meaning to discuss with you for some time."

"Of course there is," she said, and lifted the decanter. "Would you like a drink?"

"I do not drink. As you well know."

"Yes, I do," she said, and drank again.

His brows had lowered a fraction of an inch. "It's not like you to be so glib."

"What do you know of me, Jasper?"

"I know—" he began, voice momentarily sharp, but he stopped himself. "You must leave the country."

She sputtered on her sherry, then laughed, surprised. "I beg your pardon."

He glanced toward the door, irritation showing on his face for the briefest second. "It is time for you to leave Britain."

"What?" Her heart was wild in her chest. She could not leave England. This was her home, where she had found safety. Where she had found peace, learned to accept her powers. Learned to accept *herself*. Oh yes, Jasper had had a hand in that. But others had as well. Lady Beauton, as old as the river and no longer at Lavender House, had taught her how to look into others' minds. Francine had given her a glimpse of how to judge whether another spoke the truth. Even Shaleena had been helpful in some ways, but there was so much more to learn. So much more to teach. She could not leave them; anywhere else she would be naught but an oddity. A freak. "Have you gone mad?" she asked, heart tight in her chest.

He watched her in silence for a moment. "You know I am far too sensible to do something so dramatic."

"Why the devil would I leave England?"

"It is my job to keep you safe," he said. "I cannot do so if you are not safely ensconced in Lavender House."

"Safe. From what?"

"Surely you are not so naïve as to think there is no danger. You have been in the employ of the British government for some years. You think you have not made enemies?"

"I can keep myself safe," she said, and sent him a

shadowy image of herself with immobile bodies at her feet. Her eyes were glowing, her hands fisted.

He stiffened almost imperceptibly. "Your powers have increased," he said. "That I admit." He seemed to be looking back, remembering. "Perhaps you are stronger than I realized." He said the words with some regret. "But I fear you overestimate your talents."

Did he not see the image she had sent? Did he not know the power it took to project that? "And I think you underestimate them," she said. Anger was sifting through her, but she dared not let it overshadow her good sense. That she had learned from Jasper himself. "Indeed . . ." She drank again. "I believe you always have. When in truth I—" She stopped suddenly as an errant flash of bright imagery burned in her mind. She was naked, perched upon Cinderknoll's arbor while Jasper . . . Dear God, would that even be possible? she wondered.

"You are gifted," Jasper said. "You have always been, but you are not strong enough to stand alone."

"You're wrong."

"And you have no idea of the dangers that lay in wait for a woman unprotected," he snapped.

She scowled. The room went quiet. "Are you threatening me?"

"I'm warning—" He stopped. A muscle jumped restlessly in his jaw before he found his irritating calm. "You are not invincible." His face was expressionless, as if carefully chiseled from stone. "If left unchecked even Shaleena might yet be able to best you."

"Shaleena couldn't—" Maddy growled, but a sudden idea stilled her anger. "Is that why you brought her?" she asked. "So that you might remain safe from me?"

He kept his gaze steady on her. There was the barest hint of surprise in his face, as if he was shocked to learn she might believe such rubbish. "As you know, your powers have no effect on me," he said finally, but even as he spoke he glanced through the window at the arbor. The slightest tremor seemed to shake him.

And never, *never* had she felt more satisfied. Finishing her second sherry, she set the glass on the sideboard, then sauntered over to take a seat on the settee, framing the arbor perfectly in the window behind her.

"Very well, Jasper," she said, removing the short spencer that covered her bodice and carefully setting it aside. "I have no power over you. Now . . ." She watched him swallow. "Why, may I ask, do you think I should do something so foolish as to leave my homeland?" Lifting her arms, she stretched them across the back of the settee.

Jasper looked as stiff as a corpse. "Must I remind you that this is not your homeland, my lady?"

She raised her brows. "I realize that, Jasper, but I also realize you warned me never to speak of that. You said, if I remember correctly, that I was to forget I had ever stepped foot on French soil, to act as if my past had never been."

Irritation showed on his face for the briefest moment.

"The committee knows of your parlor games," he said, voice unusually rapid.

"What's that?" she asked, and lifting her skirt a bit, crossed one leg casually over the other.

His gaze remained on her face, but his jaw looked set. "The committee," he said. "I fear your adolescent pranks have come to their attention. They sent an . . ." His jaw hardened again but only for an instant. ". . . an emissary to Lavender House."

She considered that for a moment, then shrugged. "If they would like a reading, I am certain I can fit them into my schedule."

"This is not a jest."

"No." She rose to her feet, stretched, and glided toward the door. "I am sure it is not. For you do not jest. Therefore, I must thank you for the news. Now if you'll excuse me, Joseph was about to—"

He turned with her. "They believe you may compromise national security."

"What?" She was momentarily snapped out of her act.

"You're a government servant, woman. With years of training. Years of accumulated information. Are you so daft as to believe they won't complain if you begin foolishly suggesting you possess unnatural powers?"

"I'm not *suggesting* I have powers, Jasper. I *do* have powers."

"You think I don't know that?" he asked, and jerked his attention back to the arbor. "You think I don't spend every waking—" He stopped himself, gritted his teeth. "You are far too valuable, too well trained to waste your efforts on—"

"On what? Everyday people? Folks of no consequence? We can't all have seats in the House of Lords, Jasper. We weren't all born with a silver spoon."

For a moment he was silent, then: "No. Not all were so lucky as I," he said, and drew a careful breath. "But I thought, at least, that you knew better than to compromise your sisters."

Guilt sliced her to the bone, but she lifted her chin. "I've done nothing to harm the coven."

"Are you so naïve as to think the others won't be affected if you are determined to be a witch? Even Shaleena—"

"What of Shaleena?" asked the sorceress as she suddenly stepped into the room.

Madeline turned her gaze to the other. Their gazes met with a clash. Anger burned through her.

"If you are so concerned for her safety, Lord Gallo, I would suggest you do not bring her here in the future," Maddy rasped.

Shaleena smiled and crossed the room to take Jasper's arm just as Joseph strode through the doorway. "My apologies, my lady," he said. "Your guest said she felt faint. I but went to fetch—"

"I go where I please, Maddy," Shaleena said. "Surely you know that much."

A dozen feral emotions steamed through Madeline. She curled her nails into her palms. "I know you're a self-centered—"

The redhead raised one brow.

Madeline loosened her hands. "Joseph," she said. Her tone was calm once again. "I've a bit of a headache. Might you be so kind as to escort our guests from this house?"

"Certainly, my lady," he said, and lifted a hand toward the door.

A muscle jumped in Jasper's jaw, but he nodded once and moved toward the exit.

Shaleena, however, remained where she once.

"Lady Onyx," he said.

"I go where I please," she repeated, but her gaze was now leveled on Joseph. Their eyes clashed with an almost audible ring of steel on steel.

"Which is just as well," he said. "If you are pleased to leave this place."

"I will go when I am good and ready—" Shaleena began, but Jasper interrupted.

"Let us go."

She smiled, not turning toward him. "I would be happy to," she said, "but I believe this hulking underling needs a bit of an education."

"Shaleena," Jasper warned.

She ignored him completely, but gave the butler a come-hither motion with her right hand. "You think you can displace me? Come along then, hulk."

He took a step forward, but she whispered something, and suddenly his body halted as if frozen. His muscles jerked, but he remained as he was. Effort contorted his face. An arm jerked the smallest amount.

Shaleena laughed. "How unfortunate, I was so looking forward to a confrontation. Now, Maddy, I've a few things to say," she began, but suddenly Joseph wrestled himself from immobility. His right leg swung forward as if breaking free of ice. His left followed woodenly.

Shaleena scowled and raised her hand.

"Cease," Jasper hissed, but Shaleena whispered a word and sent a shock wave through Joseph. He trembled as if struck by lightning, then continued to advance.

Shaleena pulled her brows low. "Halt," she said, and again he shuddered and broke free.

"Curse these garments!" she said, red-faced, and reaching up, yanked the gown from her shoulders. Her breasts burst into view. Joseph stopped in his tracks. Madeline groaned, and Jasper swore under his breath.

"What the devil do you think you're doing?" he asked.

"Sky-clad is the way of the true—"

"Put your gown back on or I swear to God, you will not spend another night at Lavender House."

She speared him with her eyes. Spells trembled on her lips, but Jasper remained unmoving until finally she reached out and yanked her gown back over her shoulders.

With that she headed toward the door. "Another time, hulk," she said, and disappeared.

Jasper gave Madeline a look that almost spoke of apology and followed the woman from the room.

Footsteps echoed in the hall. In a moment the house had gone silent.

Madeline refrained from closing her eyes. Instead, she cleared her throat and turned toward her manservant.

His face was absolutely impassive, as if he endured the same sort of thing every day of his life.

"My apologies," she said. "Lady Onyx can be rather . . ."

He raised a brow a quarter of an inch.

She gripped her hands hard in front of her body. ". . . unorthodox," she said, and conjured a spell in her mind. She was going to have to make him forget all that had just happened. Good God, the crazy witch had frozen her manservant to the floor. What the hell had she been thinking? In her mind, Madeline conjured the thought of sleep, of slumber, of dark and distant forgetfulness. "Unusual even," she said, and spattered him with the spell.

His expression never changed. His stance remained exactly the same, unmoving, relaxed. She watched him.

"If you'll excuse me, my lady," he said finally, "I shall inform Cook that dinner shall be for none but yourself."

Madeline turned her head to watch him walk from the room and wondered what the hell had just happened.

Chapter 11

Far beyond Mayfair's glittering grandeur, the East End stretched dark and dangerous. But those elements mattered little to Madeline, for she could not be seen. 'Twas her greatest power. Indeed, it had always been. Long ago, even Ella had been awed by Madeline's stealth. There were times when Maddy had wondered if her sister had only ooohed over those gifts because her own were so much greater. But that was no longer the case. Over the past few months, Madeline's powers had blossomed, had morphed into something entirely different. None realized this. Even Ella was unaware of Maddy's abilities, for she now employed so much more than simple stealth. Standing in the darkness, feet bare on the life-giving earth, face turned toward the sheltering sky, she had invoked a simple cloaking spell that she held even now. She had drawn the darkness into her, capturing it, holding it inside, for she had a mission. While reading palms in her own parlor, she had felt something in Frederic Lambert's demeanor. It had taken her days to decipher the sensations. Indeed, even now she was uncertain of their meanings, but in that burgeoning portion of her mind where her powers grew, she had heard the restless lap of water against a wharf. By the light of a fat, gibbous moon, she had seen a shingle hanging askew from a rusted bracket, had felt fear and excitement and guilt meld seamlessly in Lambert's soul. The uncomfortable feelings had grown, had come at her during the night, had forced her out of bed. Thus she walked alone through the city, her footfalls almost noiseless as she padded, dark and silent, down the twisted, half-cobbled alleys toward the river. Above her, the waxing moon peeked from between tattered, ghostly clouds.

The wharf was far, but it mattered little. Madeline had been trained to be strong. Had been forced to be resilient, thus the miles beneath her sturdy shoes meant nothing to her.

The foul smell of fish and algae was heavy in the night air, making her nostrils pinch. Perhaps this was a fool's errand. Perhaps she should have stayed home, saved her energy, but she had so few clues to work with.

A carriage approached from the rear. The horses' hooves clicked rhythmically until the near cob, so much more attuned to the impossible than its driver, sensed her presence and shied abruptly, snorting as it forced its companion to the right.

"Steady on," called the whip, not noticing her as they sped into the darkness, hoof beats fading.

From the left, laughter wafted through the open windows of an inn, raucous and inebriated. Candlelight shone bright as gold through the uneven panes, but in Maddy's mind, she saw an etched picture of a boar's head on a slanted sign and slipped away, moving on until at long last she came to the tavern she had seen in her mind. It was old, beaten by time and leaning heavily as if against a stiff wind. The etched pig's head had almost been worn from the sign that sagged above its weathered door.

Stopping, Madeline drew a deep breath of midnight air and let her mind fill with the "feelings" that had haunted her. Again they came. The sharp tang of guilt, the acrid smell of excitement, heavy shadows, the smell of stale beer. These things could be found anywhere. At any time of day. And yet some sense older than time had brought her here.

She moved a step closer. There was only one window in the broken structure. One window, one door. Glancing behind her, she studied the night for an instant, but nothing untoward disturbed the darkness. Thus she stepped up next to the building and peered through the glass.

Inside, candlelight flickered erratically across two men. One was Frederic Lambert. He sat facing his companion, and though his expression revealed little, Madeline could feel the angst in him. Angst and excitement, melding to a powerful potion. Across the table from him, the other man felt relaxed. Confidence flowed from him. He was young, fair, and undeniably attractive.

"I believe you might be suggesting something illegal," Lambert said.

Madeline held her breath, listening, feeling.

"Am I?" asked the other, and smiled. His teeth were all but perfect. A dimple etched itself into his right cheek, and his hair was the color of autumn wheat.

"Not to mention immoral," added Lambert. "Indeed, if these deeds became known we might both be hanged."

The young man's hands were long and graceful as he fiddled with an uncut cigar. "Are you saying, then, that you are uninterested in my proposition?"

Madeline's mind was racing. Might this fellow have taken the girls? Might he be keeping them? Selling them to the highest bidder? She had sensed guilt from Lambert. But there had been more. An excitement that felt like sexuality.

"That's exactly what I'm saying, Bennington," Lambert said.

The other leaned back in his chair. His cravat was untied, his chest smooth where two wooden buttons had been undone. "Then why are you here, Freddy? You could be home, enjoying your wife's charming company."

Something dark crossed Lambert's face. A shudder, almost indiscernible, shook him, but he covered it well. "You owe me."

"But as you know, I do not have the cash readily available. Which makes me wonder why you have come, unless you wish to participate in this newest gamble."

They stared at each other, tension twisting tight until Lambert broke eye contact.

"Don't get clever," he said.

"But I cannot help myself," Bennington countered. "I *am* clever."

"Is that so?" The older man stood, poured himself a drink. Did his hand shake the smallest amount?

"Indeed."

"How so?"

Bennington smiled again. He dropped his chin, eyeing the other through heavy lashes. "Come into the other room if you dare and I shall show you."

They stared at each other, then Lambert downed his drink, froze for several long heartbeats, then stepped toward the interior door. Smiling, Bennington lifted the candle and followed him. The door closed behind them.

Madeline waited by the window, heart thumping. What was in there? Could Bennington have abducted Marie? Or perhaps he had taken them all. He was obviously in debt. Perhaps the girls were part of his scheme to repay what he owed. The idea burned at her mind. She could wait and hope the two men would leave, giving her a chance to search the room. But perhaps that would be too late. There was no way of knowing what the abducted maids had already endured. No way of knowing what they might have to endure in the next few minutes.

She could go in now, but perhaps there were more men inside. Two she could handle, perhaps, but more might be difficult even with her new-found powers.

Thus she had no choice. Time was her enemy. She would have to take a risk. Glancing about, she looked for a place to hide, for she could not cloak herself and do what she must. But in that moment a noise sounded from inside. She couldn't have said what it was. Maybe a muffled scream. Maybe a curse.

Pressing her back into the building's deepest shadows, she closed her eyes, shut out her fear, and turned down the doubt.

It took only a second for her mind to expand, to stretch, to seep softly into the darkened tavern, as if she were there herself.

It was darker than soot on the river.

Somewhere above the clouds the moon was nearly full, but it did Jasper Reeves little good. Perhaps he should have come in the morning, but he dared not wait. Madeline could very well have already reached the tavern. He knew she would arrive there eventually, for she had made inquiries about the Boar's Head. Not that he was spying on her. He wouldn't do that. Neither would he stay awake at night wondering, worrying about her next move. That would be asinine. But she would come here. That he was certain of, for he knew her well. Still, it had not been easy for him to predict when she would make the journey into this dark side of the city. Indeed, she might not come at all this night. She might, in fact, have finally realized it would be foolhardy and dangerous to travel here alone, but sleep had evaded him, scattering into a thousand broken thoughts. Thus he had come. Not because he was worried for her safety. She had made it perfectly clear that she neither needed nor desired his help. And that was perfectly fine with him. He had others to protect. Others—

Jasper's boat bumped suddenly, snapping his

thoughts to an abrupt halt. It would do him little good to overturn in these choppy waters.

Oaring his narrow vessel into the sand, Jasper became aware of a hubbub of voices as he stepped onto the beach. Silently pulling the craft along after him, he scanned the shoreline. It was scattered with wind-buffeted buildings. A crowd had gathered in the lee of an uneven warehouse. By the light of a dancing bonfire, Jasper could make out a few faces, intent and grubby in the erratic light. But in a moment the ring of spectators broke apart and two men stumbled into the breach. They were bare to the waist, one large, one average, both pale and bloodied. The smaller of the two stumbled. Someone shouted, a curse or an endearment or both. The giant glanced to his right and the smaller struck, bringing up an undercut from his hip and landing a solid blow in the other's beefy face. The big man staggered back three steps, teetered for an elongated instant, and went down.

The crowd bellowed, leaving Jasper to slip into the shadows without being seen. The ancient tavern Lambert was known to frequent was just a few blocks to the north. Jasper would go there. Would learn what he could. Would . . .

A noise rustled to his left. He paused, listening, prepared, but it was only a loose cur, nosing about in the shadows. Jasper looked beyond him, searching for the dog's master, but the skinny hound was alone. It stopped to issue a low-throated growl.

"Away," Jasper said, but the mutt stalked forward to sniff Jasper's breeches, then followed when he headed down the street.

It didn't take long to find the Boar's Head, for it was just where he had been told it would be, though it looked as if it would not remain much longer. He stopped to study the moldering building in silence. From behind, the scrawny hound trotted past and into the darkness. A tall, dark gelding was tied to a post beside the tilted front door, looking elegantly out of place against the haphazard buildings. Jasper's senses sharpened. What would such a fine steed be doing here? Perhaps Madeline *did* have reason to be come here in the dark of night. Perhaps her powers were even greater than he had—

The dog growled.

Jasper froze. Was someone nearby? Was someone watching him? He had keen eyesight, but he could see no one.

The hound growled again, and Jasper stepped forward as quiet as a thought, following the sound of the cur's rumble. And there, in the deepest shadows of the broken tavern, he saw a figure concealed against the building's rough side.

Freezing, he watched it. But it remained absolutely motionless. Who was it? Why was he there? Was Madeline here also? Was this character watching her? Was he planning some evil—

But in that instant the moon broke free of the dark net of clouds and shone like a gilded beacon on the still form's face.

He was never certain if he cursed out loud, but he knew he felt his stomach drop, felt his blood freeze. For she was there, standing amid the shadows. But what was she doing? She was facing outward, not looking inside. Why?

Glancing from side to side, he searched the darkness. When no threat revealed itself, he hurried forward.

"What the devil are you doing here?" he hissed, but she said nothing. "This is no safe place," he warned, and grasping her arm, turned her toward him. But she only stared, seeming to see something that he did not.

Worry trickled in anew, etched with caution, tinged with suspicion. "What's happening here?" he murmured.

But again she did not answer.

"Madeline," he said, and suddenly her eyes widened the smallest degree as she stared past his shoulder into the darkness.

Beside him, the dog yelped. Jasper jerked about, but nothing unusual could be seen, only the ragged cur fleeing into the night, tail tucked tight against its rump.

He turned back toward her. "What's—" he began, but suddenly she started. A shudder ran through her. She pulled in a hard breath and blinked as if just awakening.

"Jasper!" she rasped.

He watched her, questions ringing like warning bells in his head.

Her eyes widened again. Her lips parted as if in surprise at some unheard dialogue.

"Tell me—" he began, but voices flared suddenly from the beach, a mix of hot passions, reminding Jasper of the dangers looming less than a furlong away.

Anger spurred through him. Anger and dread and a dozen other emotions Jasper Reeves never felt. "Come!" he ordered, tone oddly unsteady, but she remained as she was.

"Have you done that?" she asked, voice almost raspy in the darkness.

He turned back. Her eyes looked unusually large.

"What are you talking about?"

She took a step toward him. "Perhaps you came to join them."

"Who?" He stepped onto the street and she followed, matching him stride for stride.

"Lambert and Bennington. Isn't that why you're—" she began, but harsh laughter burned the night. In the cross street, a trio of men staggered past.

The pair watched until they were out of sight.

"How did you get here?" Jasper murmured, and started forward again.

"I have very strong legs," she whispered.

He glanced at her, cursing in silence. "You walked here? Alone?"

"How are *your* legs?" Her voice was still low and throaty. He turned. The light was a little better here, and he studied her face. It seemed different in the near darkness somehow, bolder, more alive.

"Have you been drinking?" he asked.

"Are they strong?"

"Why did you come here?" he asked.

"To see what Lambert does in his spare time." Her eyes looked wide in the darkness. Wide and surprised. "He's rather naughty."

Naughty? "What's wrong with you?"

"I think I might be naïve, after all," she said, and laughed.

Jasper cringed. "Keep your voice down. This is no place to draw attention to yourself."

"Too late. I think you've already noticed me?" she murmured. Then, stepping forward, she slid her fingers into his hair and kissed him.

Lightning flared through him. The skies trembled. The world shuddered, shaking the very earth upon which he stood until she broke the contact, drew slowly away.

It took him a moment to remember he could talk. Still, he couldn't seem to be able to master his tongue. It lay dead in his mouth as a million wild thoughts took flight in his mind, strangling his breath, gripping his body. He could take her right there. On the street. In the dark. Before good sense returned, he thought, but he found his footing, drew a deep breath, and held it.

"I think you'd best visit a physician first thing in the morning," he said. "I believe there may well be something amiss with you."

She laughed. The sound was flirty, almost shy. But it was sultry too, low and suggestive and so damned seductive it twisted his senses, boggled his mind. Awakened every slumbering sense to tingling awareness.

"I fear you might be right. For one thing . . ." She stepped up close, touched his shoulder, and stretched toward his ear. "I seem to be hopelessly aroused."

Jasper stumbled backward, actually, physically lurched away like an overawed youth.

"Aren't *you*?" she asked.

"I think we'd best—"

"Have you ever done it like that?"

"*What?*"

"What of multiple partners?"

He retreated another step, stumbling a little.

"Lambert seems to have a fondness for it. Of course Bennington *is* quite attractive."

"What the devil are you talking about?" His voice sounded strange. Raspy. Strangled.

"Bennington." She stepped forward. He forgot to retreat, forgot to breathe. "He's rather handsome. And they're both hard." She blinked. "Did you know they would *both* get hard?"

"What the devil have you been doing?" Raspy again, and a little breathless.

"Watching," she said. "And it made me rather . . . Well . . ." She scowled as if searching for the perfect word. ". . . restless. Not that I wished to join them, mind. Not when you are so close and so hard and so . . ." She canted her head as if examining him. As if she could see through his clothes. ". . . so ridiculously controlled."

For a moment he actually thought he would be all right. That he had control firmly within his grasp, but then she smiled. It was a titillating meld of seduction and innocence, and suddenly he was crashing in for a kiss, pushing her up against the wall. Just as suddenly her leg was bent between his. He was already throbbing, aching, pulsing.

He grabbed her skirts, searching for release, but a voice snaked through the darkness.

" 'Ello."

Jasper jerked away, simultaneously pushing Madeline behind him as he frantically searched for the speaker. But he was not difficult to find. Indeed, a band of four was arced across the alley, their eyes gleaming in the dimness. Behind them and a little to the left, another watched.

The nearest man smiled. "Well, my merry blokes, what do you suppose we got 'ere?"

Chapter 12

Madeline came fully back to herself with a start as Jasper pushed her behind him. What the devil had just happened? Had she nearly ripped off Reeves's clothes? Nearly—

"Looks like these two was just about to 'ave at it right 'ere in our backyard," said a rough voice.

Madeline took in her surroundings with burgeoning dismay. What was happening? Who were the men ranged across the alley in front of them?

She'd been completely distracted, completely absorbed. Not unlike on the dance floor and those few breathless moments in the drawing room when the images by the arbor had seemed so breathtakingly real. So vividly tangible.

She'd caused those images herself. And yet it was not she. Not really. It was a part of her she had somehow awakened. A rudimentary shadow of her being. A shadow without constraints, without solid barriers. The part she could send into the world. The part she *thought* she could control.

"Dear Lord!" she rasped.

"What's that?" Jasper asked, not turning toward her.

Madeline gritted her teeth, remembering the men who faced them. Remembering the danger. "Dear Lord, save us," she said, louder now, but just as shaky, for surely any *normal* woman would be afraid in such a situation. "We don't want any trouble," she said.

"An excellent point." Jasper nodded, tone soft, placating. "If you're not too preoccupied, Lady Redcomb, now might be a good time to be sensible."

She shot her gaze toward him. "I've always been sensible."

"If that were true, you wouldn't be here now. Talking like . . . Talking . . ."

"Like what?"

Jasper turned toward her, scowling over his shoulder even though the quartet was approaching steadily. "Like you're losing your mind."

"So what might a fine lady and gent be doing in this shoddy part of the world?" asked the tallest of the group.

"You think I'm mad?" Madeline rasped.

Jasper was facing the strangers again. "If not, it might be wise to cease talking to yourself."

"Listen, Reeves—"

" 'Ey," said the ringleader, "I asked ya a question."

"I'm not mad." She hoped.

"Stay behind me," Jasper ordered.

"Are you joking?" She had been trained for just such an eventuality for nearly a decade. Surely he wasn't suggesting that she cower in the shadows now. Then again, it wasn't as if he had a sense of humor, and the villains were drawing nearer.

"I don't mean to be in'ospitable," said the closest fellow. He was holding something long and narrow in his right hand, tapping it against his left. "But I'm afraid we're going to 'ave to relieve you of yer valuables."

"I'll handle this," Jasper said, still not turning about as he spoke to her. "Stay behind me."

"*Behind* you?"

"Now's not a good time to argue," Jasper suggested, watching the approaching men.

"What is this a good time for exactly?"

"I want you to leave here," he intoned.

"Leave—"

"The one with the club is going to come at me," Jasper murmured. "I'll handle him. Then two will come. When they make contact you are to turn and run."

"You *are* joking," she said.

"Good God, woman!" Jasper gritted. "Could you listen to me this once?"

"This once?" She couldn't believe her ears. "I've been listening to you for eight years. Every time the world was falling apart around our heads and you gave me some weak-kneed mission. Every time I was told to cower in the background while real work was—" she began, but suddenly the man with the club attacked, rushing in, swinging wildly.

Jasper ducked, waited a fraction of a second until the attacker had swung past, then reached out with lightning speed. The man crumpled to the street and remained still. But two others were already coming, lurching toward him.

"Run," Jasper ordered, and snatching up the other's club, swung it at the first man's head. He went down with a grunt of surprise, but another was only inches behind him, and he had a knife.

Dodging in, the villain took a hasty swipe. Reeves grunted and stumbled away.

But Madeline could watch no longer. For a fourth man was lunging toward her. No time for spells. Madeline spun and kicked. Cartilage crunched beneath her heel. Her attacker staggered back, holding his nose. Arms raised in a defensive position, Madeline glanced around. The first man was still down but the second was rising to his feet. He advanced, intent, wary now, and she let him come.

"Please," she whispered, faking weakness. Jasper was crouching on the ground beside a felled body. How badly was he wounded? "Don't hurt me."

The man snickered. "Course not, missy," he said. "Not if you cooperate, leastways."

"I'll do whatever—" she began, but in that instant, he lunged toward her.

She struck him a hard blow to the throat, and he staggered backward, eyes wide in surprise, gasping and holding his neck as he dropped to his knees.

The night was silent for a second, then: "I told you to get out of here," Jasper said, rising unsteadily.

Madeline glanced around. The fifth man remained standing. He looked scrawny but unmoved in the uncertain light. "And leave you here I suppose? Alone? To fend for yourself?"

Jasper grimaced, then nodded at the villain's unconscious friends. "There's no shame in walking away, lad," he said.

The boy shifted his slight body. "Who are you?" he asked. He had a smooth voice. Melodious, almost cultured.

"It's a bit late for formal introductions," Reeves said, but Madeline was feeling something, sensing something that shivered over her skin like a silent breeze.

"Who are *you*?" she asked.

The lad turned and looked at her, seeming oblivious of the darkness. "They call me Cur."

"It has been a rather wearing day, Cur," Jasper said, and glanced at Madeline. "We shall call it a draw. We'll go our way. You go—"

"But it's not," said the other.

"What's that?" He turned slowly back.

"It is not a draw. In fact, it seems to be four to naught."

Jasper straightened and pulled in a careful breath. "You've got nothing to prove."

"Wouldn't that be for me to say?"

"Go away," Jasper ordered. "Your friends can think you fought like a lion."

There was a moment of silence as he seemed to consider his felled comrades. "What are you?"

Jasper shook his head. "I don't know what you're talking about."

The boy shifted his gaze to Madeline. "Does *she* know?"

"It's time for you to go home before it's too late. Tell your mother all about your day," Jasper said, but Cur was already shaking his head.

"One on one," he said. "Just you and me."

"Don't be ridiculous," Reeves scoffed, and turned away, tugging Maddy with him.

But suddenly the boy was in front of them.

They stopped in tandem, hearts pumping.

"Something is not as it seems," Maddy murmured.

Jasper snorted at her understatement, and Madeline glanced at him, worried. Jasper Reeves didn't snort.

"Are you afraid?" Cur asked.

"I've no desire to fight you," Jasper answered, and tightening his grip on Maddy's hand, turned as if to skirt him, but suddenly he was there again.

"But I've a wish to fight *you*," he said.

"He's gifted," Madeline whispered.

Jasper drew a deep breath through his nostrils as if tired. "Can we not simply assume you are stronger?"

The boy shook his head, eyes gleaming in the darkness. "I've been waiting a long while."

Jasper studied him in silence. The night lay heavy around them, quiet, watching. "If I agree . . ." he began quietly, then: "If I fight you, the girl goes free. Win or lose."

"No," Madeline said, but a smile flittered across the lad's face.

"I'm not an animal."

"What are you then?" Maddy asked, anger and fear fluttering through her, but the boy didn't bother to turn toward her.

"I'll have your promise," Jasper said.

"Don't do this," Madeline said, and Cur laughed.

"I'm planning to kill you," he said. "And yet you want my promise?"

"Yes."

Cur's expression sobered. "Very well. No harm will come to her."

"Win or lose," Jasper repeated.

"Don't be stupid," Madeline rasped.

"Stay out of this," Jasper warned, but Maddy set her jaw, irritation overwhelming fear.

"I'm a bit weary of staying out of things," she hissed, but in that moment Jasper turned toward her.

"Please," he said, and there was something in his voice, something so elemental and earnest that she stood and stared.

"What?" she asked.

"I am not above begging," he said.

"Since when?"

Jasper chuckled a little. The unlikely sound was eerie in the moonlight. "You are correct, of course. He is not what he seems."

Madeline scowled. "What's happening? What aren't you telling me?"

"Please go."

"No."

"Go," he said softly, "and I vow to leave you be. You have my word. I'll no longer pressure you to return to Lavender House." His face was solemn, his body still. "You'll be a free agent."

But she didn't want to be free. Never had. Not really. Lord help her, she wanted *him*. Always had.

He drew a quiet breath as if to steady himself. "The girls are still alive," he said. "You can yet save them."

She opened her mouth in surprise, but he spoke before she was able to voice a question.

"I shall make certain the committee assists you."

She remained as she was, questions soaring through her mind, but she couldn't abandon Marie, couldn't fail Bertram. Drawing a deep breath, she agreed.

Jasper nodded, face solemn as he turned toward his opponent. "Very well," he said.

Cur smiled. "You're ready?"

"Try me," Jasper said, and without a moment's notice, the boy attacked, leaping in with a kick to his opponent's head.

Jasper ducked, but instead of stumbling over him, Cur flew over top, then spun about to land a trio of punches to Jasper's kidneys.

Grunting, Jasper swung about, but the boy struck again, plowing a fist into his stomach.

Jasper fell.

Cur leaped in with both feet, ready to stomp his face. But Jasper rolled aside at the last instant. Even as he did so, however, the boy adjusted his leap and pulled a knife from some hidden pocket. For an abbreviated second his blade shone in the moonlight, and then he stabbed.

Jasper jerked to the side, but too late. The knife bit into his left arm. He jerked his legs upward, ready to thrust the boy aside, but Cur had already leaped out of the way.

"He's got premonition," Maddy rasped.

Cur glanced at her and grinned. "Is that what it's called, then?"

Their gazes met in the darkness. "You see things before they happen," Maddy whispered.

The boy straightened a little, eyeing her. "Maybe I'm fighting the wrong person," he said.

"You're going to want to concentrate on me," Jasper rasped, and gained his feet.

"Maybe the lady-bird would be more of a challenge," Cur said, and took a step toward Maddy.

"Your agreement is with me," Jasper growled.

"I felt a spark of something," Cur said, still watching her. "Was it from you?"

"Only cowards fight women," Jasper rasped, and attacked.

Cur turned like a cat, bent, and deftly tossed Jasper over his shoulder. Reeves landed hard.

Madeline refrained from calling his name, stayed where she was.

Cur shifted his knife to his other hand and advanced slowly. "You're not done already, are you, old man?"

Jasper rose. But even in the darkness, Maddy could see he was injured. He was bent, wounded. She clasped her hands to fists, kept herself at bay. Jasper straightened, stumbled a little, then made a come-hither motion with his left hand.

"You're game. I'll give you—" Cur began, but in that instant Jasper attacked again. He jerked forward, fists raised, then spun and kicked out, striking his heel to the boy's chest. Cur stumbled back. Jasper dove in for the kill, but suddenly the lad was on the ground, kicking up. His left foot caught Jasper's injured arm. Reeves cried out in pain, stumbling sideways, but Cur was already on his feet.

"Almost done, old man?" he asked.

Jasper was breathing hard. He straightened with an effort. "Not just yet," he growled.

Cur shook his head. They circled each other, cautious now, watching, waiting, and then things happened faster than the eye could see. Fists flew. Kicks landed.

And suddenly Jasper was on his back. His breath rasped in the darkness. Cur stood over him, knife to his throat.

"Not bad, old man," he said. "I almost hate to kill you."

Jasper gritted his teeth. "Go back on your promise, and I'll see you in hell."

Cur narrowed his eyes. "My promise?"

"Lay a single finger on her and you'll regret it every day of your miserable life."

The boy canted his head. "You realize you're about to die, don't you?"

"Harm one hair on her head, and I swear to God, I'll find you," Reeves rasped, "in hell or beyond."

The boy laughed, but his knife hand was steady. "Is this what they call love?"

"It's what they call a promise," Jasper said.

"You'd be wise to spend your time on prayers instead of promises, old man," Cur said, and lifted the blade.

But in that instant Jasper bucked beneath him, tossing the boy over his head. Reeves was up in an instant, twisting, dropping his knees on the boy's knife hand and gripping his throat in a death grip.

Their gazes met and clashed. Cur struggled for an instant, clawing at Jasper's coat, but there was no hope.

Madeline covered her mouth with her hand, almost screaming.

"Do you possess it?" The boy's voice was raspy, grated.

"What the hell are you talking about, boy?"

"The enchantment," Cur rasped. "Do you have it?"

Jasper shook his head and gritted his teeth. "I bested you without."

The boy's eyes gleamed in the darkness. His face was as pale as ice, but when he spoke, his words were almost steady. "Then it comes from her."

"Leave her out of this."

"The enchantment is hers," Cur said, and turned his popping eyes toward her. "I should be battling her."

Reeves tightened his grip, but Cur wriggled inexplicably out of his grip and jolted to his feet.

"We're not done here," rasped Jasper, but Cur straightened, finding Madeline in the darkness.

"Not done," he agreed, and turning, stumbled into the shadows.

"Come back here," Jasper rasped, and prepared to rush after him, but Maddy caught him by the arm.

"Let him go," she ordered.

"And give him another chance to harm you?" He jerked out of her grasp.

"Jasper!" She imbued her voice with every bit of command she could find. He turned toward her, face twisted in agony. "Let him go."

"He'll not touch you," he snarled, but she caught him again.

"He's gone."

"I'll find the bastard. Kill him. Rip out his heart. He'll not harm you." His eyes looked mad. "You'll be safe. You'll be—"

"Jasper." She caught his other arm and tightened her grip. "Cease!"

For a moment she thought he would break free, but finally he relaxed a little. Drawing a heavy breath, he watched her. "He'll not touch you," he repeated, softer now.

"He's gone."

He turned his head. The cords stood out taut and hard in his throat. His jaw tightened.

"Jasper." She drew him back. "All is well."

His eyes gleamed like a wolf's in the moonlight.

"We are safe."

He turned toward her. The madness receded slowly from his expression.

"Safe," she said again.

He reached out, almost touching her face, almost making contact before drawing back.

"All is well," she repeated.

A moment of silence hung between them, and then he drew nonchalance around him like a comfortable shrug. "Good," he said. "We'd best leave then, before you find more trouble."

Chapter 13

Jasper sat in silence in the bow of the little vessel, trying to stop the scenario from playing through his mind for the hundredth time. Yet still he saw her, frozen beside the tavern, face blank, body motionless. What the hell had happened? And how the devil had he allowed it? He should have known something was afoot long before she'd left Cinderknoll. Hell, he should have known before she left Lavender House.

"Are you all right?" Her voice was quiet. The night the same. Waves lapped steadily against the boat's weathered ribs.

She was rowing. And why the hell not? She was the one with the power. He was the one who had failed her.

"Jasper, are you—"

"I am well," he said. His voice sounded childish to his own ears. Good God, he hadn't even been childish when he was a child.

"Your arm—"

"Is fine."

"It is not . . ." She paused, drew a breath. "You were stabbed."

He snorted. Perhaps one could say he was out of sorts. Hell, if prompted, one could say he was out of his mind. Had he just fought a man for her honor? Was he that stupid? She could have probably knocked the poor lad flat with a glance. She had taken out two of them. Perhaps the boy hadn't realized that at first. Perhaps he'd assumed Jasper was the powerful one. But he'd misjudged her. Just as Jasper had. And yet, even if he had realized how her powers had grown, he wouldn't have had the strength to let her fight. The idea made his heart shudder, even knowing what he now knew. What he now suspected. He eyed her through the darkness, feeling anger well up again, though he couldn't have said why exactly.

"Let me bind it before—" she began, but he interrupted her.

"How do you do it?" he asked.

He could sense her scowl even if he couldn't see it.

"I've heard of such things," he said. What the devil was wrong with him? He should have known. Should have realized the powers she had been grooming under his very eyes. "But I've not seen it done."

She glanced over her shoulder at the river, arms straightening and flexing. "I don't know what you're talking about."

He refrained from laughing. He wasn't the laughing kind. Cool. That was he. "When I found you, hidden in the shadows, you were no more than a shell."

"What an unbecoming thing to say." She leaned into the oars.

He allowed himself to grit his teeth.

"Shaleena thought you were losing your mind." And that had been months ago. How could he have failed to see?

"Shaleena's a pain in the . . ." She paused, pursed her lips, remembered her title, her upbringing. Her training. She was supposed to act like a lady, not some foulmouthed light-skirt. She blushed at the memory of those first moments outside the tavern. Had she actually told him she was aroused? Had she kissed him? "My mind is fine," she said, and hoped she was right.

"She said she saw you once, in your chamber, staring at the ceiling, unspeaking."

" 'Tis a good thing I left Lavender then, if she made a habit of sneaking into my room uninvited."

"She said she was worried for your welfare."

She laughed. "Shaleena worries for no one's fare but her own."

"You were gone, weren't you?"

"You're not making any sense, Jasper," she said. "Perhaps you've lost more blood than I realized."

"You have learned to . . ." He considered how best to phrase his words. ". . . to separate your thoughts from your physical being."

She laughed. "How fanciful of you, Jasper."

"You can send your mind out to listen. To see."

"Perhaps you're the one losing your mind."

It was fairly likely. After all, if he remembered correctly, and he hoped to God he did not, he had been idiotic enough to ask her sister if Madeline might care. *Just a bit.*

He almost moaned out loud at the memory. Yes, he might very well be losing his mind, but he was right about this. He knew it, as unlikely as it seemed. "All this time I thought you were simply adept at making yourself unseen, that you could hide where others could not," he said.

She shrugged. "Stealth has always been my gift."

"But you've extended it. Expanded it. Now your . . . *spirit* leaves your body behind."

She shook her head. Frogs chirped from the bank.

"Why didn't you tell me?" he asked, and found that despite himself, he was wounded, for though he had forced her to believe him to be cool and unfeeling, he had wanted her to think differently. The ridiculousness of it almost made him laugh.

"I've never seen you so imaginative," she said.

"I had a right to know," he countered, nerves fraying. He was unaccustomed to feelings. Hated feelings. Oh, he had lusted for her for a long while, but he could deal with lust. Could ignore it. Ridicule it. Overcome it. "I—" he began, but stopped himself before he could spew out any kind of lunacy that would further weaken his position.

"What?" she asked, and turned abruptly toward him. "You what?"

He steeled his jaw. "I am the director of the coven."

"The director." She laughed. "You don't direct me, Jasper. You ignore me. You dispose of me."

Ignore her! Was she out of her mind? No man could ignore her. She was like sunlight in the darkness. Like music to the deaf. "I use your gifts as I see best."

"You shame me," she rasped.

He shook his head, trying to imagine what she meant. "Don't be—"

"I have powers, Jasper," she gritted. "Perhaps I'm not as gifted as my sister. Perhaps I'm not even as powerful as Shaleena, but there are things I can do. More things than you know. Hell!" She laughed. "My *shell* could do more than you know."

"So I was right!" The truth thundered in on him. "While your . . . your consciousness is wandering about, your body is left defenseless."

"I didn't say that."

He felt sick to his stomach. She had been alone there, in the shadows with a hundred lusty men only yards away. "But it's true," he said. "Had they found you, you would have been unable to escape."

"They *didn't* find me," she said. "I was hidden."

"*I* saw you."

She scowled.

"You cannot mask yourself when your consciousness is gone, can you?"

She didn't respond, and he felt like cursing. Like screaming. Like pulling her into his arms and shaking her until she vowed to remain within two steps of him at all times. Until she agreed to keep herself safe, protected, insulated from the world.

But it was his job to subject her to danger, to use her. The idea made him feel as though his skull was too tight for his brain.

"Even the dog saw you," he said.

"Luckily, I have little to fear from dogs."

He did swear now, but softly, allowing himself that tiny bit of satisfaction so that he would not explode. Would not burst into a thousand shards of frustration.

"What did you say?" she asked, voice sweet, arms pumping rhythmically.

"Nothing."

"I thought I heard you say something."

He gritted his teeth, ready to deny again, but in that moment a thought struck him. "So your consciousness . . . what do you call it?"

"I don't call it anything, because it *isn't* anything."

"It's everything," he gritted. "When it's out on its own, it's everything, leaving—"

"So my body is nothing?" she asked, voice soft, eyes wide.

He stared at her, remembering the images of her naked in his arms. Remembering how she had felt, sounded, smelled. Like heaven, like hope, like . . .

"You were different!" he rasped.

"What?"

"When your consciousness returned to you from the tavern, you were . . ." Flirty. Seductive. Irresistible. ". . . altered."

"Don't be ridiculous," she said, and continued to row. Somewhere nearby a gull called.

"You can't know how she will affect you."

"It's getting choppier," she said, but he ignored her, mind churning.

"How long has this been happening?" Holy God. He felt a little sick to his stomach. He should have known. Should have realized what she was attempting. What she was dabbling in. But he kept the terror out of his voice. "What of when your mind is out on its own? When you are nothing more than a shadow of yourself . . ." Too much emotion. He smoothed his tone. "What then?"

Emotion shifted on her face. He watched, barely breathing as he read her expression.

He was tempted to swear again, to curse like a sun-weltered smithy, but it would do no good. There were no words vile enough. "You can't always control it, can you?"

She glanced to the right, over the rough waves.

He almost reached for her then. Almost lost control, but he gripped the gunwale instead, squeezing until his knuckles hurt. "What if it doesn't return?" he asked. "What then? What if something happens and you are left alone forever?"

She straightened, flexed, rowing like a slave. "It can't leave me alone. It *is* me. My mind." She shook her head. "Just an extension of my mind."

He laughed. "That can see through walls? That can leave you alone, unprotected? Uncared for?"

"Am I uncared for?" she asked, voice so soft, he could barely make out the words. Eyes so wide and solemn he longed with every fiber to pull her close, to hold her, to tell her the truth. That he loved her.

Had always loved her. But he survived by his rules. Still, he had to look away when he spoke.

"Your sisters care for you." God, he was an empty hull of a man. And a coward. A goddamned coward. "Faye inquires about your welfare every day. I think she misses you most. Though at times, Darla will conjure your image in the flames." It was spooky as hell, and disconcerting; more than once he had nearly reached into the fire, just to touch her, just to believe she was near. Oh hell.

He almost closed his eyes to the lunacy, but managed to keep his expression stoic. "How do you draw it back?" he asked.

She was silent again. Had he wounded her? Did she hope for more? Did she care? *Just a bit?* God save him. "When you're weak. Just a shadow. How—"

"I'm never a *shadow*," she said.

"When you are without . . . your full self, then," he corrected, but didn't bother to try to soothe his expression. "How do you draw it back?"

"I told you, it's just a piece of me. Like my arm or my . . ." She paused, thinking. "It's a part of the whole of me. Who I am. Maybe who I should be. Although it's . . ." She paused, glanced away again.

"What?" He felt crazed with the need to strike something, and wished, rather desperately, that the violent little street shit named Cur would appear again. Just for a minute.

Madeline shrugged, casual, as if discussing her favorite tea. "Sometimes it seems easily distracted."

"Easily distracted." God help him.

"Yes."

He closed his eyes for a moment, calming emotions he refused to accept. "How do you mean, exactly?"

"You're bleeding," she said, looking at his arm. He didn't bother to glance down.

"What do you mean, easily distracted?"

"When it goes out, it's not . . ." Her voice was breathy. "Not fully aware. Or maybe it is simply . . . unfettered."

He thought about it, consumed it. "It's the childish part of you."

She shrugged.

"The unthinking part of you."

She didn't respond.

"You send the unthinking part of you out into the world. Into dangerous situations."

"It's not unthinking."

"Like a half-wit?"

"No!"

"What then?"

"More like . . ."

"Like an animal?"

She gave him a peeved glance from the corner of her eye. "It's just a piece of me. A portion. A sliver."

If he couldn't find the kid named Cur, maybe he could hit someone else. Weatherby perhaps. Or any of the other preening lords who stared at her as if she were part of a scrumptious buffet, complete with cherry tarts and meat pies. "What kind of animal would you say?" he asked.

Her brows dipped in irritation, but her movements never slowed. Dammit, she could probably row all night. Then when she got tired, the animal would take over. "I said, it's *not* like an animal. It's . . ." She swallowed, looking young and fragile, and so damned beautiful it made him want to cry. And wouldn't that just be damned near perfect? ". . . the part I lost."

"Lost?"

She didn't respond, but suddenly he understood. "In Marseille," he said, feeling sick. "After your father's death." Her father had been an ass, had all but abandoned them—his children, his own flesh and blood. What would it be like to have kin? Daughters. Small and strong and beautiful. To care for and coddle and adore. To look into their eyes and know you were connected by more than circumstance? More than fate? He wondered, but he set aside the thoughts, for they would do him no good. Never had. "When your sister was taken." He remembered her face and voice as if it had been yesterday. "You were just a child then." But really she was not. She was bravery and loyalty and strength, plucked from adolescence and thrust into terrifying hopelessness. Bound by honor, by famil-ial duty, she had somehow found him. Found him, braved his seeming nonchalance, and convinced him to help.

She had been forced to grow up quickly. Or so he had thought, but perhaps he had been wrong. Perhaps the child in her had only waited. Waited until Madeline came into her full powers, waited for her to reach inside and draw out the totality of herself. Waited until she could come out and play, come out and . . .

A new thought rocked him—the image of an arbor, of Madeline perched upon the cool iron, legs spread, fingers gripping the curled metal over-head while he . . .

"What are your capabilities when you . . . go outside yourself?" he asked. He was beginning to sweat. Maybe it was because he was wounded, but he couldn't actually feel the pain. Where was the damned pain?

"What do you mean?" she asked, tone cool, detached.

He gritted his teeth. "Can your consciousness
. . ." Dammit to hell. "Can it project images?"

"Images?"

Was she intentionally acting obtuse?

"Back in . . ." He drew a deep breath. "In Cinderknoll I got an image in my mind."

"What kind of image?"

Did she look pale? Did she sound strained? Did
she know exactly what he was talking about? Had
she seen them too, draped against the arbor, her
arms, slim and bare as she reached above her,
pressed against him. Had her other consciousness
sent forth the image?

"You'll have to be more specific," she said, and
in the darkness he wondered if she blushed. If she
even remembered how.

"Can it send forth *any* kind of image?"

She pursed her lips as if debating how much to
tell him. But dammit! He was her . . . What? What
was he to her? Her employer? Her protector?

"I'm not sure," she said.

"What?"

She cleared her throat. "My powers are still
growing. Still evolving. In truth, I'm not sure what
I will be able to achieve in the end."

"Does it ever send *you* images?"

"No," she said, but the denial was rushed. Was
she blushing *now*? He couldn't tell. But it prob-

ably didn't matter anyway. She had perfect control. Over her capillaries, her thoughts. Her arms. Hell, she could row until the damned cows toddled home. He gritted his teeth and glanced toward shore. "No. Of course not. We're one and the same." She laughed. "So naturally it can't send me any arbors."

He snapped his gaze to her. "What did you say?"

Her lips parted and stammered. Her eyes were as wide as the sky.

He stared at her, waiting, breathless.

"*Images!*" she rasped. "She sends me no *images.*"

Chapter 14

"**Y**ou said *arbor.*"

"No!" Madeline's heart fluttered like a frantic butterfly in her chest. What the hell was wrong with her? Maybe he had been right—maybe he *had* seen them draped against the arbor, immersed in each other, drowned in ecstasy, but if that was true she wasn't about to claim responsibility. Neither was she going to admit her own lurid thoughts.

"Did you imagine an arbor?" he murmured, and suddenly she was lost in his eyes, in possibilities. Maybe she was wrong. Maybe he did care. Maybe he wanted her as badly as she wanted him. "Did you?" His voice was deep and mesmerizing, his gaze searing, and she wanted to speak, wanted to admit the truth, but suddenly the boat bobbled wildly, shattering the moment.

"We've arrived!" she rasped, and yanked her gaze from his. Jumping into the water, she towed the vessel behind her. "Do you need assist debarking?" Her heart was wild in her heart, her breath sharp in her lungs. It was difficult to look at him, to even glance his way, lest he see the lewd, unspeakable thoughts skittering through her mind, but he only gritted his teeth and stepped over the gunwale.

Just as his foot touched the ground, however, he faltered. Without thought, without volition, she grabbed his arm.

Energy crackled between them, and for a moment she thought he would turn toward her, would act, but he did not. Instead, he closed his eyes for an instant and allowed her to help him to shore.

"I am well," he said finally, and drawing his arm from hers, turned stiffly away.

Feelings shimmered through her. Regret and uncertainty and loss so deep it wounded her soul. "You need help," she murmured.

He paused for a moment, then: "You are mistaken," he said, and continued on.

Anger flashed through her, created by frustration, spurred by rejection. "Very well then," she said. "I'll be off."

He turned, too quickly, almost falling. She instinctively reached out, but he drew himself carefully erect on his own and straightened, expression already impassive. "I beg your pardon."

"I will arrive at Cinderknoll well before dawn," she said.

There was a moment of silence. His whisky eyes shone bright in a sudden shaft of moonlight. "It seems I was mistaken," he said. "I fear I will be unable to make it on my own after all."

She scowled at him. "What's that?"

Silence again, then: "I need help."

"You need help?"

For a second she actually thought he might curse her. But finally he nodded, thus she slipped her arm through his, supporting him as they traveled the dark streets.

By the time they arrived at Lavender House, Madeline felt strangely dizzy herself. Dizzy and disoriented, for she wanted nothing more than to touch his face, to look into his eyes and admit her feelings, to chance his cool demeanor. To take the risk. But the door burst open long before they reached it, preventing her from doing anything so foolish.

"Madeline!" Faye flew toward them, tiny feet soundless and bare against the cobbles, gown flowing like gossamer behind her.

"Faye," Maddy breathed, heart filling at the sight of her.

"You've returned." She murmured the words like a child's breathless prayer. "Shaleena swore you would not but I hoped . . ." She paused, eyes going wide as she shifted them to Jasper.

"What's amiss?"

"Lord Gallo has been wounded."

The faerie-bright face darkened. Her tone hardened. "Gunshot or knife?"

"Knife."

"How long ago?"

"Less than an hour."

"I shall fetch my amulets," she murmured, and in an instant she was gone, flying back into the house.

Madeline and Jasper followed at a more laborious pace. It wasn't until they stepped into the foyer that Maddy could see the blood that had dried on Jasper's shirt. Her stomach roiled, but she kept her tone steady. She was no healer. "Just a little farther."

"I am fine," he said, tone measured, expression stoic. "You should find your bed."

She ignored him. "We'll get you in front of the fire, then—"

"I'll go straight to my chambers."

"But Faye will be better able to see—"

"My weakness," he interrupted, then paused, gritting his teeth for a moment before continuing in a carefully conversational tone. "I shall go to my rooms."

She stared at him. "You've been wounded, Jasper. Surely you can't expect—" she began, but he cut her off, teeth clenched.

"I was almost too late."

She watched him, trying to decipher his meaning. "You can't seriously blame yourself for something that never happened."

He looked at her for an instant and actually laughed. "I'll go to my chambers," he repeated.

"Don't be a fool," she said, but he had already turned away. She caught up, swore in silence, and helped him up the stairs.

His bedroom was as dark and as neat as an old penny. She wished, not for the first time that she had her sister's gift to start a fire, but she did not. Thus she deposited him in a chair before the hearth and set a match to the firewood.

"How does he fare?" Faye asked, rushing into the room, her unbound hair a wild mass of gold against her back.

"He's stubborn," Maddy said, and the fragile little witch smiled.

"That's a favorable sign at least," she said, and hustled forward. But she stopped long before touching him, eyes wide and wary. Faerie Faye had never been comfortable around men. Indeed, it had taken her a fortnight to speak to any of them. "You'll have to remove . . ." She paused, looking young and uncertain. "You'll need to remove his shirt."

"No," Jasper said, voice firm, expression unyielding.

Faye scowled, balancing a handful of stones and a wooden basin of unexplained liquid. "I truly believe it would be best if—"

"No," he said again.

Faye bit her lip and shifted her eyes away. "The wound should be washed with goat's rue and camphor before employing—"

"It's not necessary," Jasper said, and leaned his head back against the cushion.

"Well . . ." Faye glanced uneasily from him to Madeline. "I fear there is little to be done then if—"

"The hour is late. Find your bed," Jasper ordered.

"Very well," Faye said, and depositing the basin and stones on the bedstead, turned shyly away.

Madeline gave him a scalding look and hurried after the girl. Closing the door behind her, she spoke. "Faerie Faye."

The little witch glanced back, eyes troubled, and Madeline reached for her hands, clasping them gently.

"What of you?" Maddy asked. "Are you well?"

Faye smiled, but the connection of skin to skin evidenced emotions other than happiness. "Of course, now that you are here," she said. "I've been hearing wild tales."

"Rumors, no doubt."

"Oh I hope not," Faye said, and a trickle of sadness seeped through her fingertips. "Someone has to live life for those of us too . . . those of us left behind."

Madeline searched the girl's eyes, but they were bright and clear, showing no signs of the debilitating headaches that accompanied her erratic bouts of "sight." Only the physical contact proved her consternation.

"Forgive Lord Gallo," Maddy said. "He's out of sorts. His arm—"

"Does not hurt half so much as his heart."

Madeline scowled. "What?"

The girl smiled, the expression real and bright this time. "He will be well now that you are returned."

"Don't be silly," Madeline said. She felt fidgety suddenly, strangely breathless. "*You* are the healer."

"Not for him." Squeezing Maddy's hands, she sent a quiet river of peace through the connection. "Good night," she said, and slipped away.

Madeline returned to Jasper's chambers with a scowl.

He didn't turn toward her, but kept his eyes

closed, his face impassive. "Did I not tell you to find your bed?"

"You must be more gentle with Faye."

"I believe I am still the director here."

"And she's still fragile."

He opened his eyes, caught her with his gaze, dark and still and deep. "Then why did you leave?"

Because she could not be near him, could not see him and know he didn't want her. She turned away, fiddling with the amulets. "I'll tend your wound before I go."

"So you insist on continuing with this foolishness?"

"I insist on saving—" She stopped herself, closed her eyes, and took a careful breath. "I insist that you take off your shirt," she said, and turned back, hands almost steady.

Their gazes met and fused. "No."

"Why? Are you hideously deformed?"

"Yes," he said. "And I'm very sensitive about it."

For a moment she almost believed him. "Oh, don't be a child," she said finally, angry at herself for her naïveté. "You've been hired to care for those in this house. How will you do so from the grave?"

"I am not about to die."

But suddenly the enormity of the possibility rushed in on her. "What if you do? What if you expire before morning? What then will become of Les Chausettes?"

"Don't be ridiculous," he said, jaw set.

"Faye is not yet ready for the world," she said, and winced at the thought of living without him. "She has not yet realized her full powers. What will become of her? Of all of us . . . *them*," she corrected.

Their gazes clashed. He pulled his away.

"Very well then," he said. "If that is what it takes to get me a night's rest, do what you must."

Stifling a scowl and remembering to breathe, Madeline squatted before him and reached for his buttons, but in a moment she accidentally touched his chest. Feelings flared like lightning, but she ignored them, held them at bay, fought them back. She had work to do, and yet, as her fingers skimmed his skin, she felt her cheeks warm, felt her heart race.

The garment fell away, revealing the smooth, sloping muscles of his chest. Their gazes fused.

"You should sleep," he said, but his eyes were saying something else. Something. Though she didn't know what.

"Why were you there tonight?" she asked.

A muscle jumped in his jaw. "I fear I cannot tell you if you are no longer a part of the coven."

"So it was a mission?" And not on her behalf.

"Of course."

"And it had nothing to do with the missing girls?"

"I told you I would learn what I could only if you returned to Lavender House." He paused, body relaxed, but there was something deep and bright in his eyes. "Might you be considering coming back?"

Reaching out, she wrung out the rag that floated in the basin and washed the blood from his arm. "I gave my word to find Marie."

"You gave your word to work for Britain's government. To work with the coven."

"Do you think I've not done enough for this coven?"

"I am simply trying to—"

"For England?"

"You've been a good servant to this country, but—"

"A good servant!" She pressed harder against his wound, stanching the blood.

Jasper gritted his teeth.

"Is that what I am to you?" she asked.

He kept his gaze on the far wall. "What else might you be?" he asked.

"What else?" Maddy asked. Frustration burned her. Placing a hand on his chest, she leaned closer. The heat from his skin seared her very soul. His gaze, as he lifted it to her eyes, burned her heart. "Can you think of no other capacity I might fill, Jasper?"

His jaw tightened. "What would you be but an honored member of this house?"

She watched him for an instant, then rose slowly to her feet. "Until this moment," she said, "I would have never guessed you to be a coward."

He raised one brow slightly. In the firelight his chest looked broad and dark and capable. Just as she knew it would.

"Oh yes, you protected me," she said, and slowly paced the length of the room, chest heaving above her dark gown.

"It is my job," he said.

"And how much easier it is to take a blow than admit a weakness."

"What weakness is that?"

"That you care."

He sat very still. "I'm sorry if I have made you believe—"

"You desire me," she said, and pacing back to him, bent and gripped the chair beside his shoulders. "You want me beneath you. Around—" she began, but suddenly she realized the truth. It was that strange, undisciplined part of her speaking. The bold, uncensored part.

Sucking in her breath, Madeline remained exactly as she was, wide-eyed and staring. Then she rose and turned away, clasping her hands in front of her. The fire crackled.

"My apologies," she said.

He was silent for a moment, then: "Shall I take this to mean that it's becoming more difficult to control your consciousness?"

She forced herself to turn back toward him. "I am weary."

"So it's more difficult to maintain control when you're tired?"

She didn't answer.

"You didn't have this trouble at Lavender House."

She smiled a little as she retrieved a smooth gemstone and cradled it between her hands. Faye's harnessed energy hummed from it. "I did not have this power," she said, and slipping the leather cord over his neck, pressed the stone to his chest.

His eyes flickered a little. "I wish for you to return to the coven," he said, but his voice sounded strange, hoarse, strained.

"Is that all?" she asked.

"All what?"

"Is that all you want of me?" she asked, and smiled again.

"I want you to cease allowing your wayward *mind* to rule your life," he said.

She smoothed her hand sideways a bare inch, soothing an abrasion. Her fingers brushed his nipple, and she almost thought she felt him shudder.

"Is *that* all?"

He closed his eyes for a protracted second. "Perhaps I owe you an apology as well," he said.

"Most probably," she agreed, "but to what are you referring specifically?"

"The dance," he said. "At Byresdale. Below her hand, his mounded muscles looked as firm as the amulet. "Perhaps I wasn't completely prepared for your . . . for the powers you have developed."

Perhaps *she* hadn't been either. Perhaps she would never be.

His gaze seemed to be caught on her lips. "I think you'll agree that I'm generally more professional than I was on that particular night."

"Some might say you are usually more boring," she said.

He watched her, body still. "Boring is safe," he said.

But Maddy leaned in just a fraction of an inch. Beneath her hand, his skin felt as hot as a brand, as smooth as the hardwood beneath her feet. Not at all boring. "And what of me?" she asked. "Am I safe?"

His breath was coming a little faster now. A

muscle hardened in his jaw. He gritted his teeth, and then he reached out and curled his hand behind her neck.

"Jasper!" someone rasped from the doorway.

He jerked his hand away with a hiss. Madeline straightened, pivoting toward the door. Shaleena stood in the opening.

"What have you done?" she asked, and rushed toward them, breasts bouncing, eyes accusatory. She was absolutely naked. "A knife wound! I thought even you could prevent this, Madeline."

A thousand explanations sprang to Maddy's tongue, but she stilled them.

"He keeps us safe," Shaleena said, and placed a hand on his shoulder. "Keeps us focused."

For a second Maddy thought she saw him flinch, but then he froze.

"Every coven needs its master," she said, and stroked his arm. "I thought you knew that much." Her thigh was pressed to his.

Madeline felt strangely breathless.

"But I suspect I can fix this, just as I've fixed all your other botches."

Rage curled through Madeline, but she straightened her back and carefully clasped her hands. "Well . . ." She drew a deep breath, struggling for control. "It looks as if there is little reason for me to remain here."

For one harsh moment of weakness, she almost hoped Jasper would shake off Shaleena's hand, would rise to his feet, would beg her to stay, but he did not; there was little she could do but leave.

"You should have told me you were wounded," Shaleena scolded. "I would have come straight-away."

Jasper set his jaw and wished to hell he was unconscious. "I'll be fine," he said, and refused to glance toward the door, refused to think how she had looked when Shaleena had pressed against his thigh.

"I'm certain you will, now that she's gone." Picking up an amulet, she examined it for a moment, then tossed it contemptuously back among its mates.

"I'm tired," he said. "Perhaps we could discuss—"

"Not too tired, I hope," she said, and skimmed her gaze down his body.

Anger mingled with stunned disbelief. The woman was incorrigible. And possibly mad. He'd just been wounded, for God's sake. "My apologies," he said, "but this is not going to happen."

"I won't hurt you," she said, and approached him, hips swaying. "Not more than you can bear at any rate."

"Good night, Shaleena," he said.

She stopped, brows lowered, anger brewing. He refrained from closing his eyes. It was entirely possible that he wasn't up to this. Not against Shaleena. She was powerful and angry, and unpredictable. How embarrassing would it be if she raped him?

"Is it because of her?" she asked.

"I fear I've no idea what you mean."

"Is it because of that weak-spined little saint?"

He gritted his teeth, containing his anger. She knew nothing of Madeline. Less than nothing, if she believed her to be weak. "It is because I am not interested," he said.

She stared at him, then laughed. "That cannot possibly be true."

Good God. "Then would you believe it is because I am wounded?"

She smiled, softening, full hips swaying as she approached. "I could kiss it and make it better."

Or she could get the hell out of his room. "No."

Her face contorted. "It *is* because of her."

"Listen—"

"No, you listen!" she said, and poked a finger at him. "That scrawny little—"

"Watch your language," he warned. His voice sounded gravelly, angry. He didn't correct it. "I'll not tolerate abuse. Not where she's concerned."

Her jaw dropped. She breathed a snort of surprise. "She's hexed you," she rasped. "She's hexed you and you're completely unaware."

Jasper remained very still, wondering, thinking. Was it possible? Maybe. Perhaps that was why he couldn't get her out of his mind. Then again, maybe it was because of who she was. *What* she was. Gentleness. Goodness. Hope. The sound of her laughter sparkled in his memory. The memory of her smile warmed his soul.

How convenient it would be to believe she had cursed him, but the truth was more mundane, more painful. He was in love. Had been for nearly a decade. In love with a woman he would never touch. For touch was dangerous. Deadly. Made him lose control. And he would maintain control. Had vowed to do so. Had vowed to himself and to the man who had saved him.

"Believe what you wish, Shaleena," he said.

"I don't need permission," she hissed. "Not from you or that saintly bitch—"

He snapped to his feet. "Get out," he snarled.

She drew back in wide-eyed surprise.

"Out of this room this instant or out of the coven forever."

"You're making a grave mistake," she warned.

"It won't be the first," he said, and planting his palm on her back, shoved her out the door.

Chapter 15

It was dark and Madeline was exhausted. Once again an empty lead had taken her halfway across London. But she had made a promise to Bertram Wendell and she would not break a vow; she would learn what she could about Marie's disappearance. Would bring the girl home if humanly possible. But *was* it possible? She knew far too little. Though she had left Sultan hidden in a copse of maple near the millpond and traipsed to Lady Tillian's estate alone, she had learned nothing.

Neither had her suspicions about Frederic Lambert proven fruitful. He was not hiding girls away in the tavern on the Thames. Instead, he was performing sexual acts with another man.

Madeline felt herself blush. She truly hadn't known men did the kinds of things she had seen in her mind. Indeed, if the truth be told, she knew little of men. Of their needs. Of their desires. Despite her volition, or perhaps because of it, she had remained quite sheltered.

It had been two days since she had assisted Jasper to Lavender House. Two days since they had kissed, since she had felt the flame of his hands against her skin—since she had left him to Shaleena's tender mercies.

Madeline gritted her teeth against the memory. Perhaps she should have stayed, staked her claim, admitted her feelings. But she dared not. For if those feelings had been reciprocated, he would never have tolerated Shaleena's presence in his chamber. He would have expelled her immediately. Would have begged Madeline to stay, would have confessed his undying devotion in reverent tones and . . .

Whom was she fooling? Jasper Reeves wasn't the sort to spout poetry even if he *did* have feelings for her. If he had feelings at *all*. And she knew full well that such was not the case. Indeed—

A small scratch of a noise issued from the darkness, snagging Madeline's attention. Her mount was tethered not far away. She could see him watching her, narrow ears pricked forward. The sound had not come from him. She remained still, barely breathing. Had someone found her gelding? Was someone waiting for her? Watching her?

She closed her eyes, thinking, sensing, but her

thoughts were distorted, muddied by memories of
Jasper's touch, of his eyes. For a short while in the
boat he had almost seemed to care. Not about a
mission, not about power or about the committee or even about Les Chausettes, but about *her*.
Whether she was safe. Whether she was happy.

The shadow of a noise sounded in the darkness
again, so soft it was little more than a thought, yet
it snapped Madeline's mind into the present. What
was wrong with her? This was not the time to day-
dream like a foolish schoolgirl. This was the time
to prove herself. The time she had been waiting for.
The time to use the powers she had so laboriously
nurtured.

Drawing a deep breath, she closed her eyes,
gathered her strength, and sent her senses into the
darkness. For a short while all was normal. She
could hear the chirp of the frogs, smell the dank,
fertile scent of the pond, feel the warm, soft air
on her face, but in a moment all sensations faded.
Time ceased to be. Dimness filled her.

But gradually awareness found her again. Shad-
ows surrounded her, alive with life, with energy.
And then she was full, whole. Yet the image of
Jasper was still firmly planted in her head.

Madeline jerked, always momentarily disoriented when she was refilled, but the picture of
Jasper remained in her mind, and suddenly she re-

alized the truth; he was there, nearby, hiding in the shadowy foliage.

Madeline narrowed her eyes, peering breathlessly into the brush. It couldn't be. It was simply that she was still obsessing about him, she thought, but in the depths of her, she knew better. Far better.

He had followed her. But why?

The answer came immediately; since her departure from Lavender House, he didn't trust her. The pain of that realization struck her like a blow, but she shouldn't have been surprised. He had warned her, after all, told her that the committee was concerned. He had, in fact, demanded that she leave the country. But she hadn't listened. And now here he was, spying on her as if she were no better than any of the felonious individuals she herself had spied on.

But perhaps she was being unfair. Perhaps he was simply concerned for her safety. He had always underestimated her, had given Shaleena the Gavin mission not six months before.

That one had hurt. Madeline was better suited. She was the best they had at remaining unseen. And she had asked for the task. Had admitted she wanted it, but he had ignored her request. Was it because he thought her less talented? Or because she hadn't been naked?

Anger filled her. She drew herself up, ready to

confront him, but suddenly another idea drifted through her consciousness. An image of herself sky-clad beneath the waxing moon, dancing, cavorting. An image of Jasper, frozen in place, watching her, hard with desire. Desire for her. Desire that would never be sated.

She shook the thoughts from her head, but they returned with a vengeance. And suddenly she realized the images were not entirely her own. They were a product of her awakening senses. Making her consider foolish things. Dangerous things.

Maybe he really did desire her, and was lying to hide his feelings. Maybe he didn't trust her and therefore was spying on her. Either way, he deserved to be made a fool of. To be made uncomfortable. And she would look damned good dancing in the moonlight.

But that would be improper. Then again, she was a *witch*. She was supposed to be improper.

But what if someone happened past?

On the other hand—

Good God, it was little wonder he didn't trust her decisions, Madeline realized suddenly. She didn't trust herself.

Drawing a deep breath, Maddy straightened. She was gifted. She was powerful. If someone came by, what then? If she wished, she could send them scurrying for cover. But . . . She stared into the darkness, unseeing, but *feeling*. He was there. She was sure of it. Just him and the magic.

Madeline turned her face to the sky. The moon was nearly full and spilled out its silvery light like wine from a precious chalice. It was smiling. Beckoning, inviting her to play. And suddenly she was stepping out of her slippers. Her inhibitions went with them. Bending, she rolled down her stockings and pulled them from her feet. The grass felt soft and cool between her toes.

Smiling, she slipped her gown from her shoulders. The night caressed her breasts. She pushed the garment lower. Her nipples beaded in the night air. She was dressed in nothing but pantaloons now, yet still it was too much. Untying the undergarment's drawstring, she slipped it from her waist and bent, pushing it to the ground.

It almost seemed as if she could feel Jasper's start of surprise as her buttocks shone in the moonlight. But instead of hiding, instead of blushing, she stepped boldly out of the muslin undergarment and flung her clothing over a maple that bent sharply over the pond. Then, seeing how the moonlight rippled on the water, she stepped onto the limb. The fissured bark felt rough and solid beneath her feet. She pattered out over the water, reveling in the lush feel of freedom. Spreading her arms, she lifted her face to the moon. She was witch, she was

power, and the dark mystery of the glassy pool
called to her. Straddling the tree's broad trunk, she
dipped her fingers into the smooth surface. Ripples
echoed away from her hand, just as ripples of a different sort shimmied through her sensitized body.
Between her legs, she felt swollen and wet and hot.
Bracing her palms against the bark, she arched into
the maple and was surprised by the hard surge of
feelings, of primeval desire. She pressed again.

Suddenly she could actually feel Jasper's discomfort, could sense his engorged desire. And she could
think of no reason to stop. Thrusting her breasts
toward the moon, she pressed her groin against the
unyielding surface just as she thrust the sensations
into Jasper's mind.

Did she imagine it or did she hear his rasp of
primal desire? But it no longer mattered, for suddenly the feelings were everything. She moved
harder, her breathing escalated. She imagined him
against her, clasping her to him, thrusting, pulsing, needing, and suddenly she was full. With a
soft gasp, she fell against the rough trunk, sated,
heart pounding a primitive beat. A twig snapped
somewhere in the night, and Madeline smiled as
she slowly sat upright.

Hidden in the woods, Jasper was tight with discomfort, and she was glad. Rising to her feet, she
slowly made her way back along the bent course

of the tree and stepped onto dry land. But the night was hot, the air heavy. Leaving her garments where they lay, she untied Sultan and straightened his forelock. His broad brow felt hot beneath her hand and she paused, delaying for a moment, before mounting him. In a heartbeat she had urged him into the pond. Coolness flowed over her legs. The gelding puffed as the water rose higher and he lifted his heavy legs, pushing them through the languid current like a mighty dancer.

Finally, cooled and sated, Madeline retrieved her clothing from the maple. Smiling into the night, she slipped her gown over her head as she urged Sultan toward home, leaving her bodice gaping as she passed within inches of where Jasper stood watching from the underbrush.

He was insane. There was no longer any reason to doubt it. No reason to pretend otherwise.

Pacing, Jasper fisted his hands and tried to think of something other than how she had looked in the moonlight. How her breasts had gleamed, how her hair had fallen, soft and glistening down the length of her enchanting back. Of how she had felt.

But good God! He *hadn't* felt her! Hadn't touched her. And yet it seemed as though he had. As though he had been the one beneath her instead of that damned tree. Or that damned, stupid horse.

And . . . holy mother of God . . . was he really jealous of a horse?

At the thought, he actually gripped his hair in one hand, ready to yank it from his head as he remembered her moan of desire. Her rasp of satisfaction at satiation.

The memory made him ache, made him yearn, made him . . . crazed.

But no. Wait. He paced again, rapidly now, fretfully. *He* was not the one who had gone mad. *She* was. Because the Madeline *he* knew, the lovely, sensitive girl he had met so many years before, would never do such a thing. She was proper, pure, intelligent, controlled. She would *not* dance naked beneath the grinning moon. She would not bare her perfect breasts or . . .

He closed his eyes and harnessed a groan. It didn't matter what she did. His actions were *not* dictated by hers. He was Lord Gallo, as cool as a winter wind, as smooth as foreign silk.

He didn't have to think of her every moment. He didn't have to hold her in his arms, to make love to her. And he certainly did not have to follow her every move.

The idea was asinine. Eventually she would discover him, and then how would he explain himself?

Unless . . .

He stopped pacing, but his mind kept spinning.

Might she have known of his presence on the previous night? Might she have sensed him in the darkness?

But no. She would never bare herself if she knew someone watched. If she knew *he* watched. She didn't even like him. Had implied that he was less than human, so the idea that she would *satisfy* herself knowing he was hidden in the shadows was unthinkable. He felt his forehead bead with sweat at the thought. She would never have undressed, would never have bared every inch of her irresistible skin, would certainly never have mounted that damnably lucky tree, wet and hot and . . .

Realizing he had ceased to breathe, he pulled in a hard breath and paced again.

No, she had not known he was there, but perhaps that only made the situation worse. What kind of woman would bare her all where there was no one to protect her? Where anyone could happen along? No man could resist her. That much was obvious at the first glimpse of her. None could see her without needing to . . .

He fisted his hands and stopped short in the middle of the room, staring blankly into nothing. She was obviously troubled.

And it was his job to save her.

Chapter 16

"**L**ady Redcomb." The miss who spoke to Madeline was young, bonny, and smiling. "I was wondering if you might read my palm."

The green baize curtain had just closed on the first act of *Romeo and Juliet*. Which was just as well. The thought of fornicating adolescents was beginning to make Maddy feel strangely restless.

She had accompanied Ella and Drake, but stood a bit apart as they conversed in low voices.

"Tell me," Maddy said, "have we met?"

"I've not had the pleasure," said the other. "Indeed, I've only just arrived from Lord and Lady Renton's country estate. But I've heard so much about you. Might you spare a moment?"

Glancing toward Ella, Madeline saw that her sister was watching with raised brows.

Madeline refrained from clearing her throat. "I'm afraid you've been misled. My readings are no more than a parlor game."

"That is not what I've heard."

"Oh?" Ella asked, gliding over with a pleasant smile that didn't fool Madeline for a moment. "And who might you have been speaking with?"

"I heard you found Mr. Pendent's watch."

"I never actually—" Maddy began.

"And Mr. Menton's miniature."

"In truth—"

"Finding trinkets," Ella said, and widening her eyes, sounded breathlessly impressed as she momentarily placed a protective hand over her tiny belly. "You must indeed be gifted."

Madeline managed to refrain from giving her the evil eye. "I am truly sorry Miss—"

"Terragon, Tess Terragon."

"I am truly sorry, Miss Terragon, but I fear—"

"No." She paused. "*I* fear."

Madeline paused, breath held. "What's that?"

"There are rumors. Terrible rumors," she said, and shivered a little. "About girls going missing. Girls being . . ." She lowered her voice. ". . . violated."

"From whom did you hear these rumors?"

She shrugged, a casual lift of swan-white shoulders. "'Tis said a maid disappeared just a few days past."

Maddy felt her heart bump in her chest. "What are you speaking of?"

"Haven't you heard? A girl named Katherine. She was from a good family. A pastor's daughter, I believe, but she disappeared as if she had never been."

"Disappeared from where?" Maddy could feel Ella's concern, even though her tone was cool.

The girl hesitated a moment, then said, "Deptford."

Ella scowled. "The dockyards are hardly a place for the delicately nurtured."

"I wholeheartedly agree," Miss Terragon said, eyes wide. "And while *I* would not think of venturing there myself . . ." She glanced at Madeline. "I worry now about other parts of the city. Is it even safe to be seen in Hookham's?"

"I believe you can brave the lending library," Madeline said.

"But the thought of those poor girls simply gives me a chill." She turned brimming calf eyes from Ella to Maddy. "I had hoped you could spare a moment to seek my future in my palm. Ease my mind . . . so to speak."

Madeline watched the girl in silence. There was something strange here. Something not quite what it seemed. But what was it exactly?

Without sparing her sister a glance, she nodded. "Very well," she agreed, and led the girl back into the theater. It was quiet in the pit compared to the chaos in the lobby. They settled in side-by-side. Maddy drew a deep breath, took the girl's hand in her own, and caught her gaze. For three beats of her heart there was nothing, but soon it became clear that what she saw was not nothing. It was darkness. A fire flared in the blackness. Two pugilists appeared, circling slowly, heads lowered like battling bulls. Excitement swirled around them, rage, hope, desire, but in a moment the combatants were gone, replaced by an etched silhouette of Tess Terragon. The image sharpened. She stood in the shadows, body tense, face gilded by a flickering flame. A man watched with steely eyes from the darkness, and suddenly he was close. So close. Maddy almost cried out in fear, but in that moment she saw the lust in the girl's eyes. Felt the pounding excitement of her heart. Her hands were on his belt, pulling open his trousers, reaching for his—

Madeline dropped the girl's hand with a start.

"What did you see?" Tess gasped.

Maddy shifted her gaze to her lap. Embarrassed, uneasy, and oddly aroused, she cleared her throat. "The docks are no place for the gently reared."

Miss Terragon remained silent for a moment as if holding her breath, then leaned close, eyes alight. "I am certain you're right, but I must know that I will not . . . that *no one* will come to harm there."

"Harm?" Madeline couldn't say if sex was

harmful or not, despite her title as widow, despite her twenty-four years. "A union between the two of you is unlikely to be to anyone's advantage," she said.

The girl leaned back abruptly. "I don't know what you're talking about."

Sexual energy seemed to swirl through the theater, feeding on the drama, the life. "Be cautious," Madeline said. "Deptford is not a proper place for a maid of your ilk."

"And of course I will never venture there alone. But if I did, would I be safe?"

Madeline resisted rolling her eyes. "It is dangerous," she said, but the idea only seemed to excite the girl.

"Would he . . . I mean . . . is there someone there who might harm me?"

"That I cannot say."

Miss Terragon bit her lip and glanced sideways, eyes wide and blue. "Can I be honest with you, Lady Redcomb?"

No, Madeline thought. She felt tired and strangely old. "Of course," she said.

The girl leaned close. "I *did* meet a man."

In Madeline's mind, his face looked gaunt and angry. His hungry eyes burned.

"He's not like . . ." She drew a shuddering breath. "He's unlike anyone ever I've met. So different from the dandy pinks Mother parades before me. He's a *man*. His eyes are fire." She shivered. "His hands are magic."

"I rather doubt it," Madeline said, and in that moment, she realized the truth. The girl wasn't afraid at all. She simply wanted someone with whom to share her exploits, but the maid eyed her askance now.

"Surely you've known a man with magic hands."

"I can't say that I have."

"Well, you should," she whispered. "As soon as possible."

"And you should stay with Mrs. Prudeau," Maddy said, trying to hide her discomfort.

The girl jerked back. "You know my chaperone?"

Madeline said nothing.

"You truly *are* gifted."

Yes, she was, but it didn't hurt that she had seen the girl with the horse-faced matron. "She worries," Madeline said.

The girl leaned close. "What do you suppose *has* happened to the girls?"

A new thought struck Maddy with harsh resonance. "What is this man's name?"

"What man?"

She was becoming tired of the charade. "Did he know the girl who has gone missing?"

"No? Why? Grant would never hurt anyone. Well . . ." She shook her head, smiling at herself. "He's a pugilist. Not like one of those silly tulips at Gentleman Jackson's. But a street fighter. The best on the docks. So strong. Like a wild bull, and when he . . ." She drew a deep breath. "But he'd never hurt a woman."

"His name is Grant?"

"They call him Granite. Granite O'Malley because he's got more bottom than any other. But he has a poet's soul. A gentleman's touch." She had the decency to blush. "Or so I'm told."

Maddy took a deep breath. Having people know of her gifts was a strange, double-edged sword. "Has he ever mentioned her?" she asked. "The maid who's gone missing?"

The girl thought for a moment. "He was the one who told me of her. Said the docks were not a safe place for me."

Because of men like himself? "What of the other girls who have disappeared?"

"What of them?"

"Has he ever mentioned *them*?"

Tess chewed her lip and lowered her voice. " 'Tis said they were all untried."

"Did O'Malley tell you that?"

She shook her head. "It's what everyone is saying."

"What else are they saying?"

"They're all young, pretty. Innocents. Like myself," she said, and cocked her grin up another notch.

Madeline raised a brow, comfortable in her role as experienced widow.

"Do you think they are being used for unspeakable acts?" the girl asked.

"Is that what you've heard?"

"There are rumors. Whispers."

"Where?"

"I beg your pardon."

"Who whispers?"

She shrugged. "Everyone. But as you can imagine, folks on the docks are becoming a bit nervous."

"Were you there last night?"

"I never said I was there at all."

Madeline gave her a weary glance.

"No," she admitted, managing finally to look a bit embarrassed. "But I'm to meet him there tonight."

Madeline's mind was spinning, but she shifted her gaze to the middle distance and spoke in a dramatic monotone, "I think it best if you remain home this eventide." *Eventide?* She almost laughed at the word, but Miss Terragon caught her breath.

"Why? What do you see?"

She saw herself, dressed as a commoner, flirting, laughing, milling with the throng at Deptford Dockyards. "Trouble," she murmured, still not looking at the girl.

"Unspeakable trouble?" whispered the girl.

"Unspeakable," Maddy said, and left the girl where she sat.

Chapter 17

The pugilists had been stripped to the waist. Their knuckles were battered raw and their faces bloody. One was tall and fair. The other had dark hair, pale skin, and eyes that burned with fever. Granite O'Malley. Madeline recognized him from the images conjured from contact with Tess. Recognized him and refused to look away, for she was supposed to be one of the mob. Supposed to be enjoying herself, but truth to tell she did not even favor the matches on Bond Street. And this was a far cry from that carefully groomed spectacle. This was life, gritty and dark. Life she was trying to blend into. She had still not mastered her shifting potion, but she could do what every woman could. Alter her manners, affect a dialect, change her hairstyle, her clothes, her posture. She had done all those things.

Apparently a girl named Katherine Tell had disappeared from this very spot not many days before. Madeline had asked around, eager to learn more, but the maid didn't travel in Maddy's circles. Instead, she was the youngest daughter of a local pastor, a girl who tended the parish garden and cleaned the sanctuary. But apparently she had also frequented the docks.

Normally, of course, Madeline would have acquired information from Jasper, but she dared not ask him, for he seemed determined to keep her from learning the truth.

The mob surged, jostling Maddy. The tall man jabbed with his left, hitting the other square in the face. Granite staggered back, head tucked low, eyes gleaming like a devilish hound's. Did he know something of the girls? Maddy wondered. Was he somehow involved? He looked demonic. Terrible. His face was covered in blood, his eyes burned like living coals. But the crowd didn't seem to notice. They were yelling encouragement, cursing their luck. Money changed hands with the regularity of clockwork.

" 'Ey, Kath," someone said, and grabbed Madeline's sleeve.

She swung about, heart racing.

The man jerked back, beefy face surprised beneath his battered leather hat. "Oh. Me apologies. I thought ye were someone else," he said, and turned into the seething mob. Maybe it was curiosity that convinced Madeline to follow him. Maybe it was foolishness.

"'Oo?" she asked, projecting her Cockney accent through the noise of the mob.

He turned back, squinty eyes widening as he saw her behind him. "What's that?"

She hurried toward him. "You lookin' for Katherine?" she asked. It was a wild stab in the dark, but a stab worth taking.

He lowered his heavy brow and shifted his gaze from one side to the other. "What do you know of her?" he asked. His face was lined and troubled. His tunic bore a workingman's stains.

"Too little," she said.

He scowled, examining her with shrewd eyes set close on his head. "Have you heard from her? Do you know where she is?"

"No," she admitted. "But I wish to."

"Why?"

She sensed the mob around her, making certain their conversation went unnoticed. But the crowd was wound tight in its own wild excitement, leaning toward the pugilists, slavering with zeal. "I would help," she said.

The man's eyes were intense, his face hard. For a moment the world seemed to recede, then: "Meet me," he said. "In half an hour's time. Near the victualing yard."

She nodded, and in a blink, the man was gone, swallowed by the seething mob.

The crowd surged in on her. The boxers behind the makeshift ring circled. The blond man smiled and motioned in a come-ahead manner. Granite O'Malley swung weakly, and in that instant, the other hammered him with an uppercut. Granite staggered back.

Curses and jeers rang from allies and enemies. But he rallied, getting his feet under him and coming on.

Madeline scanned the mob, hoping Tess would be absent. Hoping everyone she knew would be absent. But blood sport was not for the laboring class alone. A smattering of gentlemen in frock coats were scattered throughout the crowd, and the well-dressed lady was not unseen. As for Madeline, she felt all but invisible in her faded blue frock and scuffed shoes. Able to look at faces, to try her best to determine whether she knew anyone there. To determine if they were somehow involved in the disappearance of the missing girls. But no one looked familiar, and suddenly the mob surged again. Men yelled. Women screamed. Madeline was nearly trampled in the uproar, but found her footing as the crowd lurched to congratulate the winner and berate the loser.

In a moment Granite was hoisted into the air and

carried forward on a sea of heaving shoulders. His nose looked to be broken. Blood marred his chest. But his eyes still gleamed, and as he looked down at her, she felt caught, exposed. His lips twisted up for a flaring instant and then he was gone, swallowed by the darkness.

Madeline shook herself free. She was to meet someone. An ally. Or so she hoped. But she would not go unprepared. She would be ready. Smart.

Hurrying from the crowd, she found the victualing yard. At one time it had only supplied biscuits for the seamen, but through the years it had expanded until it offered all manner of food and provisions. Now, however, all was dark and quiet. She studied it from the shadowed corner of a pickling house. All seemed well. Nothing sinister brushed her senses. Still, she waited in silence, watching intently until she saw the man in the battered hat approach the yard. He was alone. She scanned the surrounding area, but no one seemed to lie in hiding. He conversed with no one, seemed to plan no evil. Indeed, she was just about to step into the open when she heard a scuff of noise from behind. She jerked about, alert and ready. But in that instant someone grabbed her. A cloth was pressed to her nose. She struck with her elbow, but her arm never connected with flesh. It was as if there was no one behind her, and yet she was already growing faint. Golden dots flittered before her eyes. Her limbs felt weak.

Gathering all her will, she made herself go limp, but instead of letting her fall, her captor hugged her close, pulling her tight against his body. She kicked then, fighting with every skill, every well-honed instinct she possessed.

He grunted in pain. So her attacker was flesh and blood at least, she thought, and renewed her attack. Her elbow found purchase this time. She felt cartilage crunch, felt blood soak her sleeve, warm and sticky. But already she was being dragged backward, a hand wrapped tight over her mouth again.

Blackness threatened. Her will was faltering, her mind weakening. Her feet felt unattached as they dragged along at the end of her legs. Her body was as heavy as death. Still, she struggled, but he pressed his hand tighter to her face until she tipped with languid slowness into the tarry depths of nothing.

Madeline came to slowly, groggily. Her arms, she realized after a moment, were bound behind her.

A cloth had been wrapped across her eyes and tied behind her head. She wondered vaguely if it was monogrammed. Perhaps if she could remove it, she could gain a clue to her abductor's identity, but it felt snug against her temples. She was lying on the floor of a moving conveyance. It jarred her spine, rattled her body. Sitting up was no simple task, but she managed it and propped her back against a solid object behind her. A seat probably, for her feet were pressed tight to something on the far side, and she felt suddenly as if she were being squeezed from all sides, pressed tight until she couldn't breathe.

Panic scrambled her senses. Where was she? Why had she been taken? What—

But in that second she remembered who she was. *What* she was. Breathing carefully through her nose, she steadied her nerves. She was charmed, gifted. She was strength. She was knowledge.

"Hello," she said. The word sounded faint and weak, but it hardly mattered, for she knew she was alone. Forcing herself to relax against the cushion behind her, she tried to imagine her surroundings. There would be two seats facing each other. The space was narrow, most probably with windows on each side. It was dark, that she knew, for she would be able to sense light even through the cloth. But there was probably a lantern. It would be set near the window, above the seat.

Easing herself up carefully, she edged onto the cushion and scooted as far as possible to the right.

Once there, she pressed her face to the wall. It felt smooth and cool, but would do her no good. Standing, she struck her head on something hard and metallic. A lantern.

She shuffled to the side a bit, straightened nearly to her full height, and thrust her head over the top of the light. It was there that she found what she was looking for. A hard, metal cone atop the light. It was simple enough to ease the smooth peak under her blindfold, and after that it was only a matter of time before she was able to push it off.

The cloth stuck to her hair for a moment, then toppled to the floor. She blinked. The interior of the vehicle was little lighter without the blindfold, but when she glanced out the window she could see that London had been left behind. She didn't recognize the landscape, but that was hardly surprising. In the darkness, it would be all but impossible to identify the countryside just furlongs past the city's edge.

Twisting her arms, she felt a bit of leeway in the rope that bound her arms. Given enough time she could probably work out of her bonds. But how much time did she have? Would it be better to jump from the conveyance bound? The idea was sobering. The fall would be painful, possibly lethal. But perhaps that would be preferable to whatever lay ahead.

She wouldn't consider those grim possibilities, however. Instead, she thought of solutions. Possibilities. Perhaps she could step through, bring her arms in front of her body. Toeing off her shoes, she was careful not to tighten her bonds as she took three calming breaths. Then, flexing her shoulders almost to the point of dislocation, she eased her arms past her hips and tried to step through. But she was stiff from her time on the jostling floor. The muscles in her right thigh cramped, and she remained immobile for a moment, breathing through the pain until it subsided somewhat. Finally, able to wait no longer, she squeezed her legs carefully through the loop of her arms and straightened. Her moan of relief was audible, but it mattered little. The noise was drowned by the pounding of the horses' hooves, the rattle of the wheels against the road beneath them.

Drawing her hands gratefully up in front of her, she saw that she was bound with strips of linen. It had not been a hasty job. Or if so, she had been tied by someone quite skillful. She flexed her legs, trying to ease out the pain, then focused on the knot. It was placed on the outside of her wrists, making it difficult to reach with her teeth, but she managed it.

In a matter of minutes, the linens loosened. She shook off the bonds and rubbed circulation back into her wrists as she debated her next action.

Outside the window, the earth was racing by at a terrifying rate. Still, the leap would be far less dangerous with her hands to catch her. Then again, perhaps she should wait for her attacker to come to her. If she jumped, she could be injured in the fall, but with surprise on her side, she might be able to overwhelm her abductor.

But perhaps he was the same man who had taken the others. Fear shimmered through her, but she fought it down. If that were the case, if he knew the fate of the abducted maids, it was surely Maddy's duty to ascertain where they were being held, though waiting would almost certainly increase her risks and—

The carriage slowed.

Madeline's mind churned. She had vowed to help. It was her duty. Her calling. Snatching up her blindfold, she secured it about her head, then tried to retie her wrists, but her hands were unsteady. She could do no more than snag her arms loosely together.

Exhausted and shaken, Madeline settled back onto the floor to gather her strength, but the carriage was already lurching to a halt. Heavy footfalls thumped across gravel and grass. She tried to relax, to pretend unconsciousness, but her body was stiff, her mind too disoriented to send its senses out for a look at his face.

The door was jerked open. Rough hands reached for her, and she flinched despite herself.

"So you're awake then, are you, girl? Well, you can walk, or I can drag you. Alive or dead, it don't matter much to me," he rumbled, and heaved her out of the vehicle to stand upright, scared and blind in an unknown world.

Chapter 18

The room into which Maddy was shoved was dark and small. She knew that much even as she struggled to catch herself, to turn toward him.

"Stay," he ordered. "And you might yet live out the week."

The accent was coarse, the tone low and dark. Fear surged through her. She struggled to set it aside, for fear, more than anything, would defeat her.

"I know who you are," she lied.

Her voice sounded scratchy in the darkness. Hollow, empty, and bereft. She swallowed. She was no fool, no weakling. She straightened, lifted her chin, tried again.

"They call you Granite. They think you are strong. But you are not. You are weak."

He said nothing.

Was he angry? Was he plotting? Surely it would be wise to keep quiet, to allow him to leave, but knowing his identity would grant her an advantage, and the acrid taste of fear had leeched her ability to send her senses to the far side of the wall, should her captor leave.

"Where are the others?" she asked.

Still no response. In her mind, she imagined him pulling out a knife. Imagined him advancing on her. But she fought back the terror. She was strong. She could free her hands, could free her spirit.

"I won't put up with no trouble," he said, but his tone was a little less certain now, and with that realization she strengthened.

"You prey on the weak," she said.

"And you talk too bloody much."

"Girls," she said, and gathered her strength. "Children really, too young to defend themselves."

"Maybe you didn't understand me," he rumbled. "I'll be outside that door. If you are no fool you'll stay where you are. You'll do as you're told," he warned, and turned away.

She heard his footfalls retreating.

"You're a coward," she rasped desperately, but in that moment the door slammed shut, and she was left alone. Rubbing her ear on her shoulder, she pushed the blindfold up and listened, and there, at the very edge of her consciousness, she heard the creak of a carriage, the tattoo of hoofbeats.

She waited in silence. From outside came the

quiet night song of frogs. But little else met her ears.

"Is anyone here?" she asked finally.

A tiny scrape of uncomfortable noise answered her from somewhere on the far side of the door, but no one spoke. She drew a deep breath and removed her bonds. Then slipped off her blindfold. It did little good. The room was as dark as India ink. Walking carefully forward, arms outstretched, she found her way to the wall, then turned and headed in the other direction. In less than four feet her legs struck an object. Bending, she touched a surface. It was soft. A blanket?

It turned out to be a bed, a narrow pallet on legs. She searched on. In the corner was a commode. There was a tiny table near the door, but the surface was empty.

So she was alone in a small, poorly furnished room. Why? If her captor intended rape, surely she would already be in danger. But if not rape, then what? Was she to be held for ransom?

It seemed unlikely. After all, she had no husband to pay the reward. No father or sibling to mourn her absence. At least so far as the world was aware. Unless . . .

And suddenly the breath stopped in her throat.

Had someone learned her true identity? Did they know who she was? What she was capable of? If so, then they surely knew of Les Chausettes and . . . Her heart beat slowly in her chest. Maybe the abductor was targeting witches. Maybe the other girls were also gifted, and it was only a matter of time before the villains found Ella and the others. Perhaps, too, they knew of Jasper's involvement with the coven.

She closed her eyes as a new horror struck her. By trying to solve this crime she might have inadvertently involved the only man she had ever—

She abruptly cut off her thoughts and calmed her nerves. She was being foolish, as jumpy as a debutante. Forgetting her training, her skills. Silently tipping the little table upside down, she tested the strength of its legs. They were made of thick timber and set solidly into the top, but there were few things that could not be torn asunder if enough concentration was applied.

For one moment she let herself think of Ella, of her coven, of Jasper. They would not be risked because of her, she determined, and set to work.

Dawn came slowly but it made little difference, for Madeline's prison had no window. A chink in the wall told her morning had come, and though she pressed her face to that hole she could see nothing but a bland spread of woods. Her eyes felt gritty, her hands uncertain. Perhaps she should have slept, but she had no way of knowing when her chance to escape would present itself. She glanced about the room. It was much as she had imagined it. Ten feet by fourteen. The bed was adorned with nothing but a single red blanket. Looking at it made her feel weak with weariness, thus she turned her face away. The walls were rough plaster. The commode was metal. Just as she thought. No help there. No possibility of breaking it and using the shards for weapons.

But the door . . . there was a surprise. Five feet from the floor, a tiny hole had been drilled into the rough timber. Standing quickly, she examined it, only to find that it was too small to fit even her pinky into. On the far side it was covered by something that looked like a copper disk. Disappointed, but undeterred, she found that the hole had been freshly bored. The portal itself was weathered and grayed, but the wood around the tiny opening was pale and fresh. So the hole had been made recently. Less than a week's time, she estimated.

The first girl had disappeared almost a month ago. Was Maddy's abduction unrelated to the others, then? Or was she simply being held at a different location. And if so, why?

Outside her door she heard a rustle of sound. She waited in silence, breath bated. In a matter of minutes she could smell cooking. Her stomach rumbled but she ignored it.

"Miss." The voice that called to her was not the voice of the man who had dragged her here. This one was less certain, softer, with a lilt that suggested Celtic heritage. "I have your breakfast."

She said nothing, trying to place him. In polite society breakfast wasn't served until well past one. What did it say of him that he had prepared a meal just after the break of dawn?

She heard him shuffle his feet, listened as he shifted the copper blind aside so that he could gaze into her room. "You must get back from the door."

It seemed strangely difficult to remain silent; she had been taught politeness since infancy by a mother who had died too early, a mother who didn't realize that good manners could get you killed. That sometimes boldness alone could save you.

"You must back away from the door or I cannot deliver your meal."

She waited. Seconds ticked away.

"I was told not to trust you," he said.

By whom? And why? Did this mean he knew who she was? *What* she was? Or had he been told to trust none of the girls? Questions chased themselves wildly around in her head, but she voiced none of them. Curiosity could often do what pleading and arguing could not. She waited, prepared.

Quiet settled in. He shuffled his feet. "Very well then," he said, and letting the blind drop, stepped away from the door.

Five hours later she was truly hungry. She heard him cooking again, smelled side pork, and rose silently, feeling her knees groan and her muscles strain as she stood, but in a moment she heard him pace to the door once again.

"It is time to eat," he said.

Her back ached. Her legs felt stiff, and she wondered rather grittily if she would be able to move when given the chance.

"Miss?"

She felt her diaphragm rise and fall with each silent breath. For the hundredth time she wondered if she should attempt to send her senses out, but again decided she would need all her resources for the coming encounter.

"Miss?"

She waited, tensed, ready, and then the lock turned.

Clenching every muscle, readying every instinct, she lifted the table leg she had spent the night twisting free. A dark head peeked inside, and in that moment she swung with all her might. Her weapon struck his forehead with a resounding smack and splintered into a dozen shards. He staggered sideways, but she was already jerking the door open.

He lunged toward her, but she struck him with the heel of her hand. He stumbled away.

"Harry!" a voice boomed from outside.

Maddy bent, snatched a five-inch splinter from the floor, and grabbed her captor from behind. He was a good six inches taller than she but she could see past his bulky shoulder. Steadying her hands, she calmed her shuddering nerves and made certain her voice was level.

"If you've no wish to be responsible for this man's death you'll step into view," she said.

No one answered.

"I am not a violent person," she added, and steeled her will. She would kill to save herself. It was one of the coven's foremost rules. "But I will kill him if I must."

"She broke my nose," Harry said. His voice sounded nasal and quivery. "I think she broke my nose."

Blood leaked onto Maddy's hand. "I *did* break his nose," she said, gritting her teeth. "And if you do not show yourself in the next ten seconds I shall pierce his carotid artery."

Harry moaned.

No sound came from the other room. Maddy closed her eyes, steeling herself. "He'll not survive a full minute."

Sill no response.

She swallowed her bile. "Ten!" she said.

"I didn't wanna do this," Harry said.

"Nine! Do what?" she asked.

"Keep you here. I didn't want to. I just . . ." He paused, cranking his head sideways in an attempt to catch a glimpse of her.

"Eight! Where are the others?"

"What others?"

"Seven!" She held the stake very tight to quiet the tremble in her hands. "Milly, Tipper, Marie. Where are they?"

"Please don't kill me."

"Six! Why were they taken?"

"I got a daughter."

"Five! Are they still alive?"

"Please." He was starting to snivel. Becoming incoherent.

"Four!"

"Her name's Melinda. She's just a child."

Dear God, please don't make her kill some girl's father. "Three!"

"She ain't even four years of age and—"

"Two!"

"Kill him if you like," said a voice, and a hooded man stepped into view.

Chapter 19

A dozen scenarios stormed through Madeline's mind, a score of possibilities bloomed, but in an instant, in a split second of time, she thrust her captive aside and launched herself at the hooded man.

She struck him full-on. He hit the floor with a grunt, but the impact had toppled her sideways. She scrambled on top, righting herself, shoving the thick splinter up against his throat.

"Move and you've breathed your last," she rasped.

His hood was askew. Only one eye shone through the hole in the black fabric. He was breathing steadily and raised his hands in surrender.

She gritted her teeth and nodded jerkily. "Now . . . where are the—" she began, but suddenly, without the slightest warning, he jerked and she was soaring through the air. Her back struck the floor with a bone-shuddering jolt. Lightning filled her eyes. She couldn't breathe, couldn't think, and in an instant he was standing over her, reaching for her.

She gasped for air. He leaned in, but she dared not let him touch her. Snapping her knees up, she kicked upward with all her might, missing his groin by a handbreadth. Still he was driven back.

She was on her feet in a heartbeat, facing him, feet spread, arms poised for action.

His hood was crooked, yet she could see none of his face.

"Show yourself," she snarled.

He straightened slowly.

"Good luck to you," rasped a voice from the corner, and Harry lunged for the door.

Madeline didn't bother to turn toward him, but heard his erratic footfalls hustle into nothingness.

"Who are you?" she asked. Her breath was coming hard, but so was her adversary's.

He shook his head.

"Coward," she hissed, and sprang at him, trying to snag his hood, but he caught her arms. They hit the floor and rolled together.

Desperate, she drew forth all her energy, conjured an image of him drowning, and shot it into his mind.

He gasped for breath and jerked away. Rage and fear brought her to her feet. She flew at him again.

They went down together, rolling, and suddenly she was on her stomach, her face pressed to the floor, but she thrust an image into his head of another attacker approaching from behind.

He jerked around, and in that instant she yanked an arm free and slammed her elbow into his face. He toppled off balance. She twisted wildly sideways, and suddenly she was atop him, pinning him down, hand to his throat.

"Tell me where they are and I will spare your life," she rasped.

He shook his head.

"Then you die now," she hissed, but with one deft movement he knocked her arm aside and rolled. She was crushed under his weight. The tables were turned. He grabbed her arms, pinning them to the floor, and in that moment she noticed that her bodice had been torn and her breasts shone pale in the faded light.

The world went silent as his gaze lowered.

Fear gripped her throat, but she threw it off. She would use his lust, use his depravity.

Closing her eyes, she summoned all her strength and threw a picture of her naked into his mind. She felt him stiffen, sensed his arousal, and hoped. He would have to loose one hand to reach for her skirts, and when he did she would break free.

But instead of jerking up her gown, he jolted to

his feet and stumbled backward. "Good Lord," he rasped.

And in that moment she felt her breath leave her lungs in a rush. It couldn't be. *Couldn't* be.

But it was.

"Jasper?" she hissed.

He said nothing.

"Jasper?" She propped herself up on the heels of her hands. "What are you doing here?"

"Is that how you got him to open the door?"

Rising, she strode forward and snatched the hood from his head. His hair was tousled, his eyes accusatory.

She shook her head, dizzy, disoriented. "What—"

"Did he imagine you naked?" he asked. "Is that why he opened the door?"

"You abducted me!" Her own voice sounded strange to her ears. "You brought me here against my will."

"I thought I knew you," he said, and shook his head.

"You *abducted* me!" she repeated, voice rising, temper flaring as the weight of the truth settled in like an anchor.

"And I knew you would fight," he rasped. "Knew you would use your powers. I warned them that you could be difficult, but I didn't think you would bare yourself. Didn't think you would . . ."

He shook his head, swept his hand forward, indicating the whole of her.

"I broke his nose," she said, scowling at his foolishness. "That doesn't concern you?"

He snorted. "Given half a chance I'd break it myself."

She watched him. Was that emotion in his face? she wondered, but quickly returned her mind to the matter at hand.

"Where are we?" she asked.

"Well west of London. A friend's hunting cottage."

A friend? "Who were they?" she asked. "Your hired thugs."

He paced two steps and turned back. "There is speculation that the girls were drugged. It made sense to have Adams use a vapor to overcome you. I hoped you would assume, then, that he had abducted the others also. I worried that he might be too rough without the cloth to rend you unconscious. But I see now that you have no scruples."

"Me!" She huffed a breath of disbelief. "Me? I have—" she began, but she stopped abruptly. "You were afraid I . . . my consciousness would see you. That's why you wore a hood."

He drew a deep breath, shook his head as if to dislodge the images there. "I should have told them you were a witch. Should have given them a fighting chance."

"Why am I here?" she rasped.

He lowered his brows. "It's a dangerous game you play, Madeline," he said. "You should not—"

"Game! What the devil are you talking about? What are you doing here? Were you—" Terror smote her heart suddenly. Was he somehow involved with the kidnapping? The committee could be heartless. She had known that for a long while, just as she knew Jasper was bound by some force she did not understand to do its bidding. "Where are the girls?"

He said nothing for a moment, then: "I warned you not to interfere."

"Not interfere." Her heart beat heavily in her chest. "Why? What—"

"You were taken for a good reason," he said, and turned away to set a chair upright.

She shook her head. "Are you mad?"

"You should have left matters to others."

"Why?"

"This is not your worry."

"Not my worry!" This was insane. "Bertram's daughter is missing! Gone. Without explanation. Without reason."

"Things happen, Madeline," he snapped. "People suffer. They die. And there's nothing we can do about it. But I can stop *this*. I can stop *you*."

"What are you talking about?" she asked, and felt the hair rise eerily at the back of her neck.

He opened his mouth as if to speak, as if to rant, but then he drew a deep breath and calmed. Like magic, his expression returned to its usual placidity and his voice became almost bored.

"The committee has expended a good deal of time and money into your training," he said. "They've no wish to lose you."

She stared at him a moment, then breathed a disbelieving hiss. "So you abducted me!"

"It was a small price to pay to keep you from meddling."

"Meddling!" she rasped, and lowered her voice, willing herself to be calm. "Are you honestly willing to sacrifice young girls, *innocents*, to prevent the loss of your pathetic investment?"

"As I'm sure you're aware, it takes a good deal to finance Les Chausettes. Not in terms of money alone, but in time and resources. We risked a good deal to bring you and your sister here from Marseille."

She stared at him, stricken. How could she have misjudged him so completely? How could she have cared for him?

"Lest you forget, Ella would have died there," he said. "Died or been driven mad in the hospitable comfort of La Hopital."

"Is that the only reason you brought us here, then?" Her voice was no more than a rasp of pain. "To use us?"

He raised a brow. "Might you truly have believed there was another?"

Her stomach twisted, but she would know. This once and forever she would learn the truth. "So had Ella not been gifted . . ." She paused to breathe past the tight pain in her throat. "You would have left her to die?"

His face was absolutely expressionless. "Yes."

"And me?"

"The same," he said, but in that instant a tiny spark of agony flashed in his eyes, and against her shuttered will she remembered the burning sensation of his skin against hers.

She watched him in silence. Even that small flash of light in his eyes was gone now, and yet there was something . . . "I don't believe you," she said.

"I am sorry if you were laboring under a false impression, but—"

"I believe you were worried for my safety."

"As I said, the committee has determined that it cannot afford to lose you."

"So this was their idea."

"Yes."

"They found this place to hold me."

"I'm told it is the property of one of the authorities."

"And they hired the thugs who took me?"

"That was my responsibility."

"They were amateurs."

"I realize that now."

"How long were you to hold me?"

"As long as necessary."

"Which means what? Until the girls are dead?"

"Or found."

Worry skittered through her. "Do you know where they are?"

"No," he said, and again something shone in his eyes, but he shadowed it in a moment, covering it with a yawn. "Now, if we are finished with twenty questions, I believe I shall retire."

She narrowed her eyes, watching, *feeling.* "You lie," she said.

"Frequently," he admitted.

"The committee would not have had me abducted."

"You are more naïve than I thought if you believe them too kindhearted to—"

"Kindhearted!" she said, and laughed. "I would never accuse them of that. Indeed, I don't think them above killing me if they determine I am becoming too troublesome."

His right hand twitched, but no other emotion was visible. "Perhaps they are softening after all."

She raised her chin, assessing. "I believe this was your idea."

"Don't be ridiculous."

"Yours and yours alone."

"You'd best have a physician see to your head at the first possibility, Lady Redcomb. I believe you may have struck it with more force than I realized."

For a moment she doubted, but the truth was there, in the heat of his eyes. "You bound me. Dragged me into a carriage. Dumped me in the dark to keep me from getting hurt."

"You have never lacked imagination," he said. "Perhaps that is why you are able to enhance your senses and—"

"You threatened my life to keep me safe," she murmured. "Indeed . . ." She paced across the room, thinking. "You went against the committee's orders to take me. *You!* Jasper Reeves, the coolheaded baron who—"

"What the devil was I supposed to do?" he snapped, eyes suddenly wild. "You wouldn't listen. You kept risking your life, putting yourself—"

"Of course I risk my life!" she raged. "It's what I've been taught to do. What I've been trained to do."

"I know!" He fisted his hand near his head as if to drive out the demons. "Don't you think I know that? But you're not supposed to . . ." He jerked his hand at her as if simple words were not enough to convey his feelings. "Good God, you were naked."

She tilted her head, wondering if she'd heard him wrong. "What?"

"By the mill. On the tree. In the pond. On the damned . . . Devil take it!" he rasped, and ran out of words.

She watched him, lips parted, head shaking. "What is wrong with you?"

He gritted his teeth. "You were *naked*!" he repeated, voice suddenly weak.

And just as suddenly their minds were filled with the image.

There was a moment of hesitation, as if they were suspended in time, and then they were flying toward each other.

They came together like magnet and steel. She crushed her mouth to his. He was tearing at her clothes, yanking them away, mindless of the damage. He tasted of life, of scalding desire. She reached up and grasped his shirt. Buttons exploded. He growled something indecipherable and grabbed her buttocks in both hands.

Yanking at his belt, she set him free. His penis reared up, hard and eager.

He jerked her legs off the floor. They almost toppled over then, but she grasped the door frame behind his head and held on, wrapping her legs around him. She pulled herself higher, like earthen magic; he thrust himself into her, burying himself to the hilt.

She shrieked. He stumbled forward, turned, pressed her back against the wall, but she barely felt the contact. Grasping his hair in both hands, she arched against him, taking him in, squeezing around him.

He growled something incoherent. Beneath her legs, his buttocks bunched. She bucked against him. Tipping his head down, he took her nipple in his mouth.

She screamed, writhed, and exploded into a thousand sparkling shards. He growled in low, hot desire, and slammed into her once more.

After that there was little more than whimpers. Heavy breathing. Her legs felt wasted. She leaned her face against her neck, let her feet drop to the floor, and almost fell.

He steadied her, then stumbled himself.

"How did you best Harry?" he rasped.

For a moment she considered letting him suffer, but she was too tired to resist the truth. "He couldn't bear the silence." Her voice sounded rusty. "Opened the door."

He shook his head, still breathing hard. "I warned him." He closed his eyes. His chest was heaving. He had a beautiful chest, broad and dark and hard with muscle. "Where did you get the . . ." He motioned toward his own neck as if holding a weapon to his carotid.

She put a hand on the wall. It only shook a little. "I dismantled the table."

"Table . . ." He nodded with no particular rhythm. "I should have thought to remove the table."

She bent at the waist, winded like a broken steed. "Took me all night."

"You haven't slept."

"I thought someone was trying to kill me."

He looked away, still breathing through his mouth, eyes burning. "You were naked," he hissed.

She looked up at him from a canted position.

"No man . . ." He gritted his teeth, tried to calm his breathing. "Tell me the truth. Did you know I was there? In the shadows. By the mill."

So she had been right.

"Shaleena is naked all the time," she said. Her side hurt, and her voice might have sounded defensive.

"Shaleena!" He jerked his gaze away and gestured wildly with one hand. "Who the devil cares—" he began, then stopped himself and closed his eyes, seeming to find himself. "Such behavior is not advised," he said. "If someone had happened along . . . had seen you—"

"What behavior?" she asked, and straightened. Her bodice was shattered. Her breasts stood out pale and eager.

He lowered his gaze, swallowed. "If someone had seen you—"

"Someone *did* see me," she said, and shrugged out of her gown.

His jaw tightened. "I meant someone else."

She watched him, drew another breath, almost smiled. "Someone not as controlled as you?"

His jaw tightened spasmodically. He glanced away. "I would advise you to cease disrobing," he said.

"Ever?" she asked, and kicked her ruined gown aside.

He fisted his hands. "Yes."

"Even at night?"

He squeezed his eyes shut. "Absolutely."

She stepped toward him. "But how—"

"Don't . . ." He closed his eyes as if in pain. "Don't ask questions, just . . . just keep your clothes on."

She almost laughed. "Always."

He had opened his eyes but didn't look at her. "Perhaps you don't realize what you do to . . . men."

"What do I do?"

"You're quite an attractive woman."

"Am I?"

"I believe you know you are."

"How attractive am I, Jasper?"

He glanced toward her. Something akin to pain shone in his face. Bending, he scooped up his shirt. Veins bulged in the lean strength of his forearm. "Put this on," he said, and handed the garment to her.

She watched the movement. Was he shaking?

"How attractive?" she asked, and took a step toward him.

He swallowed. Almost as if he were frightened. Though he didn't retreat, every fine-tuned muscle looked tense.

"More attractive than Shaleena?" she asked.

"Shaleena," he said and breathed a laugh.

She frowned. "I don't know what that means."

"Put on the shirt," he said.

She shook her head. "Not unless you explain. This . . ." She tossed her hand toward the door frame where they had first come together. "Why this?"

His fist tightened in his shirt. "Because you are irresistible."

She scowled, trying to understand. To accept. "You seem to have resisted quite well for . . . eight years or so."

"I am sorry," he said.

"For . . ."

"For weakening. For failing."

"You have not failed," she whispered, and stepping up to him, cupped his face in her hand.

His eyes fell closed. "I am paid to resist, but you . . ." Reaching up, he captured her fingers in his own, squeezing them gently. "You are Esperanza. Hope," he breathed. "Light."

"Jasper," she breathed, and shook her head, confused, conflicted.

"Beauty. Happiness," he said, and there seemed nothing she could do but kiss him.

Their lips met like magic, as soft as a sigh. The bed brushed her knees and she settled back. He came with her, smoothing his hands up her body, kissing her with gentle reverence. Her stomach, her breasts, her throat, until their gazes met. She felt the hot length of his desire against her belly.

"Love me," she whispered.

"Madeline." Pain shot through his eyes. "I'm not capable. I'm not—" he began, but she pressed her fingers to his lips. He closed his eyes, and she eased her hand away, replacing it with a kiss.

He trembled against her, but she was already pushing his breeches down, freeing him, urging him on. And now there was no stopping.

Bracing himself on his palms, he eased into her, filling her to the core. Hot and heavy and tight.

Drawing a shaky breath, she arched against him and he pushed back until they moved in rhythm, gazes locked, hands clasped above her head.

The tension built, muscles tightened, slick and eager. Breath rasped. Madeline closed her eyes and arched against the mattress, moaning as she neared the summit, and it was then, with her breasts thrust toward the sky, that Jasper lowered his mouth to her nipple.

Madeline gasped at the shattering sensations and thrust madly against him. He growled, deep and guttural, rising on a wave of ecstasy until he exploded inside her. She shrieked as she joined him in release, went limp as he fell against her, letting his head drop. His arms trembled. He rolled to the side, easing the bulk of his weight off her. His chest felt hot and hard against her arm. His heart bumped hastily against her ribs.

Gone was the bored pink of the *ton*. In his place was this man of flesh and blood, of passion and muscle. "Madeline . . ." he rasped, tone hushed and breathless. "I fear I am not a man made for poetry and—"

But in that instant, the lone window shattered into a hundred piercing shards.

Chapter 20

A gunshot pinged from the window. Jasper tossed Madeline to the floor, then threw himself atop her. She struggled beneath him, naked and squirming, but he held her down.

Another shot sounded, but he was already lifting his weight from her. The next bullet might go through his body and into hers. Lunging to his feet, he yanked her up beside him. She galloped across the floor. Yanking the nearby table onto its side, she leaped behind it.

Safe! She was safe. All was well, he thought, and slammed down beside her, back to the table, heart pumping, chest aching as he secured his breeches.

"One gunman. Male. Out front. Another man behind the—" She stopped abruptly, eyes wide, breasts rising rapidly with each inhalation. "You've been hit!"

"There's another gunman?"

"You've been shot!" she rasped.

He didn't bother glancing at his side. It would do little good. "One in front? One in back?"

She clenched her jaw, scowled, cool under fire. "There might be more."

His gut clenched. Damn him to hell, he should never have brought her here. Shouldn't have ... But there was a whole boatload of things he shouldn't have done. It was rather difficult to encompass them all, especially now that some bastard was shooting at them.

Reaching past their defensive shield, he snagged her gown and handed it to her, mind churning as he scanned the possibilities.

She yanked the garment over her head and shoved her arms through.

"I'm going through that window," he said, nodding toward the broken pane. "I'll incapacitate the gunman and cause a distraction. When the second bas—*fellow* comes round the front of the house, you go out the back window and run. He'll be fresh, and you're tired. Don't try to outrun him. Use your wits. Don't go to the stable. Hide—"

"Are you out of your mind?" she rasped.

He stopped, anger and fear boiling like a witch's brew. "I'm a bit perturbed just now," he said, teeth gritted against the pain, "so I'd appreciate some cooperation. I'm going through the window and you—"

"You go out that window, I swear to God I'll follow you and kill you myself," she breathed.

He stared at her. Her eyes were on fire and her teeth were bared. He refrained from swearing. He'd tried it once. It hadn't helped. Besides, just because people were trying to kill them was no reason to lose one's manners. Taking a careful breath, he called up a fresh store of logic.

"I saved your life," he said, words slow, tone level, reasonable. "I saved your sister's life."

She said nothing but watched him, kiss-bruised lips pursed.

"You owe me this," he added.

She looked at him an abbreviated instant, then lunged to her feet and dashed toward the window. She was one long arch of motion, loose gown flaring behind her, and then she was through. Glass sprayed in every direction. There was a shout, a grunt. By the time Jasper had galloped to the door, the gunman was unconscious, but footsteps were thundering along the side of the building. Jasper turned, took four long, silent steps, waited two seconds for the footsteps to halt, then, reaching around the edge of the building, he snapped the newcomer out by his jacket and plowed a fist into his face.

The other stumbled back, trying to bring his blunderbuss to bear, but Jasper kicked it aside. It spiraled upward and into Jasper's hands. Knocked off balance, the gunman stumbled to his knees.

"What the deuce do you think you're doing?" Madeline rasped.

"No need for harsh language," Jasper grunted, slightly bent. His left side had gone numb.

"You're wounded," she snarled.

"Get out of sight."

"Damn you!" she cursed, and raised her pistol toward the downed villain.

A rustle of noise sounded behind them. The first shooter was fleeing toward the trees.

Jasper jerked his attention back toward the second man. For a moment he thought the villain might make a grab for his own weapon, but instead, he scrambled to his feet and raced after his companion.

Jasper cursed himself in silence. The guns were single shot, useful only as intimidation.

"I can catch him," Madeline rasped, and lurched forward, but he grabbed her arm and swung her about.

"Are you out of your mind?"

She snapped her arm from his grasp. "No, Jasper. I'm angry!"

"Forget it."

"What are you talking about? I—"

"They're already gone."

"They're slow. I can—"

"No!"

"Someone almost killed you. We need to find out why. Who—"

"No!" he said, and grabbing her again, shook her.

"You'll not risk your life again," he snarled.

She stared at him, frozen.

He drew a deep breath, grappled for calm. "I'm going to harness the team," he said. "Go inside. Lock the door."

"Is that an order?"

"If you like," he said, words terse.

She stared at him a moment, then: "You're an ass," she said, and turned jerkily toward the stable.

She had the team harnessed in a matter of minutes. In less than ten she was in the driver's seat. It took Jasper almost that long to reach her side.

"I'll take the lines," he said.

She looked down at him as if he were something she might have scraped from the bottom of her shoe. "Try it," she said.

Her breasts were all but bare, her eyes narrowed. Perhaps he could wrestle her to the ground. But in his current state, he wouldn't want to place a wager to the outcome.

Grinding his teeth, he stepped inside the carriage.

In retrospect perhaps it was best she drove; for quite some time Jasper thought he might pass out. Only the thought of her finding him limp and unconscious kept him awake, but by the time they reached Lavender House, he felt sick and shaken. Luckily, it was dark. He had almost made it out of the carriage by the time she reached the door.

"Are you well?" she asked.

"Of course," he said, and managed not to fall facefirst into the hedgerow.

"I'll assist you to the house."

He turned toward her, careful to stand perfectly erect, to use his most irritating tone. "You've made mistakes, Lady Redcomb," he said. "But I always assumed they were caused by naïveté and not illwill."

Her breath rasped a little. "What are you talking about?"

"I did not think you would put your friends at risk simply to prove your own superiority."

"I'd never risk—"

"Or perhaps you think you would be safer here at Lavender House than with your sister." She would not be. He was sure of that. Someone was trying to kill him. Someone powerful. Someone he had irritated. There were a host of possibilities, but he wouldn't think of them just now. She would be safer with Ella and her husband, for he could not protect her. Not in his present condition. The idea twisted his stomach in knots, but he remained unmoving.

"With Ella? Why—?"

"Or perhaps you don't care enough about her even to allay her fears, to allow her an opportunity to keep you safe."

"Safe from what?"

"Whoever is trying to kill you."

"You think those men came for me?"

He raised one brow. "I've no wish to endanger the rest of the coven." The bullet hadn't struck any major organs. He was sure of that. Still, it hurt like the devil. For a moment he considered passing out.

Her brows lowered, her fire-quick mind spinning. "You think—"

"Yes," he said. "And it's time you did the same or be prepared to take responsibility for the death of others for whom I thought you cared."

She stared at him for one long, protracted moment, then turned, silently mounted the carriage, and drove into the night.

Jasper closed his eyes, not watching her go. Not remembering how she had felt in his arms. Like sunlight on satin, like magic in spring. Instead, he turned, diligently putting one foot in front of the other, plodding toward the house, sweat popping on his brow.

"Reeves!"

He jerked his head up at the sound of his name and almost teetered onto the cobblestones. Ella was rushing toward him down the uneven walkway.

"Where's Madeline?" Her voice was raspy with worry.

He gritted his teeth, struggled for lucidness. "What are you doing here?"

"Where's my sister?"

Keeping his gaze resolutely on the house, Jasper lurched back into motion. "Why are you not at Berryhill?"

"Because I'm here. Have you seen her? Even Joseph doesn't know where she is."

Even Joseph. Jasper ground his teeth and reconsidered the passing-out idea. It had some merit. Unconsciousness smiled beguilingly from the shadows. "She just left here," he said. "In a rented carriage. Go." He didn't dare look at her lest he topple into her bodice. "Find her. Take care of her."

"Why?" Her tone was sharp and seemed to grate against his inner ear. "What happened?"

"She needs you." He felt sick to his stomach. "Go."

She stopped dead in her tracks. He closed his

eyes in relief, sure Maddy would be safe now, but in a moment she was beside him again. "She is well. Why is she angry?"

He had forgotten about Ella's disconcerting ways and didn't really care to deal with them just now.

"What have you—" she began, but just then the toe of his boot caught in some unseen snag and he stumbled, almost falling before righting himself with a painful lurch.

There was a moment of blessed silence, then: "What's wrong with you?" Ella asked.

"Me?" He would have laughed if he had remembered how. "Nothing. All is well."

"Are you . . ." She paused. He could imagine her puzzled expression without turning her way. ". . . intoxicated?"

He never imbibed. She knew that much. "Yes," he said.

She snorted with unladylike disdain. He should have taught her better. Had tried to do so. "I never would have suspected you were such a terrible liar," she said, and reaching out, grabbed his arm. "You've . . . Good heavens, have you been shot?"

He gritted his teeth and concentrated on the front door. It had never seemed so *wiggly* before. "A little louder and you won't need to inform the *Post*," he said, and hobbled forward.

She caught him before he fell on his face. She was

a tall woman. Tall and strong, but not beautiful like his Esperanza. Not unbearably kind like her. Not irresistible like her. Her face swam in front of his eyes. Her figure danced in his imagination. Her strong, willowy legs; her sweeping waist; her firm, thrusting bosom, accented with a tiny mole on the outside of the left breast. He had known it would be there. What did that mean? Were his imaginings of her so clear that he knew every inch of her irresistible body? Knew she was magic come to life. Hope come to earth.

"What did you say?" Ella asked.

"Nothing," he muttered, but that might not have been entirely true.

"You said Esperanza."

His head lolled on his neck. "Are you familiar with the term *witch's madness*?" he asked.

"I'm not insane," she said, and pushing the door open with her foot, half dragged him inside. "Esperanza. Hope. What does hope have to do with anything?" Her voice was a little breathy.

It was good to know, at least, that carrying him around like a newborn babe took a modicum of effort. Even for a witch. But then she wasn't her sister, was she? Esperanza could probably tote him about in her reticule.

But maybe he was a little too large to fit in her handbag.

"Am I too big?" he asked, and turned his head to stare at her sister from inches away.

"What the deuce are you talking about?"

He felt strange, otherworldly, lightheaded, but he marshaled his senses. It was what he did. Marshal. "She left the coven," he said. Because of him. Because he was an ass. Because he couldn't look at her without aching. Without knowing that he would never be good enough.

"I am aware of that," she said. "What I want to know is—"

"It's not just because she's beautiful."

"What?"

He shook his head. Ella stumbled against the erratic movement. "It is because she is . . ." He saw her face again—the determination, the loyalty, the kindness written in each stunning feature. "Magic," he said.

Ella scowled. "Are you wounded *and* inebriated?"

Maybe. Drunk on Esperanza Elixir. He almost giggled at the thought.

"What the hell has *happened* to you?" she asked.

He had touched heaven, he thought, then drew a deep, sensible breath and pulled himself carefully erect. It felt like trying to push his head through a keyhole. "If you don't mind, my lady, it has been rather a trying day. I would like to get some rest."

She narrowed her eyes. They had always had that mannerism in common. She and her sister. So strong. So capable, so discerning, but where Ella was cool and aloof, Esperanza was caring personified. Or had been until she had enhanced her senses. Now he didn't know what she was. Except irresistible. At least before, her refinement had kept him at bay. Her perfect control had steadied his own failing defenses. But now—

"Someone will have to see to that wound if you hope to get out of bed in the morning."

"Esperanza," he said.

"I fear you're losing your mind."

"I fear you may be right." He almost giggled again.

A fire was burning in the parlor, chasing shadows and light across the vestibule.

"I'm getting you to bed," Ella said, and prodded him toward the stairs. He acquiesced. Not because he *had* to, but because he *wanted* to.

Each stair, however, felt like another phase of hell. His head was pounding. His pulse was doing the same.

"I can care for myself," he said. His voice sounded childish and a little mumbly.

"Like hell you can."

He tried to give her an accusatory stare, but

couldn't quite manage it and finally settled for a snooty tone. "I believe I taught you better than to curse."

"Shut up."

"Frenchwomen." His head rolled back a fraction of an inch. "So bossy."

Darla appeared from his left, silver hair gleaming in the near darkness. "What happened?"

"He's been wounded."

"Not badly, I hope."

"Esperanza," Jasper murmured.

The older witch stopped, startled. "Is he intoxicated?"

"Not yet," Ella said, tone thoughtful, gaze piercing, then: "I'll need some supplies."

"Of course," Darla said, hands folded at the ready.

They stumbled to the bed. Ella eased him onto it, covered him up. Time ceased to be as women's voices swam past him. But he woke when Ella pulled his shirt aside.

"I'm fine," he insisted, groggy and disoriented.

"You're wounded," she said, and lifted a chalice toward him. Steam curled like dragon's breath above the vessel. "Drink this."

He tried to raise a skeptical brow, to stare her down as the situation demanded, but things were a little shady. Still, he did his best. "I would rather not be hallucinating for the next fortnight if it's all the same to you," he said.

She shrugged. "Suit yourself. I'll have Shaleena hold you down then whilst I dig out the bullet."

He felt himself blanch. Ella turned away. "Darla, fetch Shaleena, if you please." She twisted back toward Jasper, expression smug. "And make certain she is sky-clad. She's stronger that—"

"I'll remain still," he vowed.

She stared at him. "I don't like it when my patients scream."

"I swear I won't scream."

She smiled, curving up her lips the tiniest degree. "Drink this," she said, "or I swear you will."

Chapter 21

Hollycroft Manor was beautifully decorated.
Roses bloomed in every hand-painted vase.
The heavenly strains of Salieri's latest overture
floated on the air. The orange flower creams were
delectable and the sherry divine.

Madeline felt as if she were in hell. Was Jasper
truly mending? Darla had sent a note saying all
was well, and though Maddy had no reason to believe she would lie, everything was all turned about
lately. Wrong. Set on its ear.

"Lady Redcomb."

Madeline turned at the sound of her sister's
voice. To her right, a trio of ladies were draped in
vines and imitating greenery. She had no idea why.
The way of the *ton* was often inconceivable.

"My lady," Maddy said. She kept her tone marvelously light, for she was not ready to admit that
her senses were a-scatter. Was certainly not prepared to tell her sister that she had been abducted

by the cool Lord Gallo. Had been abducted, then *swived* the man. Not once, dear God, but twice. "How good it is to see you."

A pair of elderly gentleman passed on Maddy's right, wafting heavy perfume in their elegant, bewigged wake.

"Are you well?" Ella asked, maintaining the charade they had played for the past eight years. Pretending, as always, that they were no more than acquaintances.

"Of course." Madeline smiled. "Fit as a racehorse," she said, and turning toward a passing server, snagged a flute of champagne. "And what of you? You certainly look well. Motherhood must agree with you most heartily."

Ella smiled and took a sip from her own glass, but her expression was . . . What was it exactly? Conniving? "I stopped by Cinderknoll yesterday," she said.

"Did you?" Madeline tensed, waiting. "What a shame it is that I missed you."

"Indeed. I was ever so disappointed. Wherever had you gone?"

Madeline took a sip of wine, fully aware that her sister was better equipped for this sort of game than she. "I paid a visit to Biddles and Tye."

"The plumassiers?"

"I no longer cared for the plumes on my ivory

bonnet and felt egret feathers would be perfect for my powder-blue gown."

Ella eyed her askance. "It would be a shame, indeed, if one's feathers did not match one's frock."

"Ghastly," Maddy said, and faked a shudder.

Lord Weatherby passed by. Maddy gave him a nod.

"I also visited Lavender House," Ella said.

Madeline felt herself pale, but willed away the weakness and tightened her defenses. "Oh? And how are the ladies of that fine establishment?"

Ella smiled, but they were alone now and there was steel in the expression. "What is amiss?"

Madeline glanced past her sister's shoulder toward the dance floor and waved at an imaginary friend. "I'm uncertain what you might be referring to," she said, and smiled at an aging baroness. "Lady Ettington, what a lovely brooch. Is that amethyst?"

"Set with brilliants."

"Of course. How very nice."

Lady Ettington moved on. Madeline sipped her wine.

"Do you have feelings for Reeves?" Ella asked.

Madeline gasped, choking on her champagne and hoping to distract her sister, but when she glanced up, Ella was merely staring.

"What? No," Maddy said, and did her best to forget what she had done up against the wall in the cottage. And on the bed in the cottage. And what she *would* have done on the roof of the cottage given half a chance. "Why ever would you say such a thing?"

She didn't answer. "So you visited the perfumery yesterday."

"The plumassiers," Maddy corrected cautiously.

"Yes, of course. I was quite worried about you. Wherever did you go after Biddles?

Maddy's mind was racing. What did Ella know? Had she spoken to Jasper? Not that it would make a difference. He would have told her nothing. "I was busy . . . with a myriad of things."

Ella raised one careful brow. "A myriad?"

"The drapery in Cinderknoll is atrocious. I can hardly be expected to—"

"I know Reeves was wounded," Ella said.

Maddy tried to continue the ploy, but it was no use. Her heart shuddered. "How is he?"

"He will be well." Ella sipped at her drink, watching Madeline over the rim of her glass. "I gave him one of my potions to aid in the healing process."

Madeline froze. "What!"

Ella looked down at her, raised one brow. "I may have saved his life."

"What potion?"

Ella smiled, pleased to have her sister's full attention. "He had lost a good deal of blood."

"What potion?"

"A pinch of earth, a white dove's feather, the hair of a hound born—"

"You gave him a truth potion?" Maddy hissed.

"It is not a truth potion," Ella argued, letting her eyes go wide. "Forcing someone to speak against his will would be counter to my vows. Against my moral code."

"You gave him a truth potion!"

Ella smiled again, sweet as jellied wine. "What if I did? Is there something I shouldn't know?"

"Know?" Maddy felt short of breath. Crazed. The things she had done! The things she *would* have done given more time. The things she still wanted to do. "Know? No. Why . . . No. Of course not." She cleared her throat. "What did he say?"

Ella scowled as if deep in thought. "Esperanza."

"What?"

"I believe he said the word *hope* . . . in Spanish, repeatedly." She narrowed her eyes. "He seemed . . ." She paused, shrugged.

"What? How did he seem?"

"Strange."

"How . . ."

"As are you."

"I'm not strange."

"Jittery," Ella said, and canted her head as if reading her sister's mood. "I don't believe I've ever seen you jittery, sister."

Madeline glanced to the side, hoping for someone to distract them, but Mrs. Braxton had begun reciting poetry and the mob had stopped to ogle. Mrs. Braxton's bosoms were as big as haystacks. "You shouldn't call me that," she said.

"Why ever not?"

"We have sworn to forsake our old selves," she said. "Sworn to work for the good of Britain, if you have forgotten."

"I have not."

"You left the coven," Madeline said. Her tone sounded strangely accusatory.

"As have you," Ella reminded. "How exactly did Reeves manage to get himself wounded?"

Madeline covered a wince. Of course Ella would be aware of his injury. "I've been trying to discover what happened to the girls."

"The ones who have disappeared."

"Yes."

"And?"

"And he . . ." Was irresistible. She didn't know why. In years past, all the long years she had adored him from afar, she had assured herself it was simply because he had saved her. Had saved Ella. But it was more than that. It was his cunning. His bravery. The way his eyes burned with unspoken thoughts. Or maybe it was just the way he looked without his shirt. She felt her face warm. "We . . . were working together," she said.

Ella's expression was intent. "You convinced Reeves to help you?"

Maddy had forgotten to breathe. "Yes."

"Even though the mission is not sanctioned by the committee."

Madeline felt fidgety, but kept herself still, her body quiet, as she'd been taught. "A fourth girl disappeared."

"I believe her name is Katherine."

Madeline cleared her throat, remembering the man who had mistakenly called her Kath. Had that been part of Reeves's ploy? Had his scheme been so carefully orchestrated that he knew she would stop if she heard the missing girl's name? Of course it had. Trickery was his forte. But she had never thought he'd stoop to abduction.

The thought made her feel crazy. All thoughts made her feel crazy. Maybe she was crazy.

Jasper Reeves, the coolheaded director of Les Chausettes, had kidnapped her, for God's sake. And then she had . . . had . . .

Ella was watching her, head tilted slightly.

"What's going on, Madeline?"

"Nothing. I fear I must go," she said, and turned abruptly away, but Ella caught her arm.

"Go where?"

"I've vowed to find the abducted girls. To try to ascertain who might have . . ." she began, but just then she saw him. Jasper Reeves. He walked as straight as a general on parade. His midnight-blue coat was perfectly tailored to his lean form, his dark waistcoat modestly shot with silver, and his buff pantaloons snug above perfectly polished black boots. He wore the fashion of the *ton* like a royal princeling. But it was his eyes that stopped her in her tracks. Something seemed to flash in their depths as their gazes clashed, but in a moment he turned away, dismissing her out of hand.

"I must go," Maddy repeated, and hurried in the opposite direction, struggling to hide the pain of his coolness. So what if they had . . . copulated? According to her fictionalized past, she'd done so a thousand times before. Well, maybe not a thousand. As the story went, she'd been married for only five months. How many times would a person copulate in five months? Every day? Every hour? How did couples ever get anything accomplished? *Why* did couples get anything accomplished? If she were married . . .

Dear Lord. She stopped her thoughts in their

proverbial tracks. She was starting to hyperventilate. And he didn't even care. Didn't even acknowledge her presence.

Good God, he had to get himself under control. But she was here. So close. Close enough to see, to touch, to—

But of course she was here. Jasper had known she would be. That's why he had come. But he hadn't expected her to act as if nothing had happened between them. He'd expected her to be worried. Hurt maybe. Possibly angry.

From across the room, he heard her laugh and closed his eyes against the pain. Why did she have to remind him how she had felt in his arms? And why in God's name did she keep laughing? he wondered, and allowed himself a single glance.

"Lovely, isn't she?"

He jumped, actually, physically jumped at the words. Like a callow lad. Like an untried boy yearning for his first conquest. He'd had other conquests. He just couldn't remember who they were ever since the day at the cottage. Since he'd held her in his arms. Since he'd . . .

He put the fuming thoughts out of his mind, calmed himself, and turned slowly. "My lady," he said, tone admirably uncrazed.

Ella was watching her sister. Not looking at him,

but it hardly mattered. She could probably hear the sweat popping from his pores like hatchlings from their shells. "She was pretty the day she was born," she said.

Holy God. He snatched a glass from a passing server. Slowing his movements, he put the flute to his lips and pretended to drink. "I was led to believe you've only known her for the past eight years or so."

She turned slowly toward him, all poise and narrow control. "Or, more precisely, you led the rest of the world to believe as much. What's going on, Reeves?"

Maddy was laughing again. He refused to close his eyes, refused to rush across the room, snatch her into his arms, give in to the . . . Well, in short, he refused to act like a raving lunatic. "Why do you ask, my lady?"

She raised a brow a fraction of an inch. "You've been acting strangely of late. Even for you."

What did she know? He could remember so little of the night he'd been wounded, but he had a blurry memory of her appearing at Lavender House. Was that his imagination?

Had she given him a potion?

The thought struck fear into his heart.

He was healing with amazing speed. Was that because of her? But no. He had always healed quickly. Perhaps *that* was his gift. He was a cold bastard. And a fool. A man who had endangered the only woman who—

"A bit . . . nervous," Ella said, and the thoughts stopped abruptly in Jasper's head.

She *was* suspicious. But of what? Had he admitted something he shouldn't have. Such as the fact that he had compromised her little sister? The sister he had vowed to protect. The sister she adored. The sister who had, in essence, saved her life.

"My apologies if I spoke out of turn some nights past." He gave her a glance, desperately hoping she would say she didn't know of what he spoke. That she hadn't seen him for ages. But she said no such thing. What did that mean? Was she toying with him? "I fear I might have been a bit . . . inebriated."

She smiled. Her expression was sweet. It made his hair stand on end. Ella was not sweet. "I meant you're acting strangely *now*. The other night you acted little differently than any other wounded man might have."

So she *had* been there. The memories sharpened a smidgeon; still they were vague, like spring mists over Highland fen. Had she given him something? Had he spilled secrets best kept to himself? Best thought about alone in the heat of the night when

Esperanza danced through his mind like a ray of golden hope.

Had he referred to her as hope? Had he told her sister how she had felt in his arms? In his dreams? In his bed.

"I'm not acting strangely at all," he said, and drank in earnest. It hardly seemed to matter.

"As is she," she added.

He didn't turn to look, but she was laughing again. He took another drink. "Perhaps she's been drinking."

"I'm sure you're wrong."

"Oh, how do you know?"

"Because . . ." She stared at him pointedly. "If she had you would have chided her long ago. Les Chausettes do not imbibe."

He lowered his glass. "She's no longer with the coven." That knowledge was still a raw open wound, eating its way through his entrails, devouring his soul.

"And tell me," Ella said, "is that why you're acting so peculiar?"

"My lady," he said, and bowed. He was an exemplary bower. And wasn't it odd that the *ton* put so much stock in such things? Fanning, for instance. Or how one sniffed snuff just so from the back of one's hand. "You seem to have an extremely vivid imagination."

"Yes I do," she said, and smiled. "But I believe you do too."

"I fear you're wrong there. My forte lies in planning," he said, and took another drink.

"Then how did you know of her mole?" she asked.

He coughed, choking on the champagne that insisted on eating its way through his larynx, because he knew exactly what she was talking about, could see the tiny mark nestled against the satiny silk of Madeline's left breast. "I beg your pardon?" he said. He didn't rasp. God knew he wasn't a rasper. He was a bower. Ask anyone.

Ella leaned close, face intense, eyes snapping with sudden heat. "If you harm her in any way you shall spend the rest of your days searching for flies."

He looked at her. "Flies?"

"For your dinner," she said, and turned away.

He watched her leave. He was quite certain his composure was firmly in place, but his mind was scrambling. It wasn't smart to anger a witch. Very foolish, in fact. Suicidal, in fact. But how much worse to vow to care for a witch. To promise to keep her safe and uncompromised, then sleep with her. To feel her move beneath his hands, to watch her come and know . . . Absolutely *know* that he would never be the same. Never be able to forget, to function, to focus on duty, on vows made in good faith. Dear Lord, he was a government man, sworn to serve and protect. Sworn to—

"Lord Gallo, you look quite dashing this evening."

He turned to find Merry May beside him, but he failed to care. For Esperanza was touching Lord Moore's hand. Was letting him kiss her knuckles.

Why? Did she suspect him? Had Ella told her he sat at the head of the committee? Had she told her the earl couldn't be trusted? And was she correct?

Perhaps Jasper shouldn't have gone to the committee, shouldn't have beseeched them to investigate the disappearance of the girls. Maybe that had only drawn attention to Madeline's actions. Maybe he had inadvertently increased her risk. Maybe it was the committee itself that had sent hired killers to the deserted cottage. The idea made his heart lurch, but he calmed himself. She hadn't been injured. Hadn't appeared to be their target. Only *he* had been wounded.

But why? Jasper had been rather insistent that Les Chausettes be allowed to find the girls. In fact, in an unacceptable bout of zeal, he might have issued threats. Moore had been angry, had reminded Jasper of debts unpaid. Reminded him of a scrawny boy found in Newgate's seething hell.

But Jasper hadn't forgotten. Would never forget.

Neither could he forget Madeline's fierce bravery, however. Her determination, her passion, her vow to find Wendell's lost daughter.

He ground his teeth, loyalties straining even as Moore stroked Madeline's hand.

"Lord Gallo?"

He turned back toward May, smoothing his motions.

"Are you quite all right?" she asked.

No. He sure as the devil was not all right. He was exploding inside. Dying. "Yes. Of course."

"You look a bit . . . distressed," she said.

"Not at all," he argued, but suddenly his glass shattered in his hand.

She raised a brow.

He stared at the broken flute, bowed. "If you'll excuse me, my lady. I should"—what should he do?—"speak to our hostess regarding the inferior condition of her stemware."

"Of course," May said. There was humor in her tone, but Jasper failed to care.

In a moment he was at Madeline's side. Moore had left her, but another man had already taken his place.

"Lady Redcomb," Jasper said. His tone was decently steady. She was dressed in a mint-green gown that accented the rich tone of her skin, hugged the high mounds of her breasts. He was sweating like a stallion.

"Lord Gallo." She turned with the smoothness of a royal swan, still smiling as she pulled her hand from her latest admirer's hand. "Lovely party, is it not?"

Lovely party? That was *his* line! He was the polished one. The cool one. The master. But his world had been blown apart. He could think of nothing else but how she had felt beside him, around him, drawing him in, pulling him apart.

"Quite nice," he said.

She smiled, but it was a little different than her usual kindly expression. It was almost pitying, as if she knew that inside his head was a blithering idiot. As if she realized he had not had a coherent thought since she'd left his arms. As if she felt sorry for him. She turned gracefully away. "The punch is exceptional. Don't you agree, Mr. Haviard?"

"Not as exceptional as you, my lady," Haviard said, double chin wobbling.

"You flatter me," Madeline said. "But I'm not adverse to a bit of flattery no matter how feigned or faint."

"Feigned! Not at all, my lady. I am the very model of sincerity."

He was the very model of English aristocracy,

Jasper thought. Preening, pampered, and overfed. Not good enough to lick Madeline's dancing shoes. "Look," Jasper said, tone carefully bored. "It appears as if they are about to serve the Shrewsbury cakes."

"Shrewsbury cakes?" Haviard asked, nose all but twitching.

"Fresh from the ovens," Jasper added.

"Hollycroft is famous for their cakes."

"Is it?" Jasper asked.

"If you'll excuse me," Haviard said, and bowing, scuttled away.

"Well . . ." Madeline smiled. "I myself am something of a Shrewsbury cake aficionado," she said and turned, but he caught her arm.

"Madeline." Electricity raged through him, but he held on, letting the voltage fry him.

She raised a brow. "Yes?"

He needed her. Wanted her. Ached, truly, honestly, physically ached for her. He took a careful breath through his nostrils. "I would like to commend you on your maturity."

"Maturity?" She canted her head a little.

He nodded and didn't think of how she had danced in the moonlight. Had arched against the tree. Against *him*. "You are a credit to Les Chausettes."

"But I am no longer a member of that esteemed society," she said, and took a drink of punch. "Indeed, last I visited, I was not even allowed into the house."

For a second, a fractured instant, he thought he saw anger flash through her and desperately hoped he was right. Rage would be so much easier than this smooth nonchalance.

"About that night . . ." he said.

She smiled. "What about it?"

What about it? It was spectacular. Unforgettable. Life-changing, despite his wound, which seemed all but insignificant in the radiant light of her beauty. "I wish to apologize."

She was silent for a moment. "Anything else?"

A thousand words swelled in his throat. He swallowed them. "As you know, I am not a man for flowery prose."

She was watching him closely.

"Not one for sentimental songs, weepy poems and—" He was starting to babble. Babbling was for idiots. He had to be careful not to babble. Dammit. He was even babbling in his head. "I am certain you are aware of that," he said, and wished rather fervently that he had never caught her eye. Never seen her from across the room. "Nevertheless, in regards to . . . our time together . . . I wished to say that I realize I shouldn't have . . ." What? What shouldn't he have done? He wished, in fact that he had done more. Was still doing more. "It was not my place."

"Wasn't it?"

"I was hired to protect." It was against his policy to speak of Les Chausettes in public. But that was certainly the least of his crimes of late. "I should not have taken advantage."

For a moment she only stared at him, and then she smiled, perfectly serene, perfectly poised. "Please, think nothing of it," she said. "I assure you, I will not."

Chapter 22

Madeline's heels clicked against the marble floor, seeming to echo in the emptiness of her soul. Behind her, Jasper watched her retreat.

So he regretted their time together. Regretted it! Apologized for it. When all she could think of was how he had felt against her, inside her, around her. She was flushed, crazed, but kept her head high, her movement cadenced. She had to leave. Had to hide before he realized he'd torn her world asunder, but from across the room she saw Tess Terragon speaking with her chaperone, and in that instant, she remembered her vow. How weak she would have to be to allow a man to come between her and her mission. How much better to move on, to find Marie, to do what she had vowed to do.

Tess turned toward the window. Her expression was solemn, but she was still safe, had not been drawn into the dark underbelly of London. What of Grant O'Malley though? He had had a dark aura to him. Was he somehow involved in the abductions? Was Tess? Probably not, but perhaps the girl could shed some light on the situation.

Pacing across the floor, Madeline approached the maid.

"Miss Terragon, isn't it?" she asked.

The girl turned to her, expression somber. "Lady Redcomb," she said.

"Lovely party, is it not?" Madeline asked.

"Yes, certainly," Miss Terragon said, "but I fear I'm feeling a bit unwell."

"Unwell," said her chaperone, long face disapproving. "What say you? You look fit as a thistle. You but need a bit to drink. Go fetch us some punch."

For a moment Madeline thought the girl would refuse, but she only nodded and turned away.

"I could use some refreshment myself," Madeline said, and left with her. "We need to speak," she said, nodding to a passing couple.

"About what?" asked Tess.

"Missing girls," Maddy said. "What do you know of them?"

"Nothing." Tess stopped suddenly, eyes wide. "Why would you think—" she began, but Madeline took her by the elbow, urging her on, nodding to Haviard as he spooned down his cake.

"How is O'Malley involved?" Madeline asked.

"I wouldn't know." Her tone was cool, her mouth pursed.

Madeline narrowed her eyes, thinking. "What do you mean?"

"I mean I know no one by that name."

"I thought we had gotten past that some days ago."

"I told you I've not been to the docks. Have not—"

Madeline caught her arm. "This is not a game, Tess. Not some sport you can—"

"He refuses to speak to me," she snapped.

"What?"

The maid glanced toward the door, eyes brimming. "Said he was seeing another. A serving girl, I believe he said."

Images loomed in Madeline's head. Memories of O'Malley's eyes burning as he gazed at Tess. "I'm . . . I'm sorry," Madeline said.

"Well . . ." The girl's lips smiled. Her eyes did not. "He was only a distraction."

That's what Madeline had originally thought, but now she wondered. "Best to be rid of him," she agreed.

"I am certain you're right. Now if you'll excuse me," Tess said, and lifting her embroidered hem, hurried away.

Madeline's head was reeling. Had she misjudged the man so completely or was the girl lying? Then again, perhaps neither was true. Perhaps O'Malley had felt a need to be rid of Miss Terragon for his own depraved reasons.

Another trip to Deptford was called for. She would go there soon.

"Lady Redcomb, you look quite as fetching as ever."

She glanced to the right. "Lord Weatherby," she said, surprised by his appearance. Judging by her last conversation with him, she had been certain he would be too busy with his *entertainments* to waste his time here.

"Might you care to dance?" he asked.

No, she thought, but she had made a vow to Bertram. Had come here with a purpose. "I've been waiting with bated breath for someone to ask," she said.

He took her hand with a smile. His skin was warm. She caught an image of him. His chest was bare, his expression agonized.

Chatter swirled around her, breaking into her thoughts, but she tuned it all out, concentrating. It was dark in Weatherby's chamber. Someone was breathing heavily. The image expanded slowly. His wrists were bound. His member was hard. Behind him stood a woman, skinny with raven-dark hair and a riding crop. Beneath the glossy wig, she looked a bit like the irritating Lady Tillian, Milly's former employer, but her nipples had been painted a garish—

"I'm afraid we must part," Weatherby said.

Madeline jerked at the intrusion as he handed her into the contredanse line.

The woman next to her looked concerned. "Are you quite all right, my dear?"

Madeline nodded blindly, heard the caller begin his chant and wheeled away. Following her feet through the well-known steps, she wiped the disturbing image from her brain, cleared her head, filled her psyche with freshness, and touched a score of hands. It was a study in concentration, for each contact was fleeting. Yet she was determined to learn, to accomplish, to scour the foolish thoughts of Jasper Reeves from her mind.

Thus she forced all her energy into the moment. Emotions flowed past her senses. Desire. Loneliness. Love, unadorned and unrequited. She drew a deep breath, and refocused.

Her hands brushed a half-dozen others. Images flew through her mind too fast to catch hold of. Thoughts flowed more freely now. Faces, meadows, a bell tower. Then darkness.

It came on her suddenly, freezing her heart, stopping her thoughts. The place was black and quiet. There was fear in the air and . . .

"My lady."

She came to with a start and drew a deep breath. The room settled around her. She was standing outside the bevy of dancers and glanced up, gathering her bearings.

"Lady Redcomb."

She concentrated on the face near hers. Lord Weatherby looked worried. "Are you quite all right? You look as if you've seen a ghost."

"Oh." Perhaps she had. Where had the darkness come from? Whom had she touched last? "I am well. Just a bit light-headed."

He moved closer, steadying her. Feelings emanated from him. She let him move closer. "Perhaps you should lie down for a spell."

"I'll be fine in a second."

"I've a place not ten minutes' ride from here," he murmured, and into her mind came the image of his bed, filled to brimming with a half-dozen writhing, eager bodies.

She jerked at the picture in her head and pulled away.

"No room there," she rasped, and hurried through the crowd toward the dance floor.

The music was just winding down, the dancers wandering off, smiling, laughing.

Whose thoughts had she felt? She skimmed her gaze over the happy faces, then stopped abruptly. Lord Moore stood near the arched doors, face solemn as he spoke to a servant in bright livery. Might he be the culprit?

Then again, Lady Evereld looked enraged. Might the feelings have emanated from a woman?

"Are you certain you're quite well?"

She forced herself into the hard present, turned.

Lord Weatherby was standing close beside her again.

"I beg your pardon?"

He raised his brows. "You sound absolutely breathless."

"Oh, I . . ." Lord Moore was walking away. Lady Evereld's expression had softened. "No. I simply became a bit dizzy on the dance floor."

"Dizzy," he said.

"I fear so."

"You look more . . . exhilarated." There was something in his tone.

"Exhilarated, my lord?" she said, and focused on him.

He raised his brows. "I've seen that expression before. Flushed cheeks, flared nostrils, dilated pupils. Almost as if you were . . . excited."

And suddenly, try as she might, she couldn't keep her thoughts from what she had done with

Jasper just a few days before. How he had filled her. How she had pulsed around him, hugging him, drinking him in. How he had throbbed and—

"Perhaps you were imagining . . ." Reaching out, Weatherby touched her arm. Uncertain images mingled erratically with memories. "A horse race," he said, and leaned in.

Images again. Not darkness now. But rancid tension. She pushed the thoughts of Jasper behind her.

"I fear I am not an equestrienne, my lord," she said, but could not seem to forget how the gelding's withers had felt beneath her. Which naturally led her to the thought of Jasper watching from the woods.

"No?" He smiled. "Perhaps you were imagining a rousing game of cricket then?"

" 'Tis not a game I particularly favor."

"Oh?" He moved closer, brushing her thigh with his crotch. His member was hard. "What, then, *do* you favor, my lady?"

She struggled to slam the searing memories of Jasper from her head. To replace them with Weatherby's images.

"Lord Weatherby," said a voice, and the baron moved away, breaking contact.

She came to herself with a start.

"Lord Gallo," Weatherby said. "I heard you have organized a match for my bays."

"Only just," Jasper said, but for a moment his gaze seared Maddy's. She felt her heart rate speed along and hated herself for the weakness.

Jasper turned to Weatherby. "And what of you? They say you are planning a trip abroad."

"I should be home overseeing the packing even now, but Lady Redcomb here looked so flushed I felt compelled to make certain she was well."

"Flushed?" Jasper said, and turned toward her.

"Yes." Weatherby's tone was dry. "Feverish almost."

Jasper said nothing. His brows lowered the slightest degree. She refused to turn away, but it was a close thing.

"I thought perhaps she should accompany me to my house."

Jasper faced him slowly. "I did not realize you had training as a physician, Weatherby."

They stared at each other a moment, and then Weatherby laughed. "Indeed I do not," he said. "I had something else in mind."

"Did you?"

"Yes indeed. In fact, you're welcome as well, Gallo."

And then the image spun back into Maddy's mind. A darkened room. A dozen naked people, all writhing and sweating and moaning. Weatherby was sandwiched between the Earl of Dundness and a lady with white-blond hair.

She jerked her gaze to Jasper, but he didn't glance her way. "My thanks for the invitation, Weatherby, but I feel a bit of a sniffle coming on," Jasper said. "I fear I am for Bedfordshire, as the saying goes. A bit of milk toast and hot tea before I turn in, I think."

Weatherby nodded, bowed brusquely, almost smiled. "And you, my lady?"

She tried to answer, but the image in her mind was as bright as a beacon. One of the men near the window was as fat as a gourd. His erection only just jutted past the bulge of his belly and there seemed to be—

"I think perhaps Lady Redcomb, too, might benefit from some rest," Jasper said.

Weatherby raised his brows, figuring. Shifting his gaze to Maddy, he reached for her hand. The images flared again.

"Some other time then," he said, and brushing a kiss across her knuckles, moved away.

Madeline's knees buckled. Jasper wrapped his arm around her back and moved her to a nearby bench.

She struggled to breathe normally, to get her bearings.

"My apologies," he said, voice low, breath soft against her ear.

She inhaled carefully, grasping for normalcy. "For?"

"I didn't mean to interfere."

Didn't he? He always had in the past, but then she had been a member of the coven. Maybe everything had changed. Maybe she was nothing to him now that she was no longer part of Les Chausettes. Now that she was only his lover. But perhaps she wasn't his lover at all. Perhaps that wasn't the word for it. After all, he looked as cold as a winter blast. As . . .

"Perhaps I can catch him up if you're still interested in his offer," he said.

She felt lost, disoriented. "What offer is that?"

A muscle danced in his lean jaw. "To join him."

"You were invited as well."

"Unfortunately I'm not particularly interested in orgies."

She opened her mouth, stunned by the word. "Is that what that was?" she whispered. "An orgy."

If she hadn't known better she would have sworn she heard him swear.

She felt a little dizzy. "He was squashed between two—"

The muscle jumped in his jaw again. "Perhaps it would be best if you went home."

"I think there might have been a bullock," she murmured.

He reached for her arm, tugging her to her feet, but suddenly feelings overwhelmed her. Hope and need and desire so hot it seared her. She pressed up against him. He growled something low. His body felt like heaven against hers, his arms like magic.

Oblivion loomed.

"Lord Gallo," said a voice.

"Lord Moore," Jasper rasped, and jerked away.

Chapter 23

"**I**s there a problem here, Lord Gallo?" Lord Moore's voice was low, quietly commanding.

Jasper voiced a dozen inventive curses in his mind and faced him, hiding Madeline behind him. "Not at all, my lord." Good God, there was something fundamentally wrong with him. He knew better than to touch her. *Far* better than to do so when the head of the committee was in view.

"I thought I heard you . . . it almost sounded like a growl. I feared you were ill," Moore said.

"No. Indeed not. All is well."

Moore tried to glance past him. But Jasper moved imperceptibly to the right. The earl moved too.

"Lord Moore," said a voice.

Jasper glanced up. Sir Drake stood not four feet away, looking large and formidable.

"I've a question for ye, my lord," Ella's husband said.

"Oh?"

"It's of a private nature," Drake added, and lifted his hand to indicate a distant corner. "If you dunna mind."

They moved away.

Jasper drew a deep breath and turned back toward Madeline, determined to behave, to act normal, decent. He was certain he could manage that much. But she was just as irresistible as before, just as hopelessly alluring. He moved toward her, drawn against his will.

"What the deuce is wrong with you two?" someone hissed.

They jerked toward Ella in unison.

"Nothing." They breathed the word in tandem. His voice sounded hoarse. Hers raspy.

"Nothing?" Taking each of them by an arm, Ella yanked them apart. "You look like you're going to rip each other's—"

"We were having a bit of a disagreement," Jasper said, and refrained from closing his eyes against his own burgeoning stupidity.

"A tiff," Madeline said. Her voice was breathy. The sound of it made him want to scoop her up, drag her to him. He felt his nostrils flare.

Ella glanced from one to the other. "You can't possibly be serious."

"Gallo believes Napoleon to be all but a saint," Madeline said. "I disagreed."

He could smell her. Goddamn if he couldn't. But it wasn't perfume or toilet water or any manmade essence. It was *she*, the core of her, the spirit of her. It was driving him mad, like a buck in rut. Still, he managed to speak. "I but said I think him a fine strategist," he said.

Ella's expression was still deadpan. "What do you think you're doing?"

"Nothing."

"Nothing."

"Well, perhaps then you could refrain from doing nothing in front of the head of the coven's committee."

"The head of . . ." Maddy asked, then widened her eyes and shifted them toward where Drake had engaged the other in conversation.

Ella raised her brows.

Jasper ground his teeth. "No one knows who sits at the head of the committee."

Ella smiled.

"But Lord Moore," Madeline murmured. "I thought I felt . . ."

They turned toward her in unison.

"What?"

"What?"

"I believe I'd best go home now," she said, and turned away.

* * *

The night was endless. The following day was no better. Jasper tried to keep himself occupied, but thoughts of her plagued him. He was constantly hard, constantly irritable and rattled and edgy. What the hell had she done to him? This wasn't normal. Not even for ordinary men. Men who hadn't spent their lives controlling every bodily urge. Or at least, he hoped not. He rolled onto his side and tried to sleep. If this was normal, he would have to spend a great deal more time feeling sorry for the average randy fool. But no one endured this. He was sure of it. If they did there would surely be people coupling on every street corner in London.

So had she hexed him as Shaleena suggested? Was that it? It didn't seem likely. She'd taken an oath to protect and serve, but she had also vowed to care for her coven sisters. And she had left them with barely a backward glance. Therefore all bets were off. She'd broken their pact. She didn't care for them. Not her sisters. Not him.

Angry, he jerked the sheets aside and rose to his feet. His erection bobbled erratically as he paced toward the door. He would go to Cinderknoll immediately and ask her what she had done. Find out—

But he stopped at the door. He couldn't go to her house. What about the arbor? They hadn't tested the arbor and he'd never be able to control himself until they had. Turning mechanically, he paced dismally back toward his mattress. The blankets were warm, the mattress soft. It looked like hell. Scrubbing his face, he tried to think. Surely he had bigger problems than his own swelling arousal. England was at war. Innocent girls were missing. Why? How? He had to figure it out, for until they were found, Madeline would risk her life. And it was his job, his appointed task, to keep her safe.

Maybe that was all there was to it, then. The only reason he was obsessed with her. Duty. It was as strong as an obsession in him. He could not fail in his responsibility. Perhaps he should go to her right now. To make certain she was well. He jerked toward the door, took two long strides, and stopped.

Hell, he couldn't control himself in a crowd. What would he do in private?

Turning back toward his bed, he crunched his hands to fists.

In his mind she watched him with coy eyes, egging him on, drawing him near her. He remembered the smell of her skin, the soft symphony of her breath. The feral feelings that had curled dangerously in his gut when she had touched Weatherby.

Jasper gritted his teeth at the thought. The bastard had propositioned her as if she were some backstreet strumpet. Didn't he realize what she was? That she was pure? She was . . .

He loosened his fists and remembered to breathe. She wasn't innocent, he reminded himself. In fact, she was as hot as a smithy's forge. Eager, ready, waiting for him to—

He pivoted toward his door before he was able to stop himself. Goddammit. He couldn't go to her. What if she was feeling amorous? He'd never be able to stop himself.

But in the end that was the very argument that made him go. Because if there was a God in heaven, he wasn't going to make her share her amorous feelings with anyone else.

The streets were dark, but it didn't matter. It was as if he could smell her, could taste her on the wind.

He left his mount beside the walkway, strode toward the house on the hill, and suddenly her door burst open and she appeared, limned by the mellow flame of light behind her, her face barely visible in the darkness.

"What are you doing here?" she asked, voice hushed, dark hair a midnight tangle about her shoulders. She looked young and bright and as innocent as a dream.

A thousand emotions swirled inside him. Need, desire, and jealousy all whirling in confusion. He

kept himself from grabbing her, from pulling her
to him, but only by the nearest measure. Only by
the strictest control. "I came to speak of your conduct," he said.

She lifted her chin a notch, voice barely audible.
"My conduct."

He thought of Weatherby's expression as he had
leaned in. Like a hound on a hot scent.

"Les Chausettes do not flaunt themselves," he
said.

She gave him a level stare. "Surely you cannot
be serious."

He ached, *ached* from his sternum to his knees.
"I am quite serious. As you know, the coven has a
strict rule to act inconspicuously."

She was standing very still, very straight. "Even
if I were still with the coven, which I am not, I do
not believe I did anything wrong."

"You looked ready to take Weatherby up on his
offer where he stood."

She stiffened for a fraction of a moment, then relaxed and smiled, quietly amused. "Perhaps I don't
have your aversion to orgies."

Something danced in his gut. Something pulsed
lower. He tried to ignore both. "You mustn't trust
him," he said.

"Perhaps I'm not looking for a man to trust."

In the moonlight, her night rail was all but

translucent. It was tied primly at her throat, but below that he could see the dark thrust of her nipples against the pale fabric. Or maybe he just imagined. He had a great imagination. It might be the death of him. "What *are* you looking for?"

She turned toward him. Moonlight gleamed on her throat. His felt dry. She looked up at him through her lashes, darkly alluring. And suddenly a flash of an image tore at his mind. It was them, together, wrapped in ecstasy. "I thought maybe you had figured that out by now," she said.

He steeled himself. It was more difficult with some parts than others. "Are you saying what I think you're saying?"

"That depends on—" she began, but suddenly he lost control. He lurched toward her. Logic told him she would flee for safety, but instead, she was flying toward him.

Before it seemed possible that she had reached him, she was straddling him, gown rucked up, legs wrapped around him, lips crushing his.

He stumbled backward, found his footing, grappled with her ass. There was bare skin. How had his breeches come undone? It didn't matter. Few things did. He groaned into her mouth. She lifted herself by some kind of magic, and jammed around him.

He growled with animalistic zeal and drove into her. She shrieked, grabbed his hair, jerked his head back. He pressed home again and licked her neck. Her breasts were hot against his bare chest. How the hell had it become bare? He didn't know. Didn't care. Couldn't think. She was swallowing him up. Eating him whole. He jerked again. She answered back, giving just as she got, riding him hard, smacking against him. Tension towered like a flame, burning him. She leaned back, arching into him. He found her breast with his mouth through the sheer fabric of her gown, and she shrieked as she came, trembling around him, forcing his own growling release until he was drained, beaten. He staggered, keeping his balance but just barely. She dropped her forehead against his. Their breathing melded, hard and heavy.

Then she released him, letting her feet slip limply to the ground. Her hot breasts crushed against his chest. One tie had been torn from her gown. He'd lost a few buttons, possibly some body parts. Maybe his mind.

But eventually good sense returned, trailing in like tattered mist, blowing back in unpredictable waves.

He closed his eyes, fighting to breathe, and glanced at her from the corner of his eyes. She was bent at the waist, wild hair even wilder, white gown billowing. Young once again. Young and gorgeous and innocent.

Shame struck him.

"I'm—"

"Apologize, and I swear to God . . ." She took a moment to breathe. ". . . you'll spend the rest of your life as a rock."

She couldn't do that. Couldn't turn him into an inanimate object. Could she? No. "I was supposed to—"

"What?" She stared at him with wild eyes. "What were you supposed to do?"

"Protect you."

She drew a deep breath. "I don't feel too damaged."

He winced, felt the worry in the core of his being. "Did I hurt you?" He stepped up close, needing to touch her. "I—"

But suddenly her hand was on his face. Desire roared through him once again. "Did I hurt *you*?" she whispered.

Caring drowned him. So much more dangerous than passion. So much more deadly. "I think I might be dead."

She smiled a little, let her hand drift down his body, brushing her knuckles along the ridges of his abdomen and lower. He shivered as she took hold of him. He was hard again. Or still.

God save him.

"Not dead, I think," she said, but he could barely make out her words, for her lips were moving, taunting, so close to his he could hardly breathe.

She leaned forward, kissed him with hot slowness on the corner of his mouth. He throbbed in her hand and closed his eyes to the piquant sensations.

"Tell me true," he said. "Have you hexed me?"

"Are you imagining us naked?" she whispered.

"Always."

"Is there an arbor?"

"Sometimes."

"What is there the rest of the time?"

He pressed up against her. She released him and wrapped her arm about his neck. He grabbed her waist, slid his hand lower, feeling the sharp curve of her hip, the soft swell of her bottom. "Ecstasy."

"How terrible." The words were a breath against his soul.

"It is." He gritted his teeth. "I can't think. Can't . . ." She tightened her grip. Had anyone ever died of ecstasy? Would he be the first? "I want to make love to you," he rasped.

"I think we may have just—"

"In a bed."

"So you're a romantic after all," she said, and pulled him tighter against her.

He was rewarded with the hard feel of his throbbing desire against her ever-softness. "A nice mattress. An aged bottle of wine."

She smiled. He curved his hand down her buttocks and kept from pulling her legs up around him. He was making a point. What was his damned point?

"Music," he said, and kissed her. She tangled her fingers in his hair and kissed him back.

"I thought you were not the sort for dreamy ballads and teary poems," she said.

He drew away a scant inch, barely breathing. "You know I am not. But sometimes when you're near . . . It seems an occasion for—"

"I want it again," she whispered, then lowering her head, tasted his nipple. He shut his eyes and tried not to cry. Between them, desire danced like a wild pixie.

"Madeline—"

"Here."

"It's my job to—"

"And you do it so well," she murmured, and lifted her gown. The hem brushed her thighs, rustled over the dark mound of her hair, eased higher, titillating her nipples as the moon—

A noise rustled behind him. He froze, listening. Madeline remained absolutely unmoving, eyes wide in the darkness. And he knew; someone was watching them.

Chapter 24

Their gazes met and clashed.

"How long has he been there?" Jasper hissed.

She shook her head, eyes gleaming in the darkness. She'd been unaware of an intruder. What did that mean? Fear for her shivered over him, but he would keep her safe. This time he would not risk her, no matter what watched them from the darkness. "Have you a pistol?" he whispered. "In the house?"

She nodded once.

"Fetch it," he said.

She remained as she was, watching him, but he spoke again before she could refuse.

"I've no desire to be wounded again."

She nodded finally and he kissed her, then turned, shielding her retreat to Cinderknoll. But his precautions would not be needed. She was nothing if not stealthy.

"Who goes there?" he asked. His voice was little more than a murmur in the darkness. But it would be heard. He was certain of it. Felt it with that odd sense that had gained him his position with Les Chausettes.

But no one answered.

"I know of your presence." He stepped forward. "I know you have powers. Come forth."

Nothing.

Jasper closed his eyes. He had no *real* supernatural gifts. No abilities except those learned on the moribund streets of London's East End. Abilities to listen. To watch. And to believe. Even if circumstances seemed unbelievable. Or maybe especially so.

Whoever was out there was not simply passing by. He was there for a purpose. Jasper was certain of that. The intruder had found a spot in the darkness. The best hidden place in the yard, most like. And that site would be near the shrubbery that towered and bent like giant birds of prey over the shadowed turf. Jasper moved straight forward, hoping to draw the other out.

"If you would speak to me, do so now." From off to his right something shifted quietly.

Jasper took another step. "Why are you here?"

No one answered.

"If you have come to harm the lady I would

suggest you consider carefully before doing so." He felt his skin tingle at the thought, felt his innards tighten, but steadied his nerves. "She is well guarded, carefully protected. If you harm her I will take pleasure in killing you at my earliest possible opportunity . . . if she does not do so first.

"But if you have come for me . . ." He canted his head a little, testing the silence, "then I would suggest you make your move now." The brush scraped off to his right again, but in that same instant he sensed someone behind him. Pivoting about, he prepared to attack, but suddenly there was a bump, a grunt, and the sight of two bodies stepping onto the lawn. One was a man standing upright, watching him, still, face pale in the moonlight. The other was Madeline. She was pressed up behind the narrow interloper, who stood with his chest thrust out in an irregular manner, as if trying to escape some unknown pain from behind.

Jasper stifled a sigh. "I thought you had gone to the house," he said.

Madeline's eyes were alight, the intensity of her face just visible past the other's shoulder. "He wasn't *in* the house. He was in the horse chestnuts." She made a slight movement. The other grunted, then stiffened in pain.

"Who are you?" she asked.

The trespasser didn't answer. A frayed hat was pulled low over his eyes.

"Why are you here?"

"I 'eard you 'ad a fortune inside," he said. His voice was nasal and whiny.

Simple theft? Really? Jasper wondered. "How did you get so near without us knowing?" Jasper asked.

"P'raps you was preoccupied," wheezed the other.

Jasper caught Maddy's gaze. She stared back. There was something familiar here.

"Who are you?" Jasper asked.

"I'm no one of import, guvnor. If you'll but find it in yer heart to let me go I'll not—"

"Cur!" Maddy rasped.

Jasper scowled. Beneath the shadow of the boy's ragged hat, his face was almost unseen, but his unique imprint of power could not be mistaken for long.

Jasper drew a careful breath. "How did you find us?"

There was a moment of silence. "I don't know what yer talking about, guvnor. I'm just—" he whined, but Madeline tightened her grip.

"Holy bones, ease up, woman," he said, voice restored to normal. "You're breaking my bleeding arm."

Jasper scowled, almost as peeved with the boy as he was with himself. "If she goes into the house will you leave her be?" Jasper asked.

"Oh for heaven's sake! I'm not hiding in the house, Reeves," Madeline said.

"I want you to fetch a weapon so that—"

"You want me to hide like a child!" she snapped.

He realized that he was actually trembling. Shaking like a frightened hare. "You're *acting* like a child."

"And you're acting like a—"

"Who *are* you people?" rasped the boy.

Jasper turned toward him, trying to shut the frustration and fear from his mind. "I'm willing to pay to keep you quiet."

"Yeah?" The boy was watching him carefully, though his position in front of Madeline could not have been a comfortable one. "And what is it you want hushed?"

He hadn't asked what the reward would be, Jasper noticed, which meant he didn't care, though it seemed likely he owned next to nothing. "The lady is promised to another," he said. "I should not be here." That much, at least, was true enough.

"Who is she promised to?"

"That doesn't matter. All you—"

"You didn't ask how much," Maddy said, and twisted up the boy's arm.

"What's that?" The lad's tone was breathy, pained.

"You forgot to ask how much," she said. "Which makes me think perhaps you're not quite what you seem to be."

"I was scared. I wasn't thinking—"

She jerked his arm again.

"How much?" he squeaked.

"Why are you here?" Madeline growled.

"Please, my lady," Jasper said, peeved, though he managed not to show it in his tone. "I'll ask the questions if it's all the same to you." It didn't seem right that she kill the boy before he had a chance to explain himself. "What is it you want?"

"Who sent you?" Madeline asked.

"Do you make a habit of having women fight your battles?" Cur grunted.

"Only when I have to," Jasper said. He was tired. And frustrated. And damned angry at himself for allowing circumstances to get out of hand . . . again.

"I don't want to break your arm," Maddy hissed.

"Works out nice, then," Cur breathed. " 'Cuz I don't particular want—" but in that instant Madeline gasped and shoved him forward. He stumbled, righted himself, then edged to the side, rubbing his elbow.

Her eyes were huge and rimmed with white in the moon of her fragile face. Her lips were slightly parted. Light gleamed on her teeth.

Jasper snapped his gaze from her to the boy, feeling lost, left out of a world they shared. "What happened?" he asked, but she didn't seem to hear. Instead, she kept her attention on the lad, breasts rising and falling with each rapid breath.

"Did it already take place?" Her voice was a rasp in the soft darkness.

The boy shifted his gaze to Jasper, still rubbing his arm. "What is she?" he asked, and jerked a nervous nod toward Madeline.

"She's a woman of passion. Apparently," he said, tone as dry as he could make it considering the circumstances. "You'd best answer her, lad."

"Can she see inside me head?" Cur asked.

"Did it already happen?" she snapped again, and took a step toward him. "Was she already taken?"

The boy stood his ground, which meant he was either extremely brave or extremely stupid. "Not so's I know."

"How did you learn of it?"

No response.

"Do you care to explain, my lady?" Jasper asked.

It was his patient tone. He loved his patient tone, though sometimes people seemed to want to poke him in the eye at the sound of it.

She straightened, took a careful breath. "He knows of another girl," she said. "Another one that has been taken. Or *will* be taken."

Jasper scowled. "And what made you think that would be of interest to us, lad?" he asked.

The boy shrugged, looking winded, unsure, and cocky all at once. It was not a simple feat. "I had me a feeling."

"How do you know about the girl?" Maddy asked.

"Pegs told me."

Madeline narrowed her eyes. Jasper kept his patience, or at least the semblance of patience, which was more and more often the best he could do. "And who is Pegs?"

"Friend, pickpocket." Cur shrugged as if there might have been many definitions for this particular acquaintance. "He was having himself a pint, waiting for others to get sauced. They was talking. Didn't know he was listening." He paused. They waited.

"And what is it they said?" Jasper asked. His patient tone was, perhaps, fraying just a bit around the edges.

The boy shifted his gaze to Madeline, cautious now. Apparently he was not unable to learn. "How did she find me in the dark?"

"The lady possesses excellent eyesight," Jasper said.

"I was well hidden. She couldn't have seen me. Yet she found me. Reached out. Knocked me off my feet before I could—"

"What did they say?" Madeline asked.

The boy kept his gaze carefully on Jasper. "I wanna be like her," he said.

Jasper glanced at her. Even in the darkness she was all but irresistible. Beautiful. Rare. Glowing like a beacon. Hot and rarefied and solely herself, she was sex personified and so much more. Desire reared its ugly head. "It seems unlikely."

"I can do some things," the boy said.

But he probably couldn't make Jasper willing to give his life just to see her smile. He drew a careful breath. "How did you find her?" he asked. "We didn't give you our names."

"Like I says, I can do some things."

Jasper narrowed his eyes. A male witch? It was rare. "Such as—"

"Dammit!" Madeline stormed, hands fisted, dark tendrils of hair flowing in an unfelt breeze. "What did they say?"

The boy straightened, chagrined but game. "If I say, will you teach me?"

Jasper clenched his teeth. Since the very first, his most important task had been to keep the coven secret. "I'm afraid I don't know what you are referring—"

"Yes!" Maddy snapped.

Jasper cursed under his breath. What had happened to the compliant girl he'd fallen in love with even before they'd left Marseille? "My lady, if you would be so kind, I would greatly appreciate the opportunity—"

"But if you lie, I'll know," Madeline warned.

"How?" Cur's voice was hushed.

Madeline's was the same. "Do you really want to know?" she hissed, and took a threatening step forward.

The lad jerked back, eyeing her cautiously before coming to a decision.

"They said they already had five of them," he said. "That they just needed one more."

"Five!" She paced rapidly back and forth. "One more than we heard of." Stopping abruptly, she jerked her gaze to the boy. "How do you know they were talking about the missing girls?"

He watched her with hard focus. The world quieted. "They was."

She held his gaze a moment longer, then nodded, seeming to understand what others could not. "What else did they say?"

"That Lord Bee says there was a likely possibility. A pretty thing. Worked at a pub."

"Lord Bee?"

He shrugged.

She scowled. "What pub?"

Cur shifted his eyes back to Jasper. "Are there more?" he asked.

"What pub?" Madeline snarled.

"Like her," the boy said. "Are there more can do the things she can?"

"I fear I've no idea what you're talking about," Jasper said. "But if you would kindly—"

"Yes," Maddy rasped.

Jasper ground his teeth in mounting frustration. "Thank you, Lady Redcomb, but perhaps you could let me—"

"I was right," the boy hissed, and stumbled back a step. "I knowed I was right."

"Congratulations," Madeline said.

Jasper felt like hitting something.

"Jesus save me," Cur breathed, then: "Can you turn that rock into a keg o' beer?"

"I can save the girls." Madeline's voice was little more than a dark snarl.

"How about a loaf of bread?"

She ground her teeth and stared through him. "I can make you wish you'd never been born."

Their gazes locked. The boy weakened. "I don't know," he said. "I don't know which pub."

"What's the girl's name?"

"They called her Rebecca."

"Where is this pub?"

"Don't know that neither."

"How did the men look?"

"I wasn't there."

"You must know something."

"There was two of them. Pegs says they looked able to take care of themselves."

"How well did they know this girl?"

"Can't say for certain, but I got the idea that they only heard of her through hearsay."

"So they don't know her well," Madeline mused. She was pacing, her night rail flaring behind her. "Then there's no reason to believe I couldn't—"

"No," Jasper said, and found that his voice was marvelously steady, despite the fact that his heart had quietly died in his chest. "No." He said it again, more forcefully this time. "You are *not* going to impersonate her."

She turned toward him, breath held, radiant in the darkness. "They'll die," she said. "If they haven't already, they will soon, and their deaths will be on my hands. On my conscience."

"No!" He felt panic rise like billowing smoke, felt it choke his soul. "I'll not let you—"

"Not let me!" She shook her head in wild bewilderment. How could he fail to understand? She *needed* to do this. Was born to do this. "You're not my master, Reeves."

"No. I'm the man who—" He stopped himself, for even now, even knowing he could lose her forever, he could not say the words aloud.

"What are you?" she asked, voice low.

"I'm the man who keeps you safe," he said. "Who keeps you from doing something idiotic. Something that will get you—"

"So that's what saving lives is now? Idiotic?"

"It is if you sacrifice . . ." His heart was racing in his chest. His hands felt clammy. He couldn't lose her. Couldn't watch the woman he loved die. He had done that before. Would do whatever it took to keep it from happening again. "Don't try it, Madeline. Don't make me stop you."

She raised her chin. "You have always underestimated me."

"I've always kept you safe. Kept you alive."

"Is that what you believe? That I can't think on my own? That I'm too foolish, too weak to manage without you?"

He stared at her, sick, broken. "I don't think you're foolish," he said, and knew immediately that *he* was the fool. "I didn't mean that as it sounded."

"Yes." She was very still. "I believe you did."

He fisted his hands, wanting to grab her, to hold her safe forever. But his very existence had long depended on his ability to be removed from emotion. Above it. Beyond it. He was not the type to burst into foolish song, to declare undying devotion. To shout or curse or laugh. For as long as he remembered he had taken pride in his ability to remain cool when others did not, and now, when his very life was hanging by a breath, he found he could not change, could not tell her the truth, that he loved her, could not live without her. Did not *want* to live without her. "I've no wish to see you hurt, Madeline," he said, tone so damnably placid he despised himself.

"And I've no wish to see you at all. Not anymore," she said, and paused, letting the world go ghostly silent. "Though I love you."

The impact of her words struck him like lightning, searing him, torching his senses. He opened his mouth to speak, to admit the truth, to save his very soul, but he could not.

Her lips lifted in a wistful smile. "I have loved you from the first," she said. "For saving my sister. For saving *me*. For allowing others to believe you are naught but a foolish fop." She laughed softly at the idea. "When you are saving the world a little bit at a time." Her smile drifted away. "But I cannot live like this. Near you . . . but not. Wanting . . ." She paused and drew an audible breath. "Good-bye, Jasper," she said.

And suddenly he knew. *Knew* he must stop her immediately, before it was too late. Before he lost her forever. He stepped forward to do so, to admit the truth, to save her. To save *himself*. But in that instant she was gone, disappeared, leaving nothing but a dark hole in the blackness of his life.

Chapter 25

"**W**hat'll you have, gents?"

The Black Stag was crowded. Madeline swiped a sticky rag across a well-worn table and gave the newest pair of patrons a sassy glance past her red-blond curls. The curls that looked exactly like Rebecca Almay's.

It had been three days since she'd last seen Jasper. Two since she'd spoken to Pegs. The same since she had first met Rebecca.

Madeline had dared not return to Cinderknoll, for Reeves would surely go there. Instead, she had followed Cur to a dilapidated cottage near the docks. The boy had raged against her presence there, had insisted that she leave. She had raged back, and it had been during that wild fray that she had fully realized her powers.

Who could have guessed that allowing her *lost child* free rein was exactly what was needed to complete the shifting potion she had been laboring over for so long? Who could have guessed that Madeline but needed to employ the entirety of herself to obtain her full potential? The wild and the tame. The light and the dark.

Not she. But standing over an iron kettle in Cur's shabby kitchen, she had allowed herself to be whole, to run free, to make suggestions, to pluck a strand of the boy's hair. To blend a host of unlikely ingredients.

"Nightshade for hiding, garlic for healing, tailwort for courage, brimstone for sealing."

The words had come easily to her. All but unbidden. And suddenly she had been transformed, shifted into the boy's image.

He had been agog, staggered, stuttering. And more than a little wary. She had barely been surprised, for she had waited all her life.

Although she'd had little enough time to study Rebecca's mannerisms and habits, she'd discovered the girl to be a quick-talking lass with a brassy attitude and enough self-awareness to save her charms for all of her nineteen years.

In the end it had been fairly simple for Madeline to obtain a drop of the maid's spittle. Hurrying to Cur's ramshackle hut, she had mixed the liquid with a bit of ground cinnamon for color, a dusting of lemon balm to soothe, and a dozen other carefully garnered herbs.

And thus Madeline now stood in the midst of the bustling tavern—young, fair, and buxom, an intoxicating potion for the pub's earthy patrons.

Yet the two newcomers barely glanced her way.

"I'll 'ave a pint," said the man nearer the hearth. He was squat and grizzled, not unlike half the men in the crowded room.

"Same for me," said the other, and Madeline's heart beat like a puffing billy. There were no "clever" quips from these two. No pinching, no grabbing as she'd endured from the Stag's other customers for the past two nights.

Why? Were these the men for whom she'd searched, for whom she'd scoured Pegs's gin-fogged memory?

Rebecca, meanwhile, had remained at home, happy to believe the story Madeline spewed about needing to *live* the part of a barmaid to make her time on the stage more believable. Happy to take the exorbitant sum Maddy offered for her garments.

"'Ey Becca," chirped a balding miner and grabbed her skirt, reeling her to a halt before she could hurry to the keg behind the bar. "'Ow 'bout tonight, luv."

"I'm not the sort," she said, and glanced again toward the newcomers. The taller of the two was watching her from the corner of his eye.

"Oh come now, just one little toss. I tell you . . ."

The miner leaned close in conspiratorial drunkenness, his fist still wrapped in her gown. "I got me a tool big as a stallion's."

Madeline pulled her gaze from the two near the hearth. Smiling, she tossed her fair curls over her shoulder and bent close to his ear. "Touch me again and I swear you won't," she said, and taking hold of her skirt, yanked it from his hand. He toppled sideways, falling with a clatter onto the floor as she strode to the bar amid cheers and hoots.

But the two newcomers said nothing as she delivered their beer, nothing as she took their coin.

She hurried through the rest of the evening, but little changed. At least she hoped to God it did not, for in truth she had no way of knowing how long her shifting spell would last. The moon had been waning when she'd consecrated the potion, not at its strongest.

But the patrons seemed to notice nothing unusual as they finally began filing out, some stumbling, some dragged.

It was well past midnight when the twosome by the hearth left.

Madeline's spell was beginning to fade. She could feel the effects giving way, could feel herself return. Glancing into a pewter mug on the mantel, she saw that her hair had begun to darken, her skin to regain its usual pigment. Time was running out.

If her instincts were correct, the thugs would be waiting for her outside, hiding along the shadowed path somewhere between the pub and Rebecca's home. Maddy dared not disappoint them.

For one trembling moment she wished she had asked for her sister's help, but she had not, had intentionally blocked all contact with her, in fact. And maybe that was for the best. Ella was with child, after all, and should be concentrating on the new life growing inside her instead of worrying about the evil wrought by others. Besides, after all these long years, it was time that Madeline stood on her own, that she proved her mettle, to herself if to none other.

Stripping off her apron, she dropped it on the nearest table and glanced breathlessly toward the door.

"And where might you think you're goin', missy?"

Madeline turned toward the proprietor. He was a stout little man with stumpy legs and a dour expression. "I was wondering if I might leave early this night."

"Early?" He scoffed, face flushed, expression perpetually angry. "These tables ain't likely to clean themselves, now are they?"

But there was no time to lose. She felt it in her trembling soul. "I fear I'm feeling unwell, Mr. Goodwin."

"*Mr. Goodwin*." He snorted and bobbled his head. "Feeling *unwell*. I don't pay you good brass to go puttin' on airs." His scowl increased, wrinkling his face like a worried hound's. "And another thing, I expect you to be nice to my customers. Show a bit more . . ." He fluttered a hand near his chest, then paused and squinted. "What the devil have you done to your hair?"

Dammit. She must be changing faster than she had realized. Before she was ready. Time was running out. Searching her inner depths, Madeline found Rebecca's bold character, siphoned it quickly through her burgeoning powers, and adopted it like a second skin. "Listen, you stumpy little hint of a man," she said. "I'm bleedin' like a stuck pig and got cramps ripping my insides out like a claw. So if you don't want to be cleanin' blood off your filthy floor from now till dawn, you won't make no trouble for me."

For a moment Madeline thought he would argue, but he crumpled like a house of sand, muttering dire warnings about tomorrow and joblessness as he retreated sulkily into the kitchen.

Relief swirled with fearful disappointment, but she turned toward the door. Still, it was harder than she thought possible to force herself to lift the latch and step outside.

The night was deep with expectancy, still and dark and waiting. Or did she only imagine the breathless anticipation that permeated the air, as heavy and thick as wood smoke. Perhaps nothing would happen. Perhaps it was her overdeveloped imagination that made the men's behavior seem unusual.

It wasn't far to the cottage Rebecca shared with her mother. No more than three furlongs, but the way was hidden in shadows.

The short hairs crept up like tiny soldiers along her arms as she made her way down the darkened street. Her breath came in sharp, raspy gasps, sounding loud to her own ears. Yet nothing happened. All was quiet. She approached the mouth of an alley and had to employ all her foundering courage to force herself to step into it. This would be a prime location for an attack. Her footfalls echoed on the packed clay. Something creaked off to her right. She started, but it was only a lone cur, watching her from beside a broken barrel.

The alley narrowed. Her steps slowed, her heart raced along at breakneck speed, but no sinister character stepped from the darkness. No hands reached for her. She passed out to the open street. Relief melded oddly with disappointment, making her stomach churn. The cottage was just ahead. She had failed. She would have to brew the potion again tomorrow. Would have to—

But suddenly something rustled ominously beside the trail. She twisted about. Too late. A hand was already covering her mouth, yanking her backward. Instinct and panic made her swing her elbow and try to shout, but the world dipped abruptly beneath her feet, and suddenly she was falling, spiraling dismally into blackness.

Chapter 26

"What happened?" Ella's body was absolutely still, her eyes wide and staring. Jasper faced her, breath held. He had not yet reached her door before she'd confronted him on the cobbled walkway, and even now he found there were no words. "What's happened to my sister?"

"She's gone," he said, and felt a lifetime of fresh pain squeeze his heart. "Last night. She—"

"Where did she go?"

He shook his head. Agony had etched itself into every fiber of his being. She was gone. Endangered. "I don't know."

"What do you mean you don't know?" She took one stilted step toward him. She was not beautiful today, only worried and angry and dangerous. "You're the director. You always know. It's your job to know."

Guilt gnawed at him, but it would do him no good. He forced it behind him, entrails twisting like vipers. "You've not heard from her then?"

She shook her head, clasped her hands. "No."

"But you sense her," he said. His voice was steady. He would not allow her to see his hands.

"Not since yesterday."

His mind crumbled. His muscles twitched with fatigue, with terror. He had spent the night searching for her, but to no avail.

"Try again," he said, but Ella shook her head.

"She's blocked me."

"What?"

"I can feel nothing."

"Try again!" he repeated. The panic was rising, threatening to drown him.

"It will do no good, Reeves. She has become increasingly powerful since leaving Lavender House. If she does not wish to be—"

"Please," he rasped, and reaching forward, handed her a narrow strip of white fabric.

She scowled as she took it, then speared him with her haunted emerald eyes. "A tie from her night rail?"

Guilt again, as sharp as the cut of a whip, melded with worry, fused with fear. "Please," he said, and she closed her eyes.

* * *

Jasper flexed his hands, opening the abrasions that crisscrossed his knuckles. It had been two days since he'd seen Madeline. Two days since he'd driven her away.

"You spoke to Miss Terragon?" Faye's voice was little more than a hushed murmur. He stood in her bedchamber, where he had never before been. Where she resented him being. She looked very small, huddled on the bed, blankets pulled tight to her chest.

"Yes." He had seen Miss Terragon and Madeline speaking some nights before, and though it had seemed an unlikely lead, he had followed it to its disappointing end. "There was no help there." Even though he had garnered Granite O'Malley's address. Even though he had gone to the pugilist's cottage.

Men who earned their living by brawling did not take kindly to accusations, it seemed. Jasper flexed his hands again and refrained from touching the seeping bruise on his left cheek. It would do no good. For there was no good to be had. Not until she was returned. Not until she was safe.

"I have spoken to her sister. I have questioned her staff." Not to mention Mr. Wendell, the committee, and every soul who had crossed her path in the past fortnight. Nothing.

Faye shook her head. Wisps of golden hair fluttered on a breeze that could not exist. "I fear I cannot help you, my lord. She—"

Impatience slashed him. He took a taut step toward her, restless and agonized. "There is someone I would have you find," he said.

She leaned away the slightest degree. Her wary expression made her elfin features seem all the more fragile. "I am sorry," she whispered. "I've not the capabilities to see her if she does not wish to be—"

"It's not Madeline."

"Then—" she began, but suddenly her expression went blank, her gaze distant. "Are you looking for . . ." Her brow wrinkled. "An animal?"

His heart shuddered in his chest. His breath quit in his throat. "A Cur," he said.

"Where is she?" Jasper's voice sounded odd to his own ears. Rusty, unused. His eyes felt gritty, his limbs heavy, his mind old beyond time.

Cur stood in his own kitchen, eyeing Jasper like a wary hound. Apparently he had not been expecting company. At least not the kind that walks in without an invitation, without warning. "How did you find me?"

"Magic." It was the truth. Yet it was also an answer he would not have considered giving three days before.

"Magic should get you out, then." The boy's voice was combative, menacing. And he had some powers. Of that, Jasper was certain. It was simply that he failed to care.

"She was here," Jasper said. "That much I know."

"What if she was?"

He hadn't asked who. Jasper's heartbeat sped up, rebounding against his ribs.

"You'll tell me where she went."

The lad smiled, but the expression was flinty, making him look old beyond his hardscrabble years. "It might be you got me confused with someone else, old man."

Jasper scowled. Fatigue lay like a desert behind his scratchy eyes.

"Someone who takes orders from the likes of you," the boy explained.

"I've met your kind before."

"That I doubt."

"I realize your life has not been a simple one." He was using his patient tone, but he was not patient. Indeed, he barely felt human. "But if you'll—"

"The unfortunate truth is I don't much care what you realize." Cur circled, tilting up his nose slightly as if testing the evening scents. "I think it best that you leave."

"I'm afraid I can't do that." Neither could he

be the man he had been just days before. Cold. Controlled. Bereft. Love had changed him. There was no going back. There was hope, or there was death. He would settle for nothing less. "Not until I learn the truth."

But Cur lowered his head and snarled. "Get out of my den."

"Your *den*?" The boy had been right. Jasper had *not* met his kind before. Still, he straightened his back and watched Cur circle. "Do your best then, lad," he said, and braced for impact.

Chapter 27

The world swayed. For a moment Madeline tried to open her eyes, but her lids were heavy, her stomach queasy, and she slipped, falling sharply back into oblivion.

She half woke several more times during the night, but the world was an uncertain place, reality unreal. When coherence finally found her, her spine felt bruised, her head swollen. She moaned and tried to cup her head in her hands, but her arms refused to obey her commands.

Panic smeared her. Where was she? What was happening? She had been working at the Stag as usual. Stumpy hadn't wanted to let her go early but . . .

Wait. The thoughts became muzzy suddenly as if they were only dreams. As if they were someone else's.

Misty memories flooded in. Her sister's face. The smell of cloves wafting through Lavender House.

The sizzling feel of Jasper's gaze on her. Who was she? The pale barmaid with the buxom form or the dark-haired government servant sworn to do as she was told? To keep the peace, to maintain order.

Or was there another option? A gifted, well-trained witch who followed her own course. Who set her own standards.

Recent memories flittered erratically through her bruised mind. Arguments, risks, conquests. Drawing a deep breath, Madeline steadied her thoughts and opened her eyes, but it did little good. Something scratchy covered her head. It smelled of horse sweat and moldy rye.

"Looks as if she's comin' round," someone said. She remained still, trying to place the voice. Her head was throbbing, making thoughts come hard and slow. But she had no time for weakness. Taking another careful breath, she tried to remember back. Someone had covered her mouth. She'd smelled a sickly sweet odor.

So she'd been drugged. Again. But with what? And who could obtain such a drug? Besides Jasper.

Rage swamped her, washing in on a wave of fear and disorientation. If he had nabbed her again he was going to regret his actions for as long as he breathed, she vowed, but she calmed herself with an effort. This was not Reeves's doing. She was certain of it, could sense it. Anger coursed through her again, undiluted by the knowledge that she would resent either his presence or his absence.

Something bumped, rocking her world, making the earth quake. It wasn't until that moment that she realized she wasn't on earth at all, but on the water, in a vessel of some sort.

"Let's 'ave us a look at ya then," someone said, and yanked the sack from her head.

Light burned her eyes, gleaming through a slice in the clouds near the western horizon. She squinted against it, raising her arm a bit in an effort to shield her eyes.

"Good mornin', sunshine."

She turned breathlessly toward the man in the aft of the vessel. He was the shorter of the two she had served in the pub.

"Ay, she's a pretty one all right," he said.

The other man grunted. "Not like those ugly 'eifers we nipped some days past, then."

So she'd guessed right; these men were the abductors for whom she had searched. She felt breathless with the knowledge. Breathless and nauseous. "Where am I?" she asked. The fear in her voice was as real as the weathered timbers that heaved against her spine, ground into her supporting elbows. The men looked huge. Huge and terrifying. Did that mean she had retained some of Rebecca's character, or was it Madeline herself who was intimidated? And what of her physical appearance? Had she retained the blond hair and pale eyes of Rebecca, or had she reverted back to herself?

"You're in luck is where you are," said the nearer fellow. " 'Cuz you're gonna get yourself a posh new 'ome. Ain't that right, Robby?"

Robby grunted, ruddy cheeks rough with stubble.

"Almost seems a shame, though, to send away a pretty thing like 'er," he said, and touched her face.

Madeline shrank back, mind churning, caught between terror and hope. Her plan was working, but she might not survive the day. "What do you mean? What are you talking about?"

"Look yonder," said the nearer fellow, and grasping the front of her gown, hauled her to her knees. They ground against the bottom of the boat, aching on contact. Castle ruins loomed against the moody gray of the sky. They looked broken and foreboding. " 'Ome sweet 'ome."

She scanned the horizon for clues to her whereabouts. But she had no idea where she might be. There were no landmarks she could distinguish. No buildings she could recognize, and beyond that nothing but water.

"Don't go gettin' too comfy, though, 'cuz it sounds as if you'll be afloat afore noon tomorrow."

Madeline shifted her gaze from one to the other, garnering details. Robby was squat and grizzled. The other was missing an incisor. His balding pate gleamed dully in the gloomy light.

"What do you mean?" she asked. Her voice was a coarse blend now, a rough amalgamation of hers and Rebecca's.

"We got us a curious one 'ere," Pate said, and yanked her to her feet by one arm. Fireworks exploded in her wrists. Her head swam, but she was already being dragged over the gunwale toward shore. Water splashed up like yipping terriers. Waves sloshed against her legs, soaking into her borrowed skirt, making it heavy and ungainly as it flapped between her wooden legs.

"What do you mean? Why are you doing this?" she rasped.

"Well, it ain't for sport. Although, with you . . ." He grinned into her face, wide enough to show the site of a missing molar. "I wouldn't mind me a little sport. You coming, Rob?"

His partner didn't answer, but stepped into the water behind them. Madeline turned toward him. He seemed different now than he had only minutes before, smaller, less powerful somehow. Was she losing her mind?

But no. Memories of herself, of her abilities swirled within her. The shifting potion must be working its way through her system more quickly now that she was coherent. Nevertheless, she kept her voice breathy, her eyes wide, befitting a frightened maid far out of her depth.

"I've done nothing wrong," she gasped. "Why are you doing this?"

"Way I hear it, that's just the reason you're here, aye, Robby?" Pate said, and yanked her after him. The ground felt only marginally firmer than the frothing waves.

"What do you mean? What are you talking about?" It was difficult to talk while being dragged along. Even more difficult to think. To decipher who she was. What she was meant to do.

"They're only paying for untried girls, I'm told."

"They? Who—" She staggered to a halt, gasped as the meaning struck home, unsure whether her actions were planned or real. Rebecca's, her own, or a bewildering meld of the two.

"Lads in Cairo or some such. Guess they got them a taste for fair-haired maids what ain't never been tipped."

They were shipping the girls to Africa before noon. That gave her very little time. Too little time to work from the inside. She'd have to escape now, hide until dark, and somehow find a way to free the girls before morning.

She glanced ahead, scanning the landscape. There was a copse of scraggly woods between her and the castle. Robby was lagging behind. She'd take Pate down once they reached the trees, then she'd dodge into the underbrush and avoid Robby. Darkness would simplify her escape, but she could hardly wait for that eventuality.

"I got an uncle," she said. Focusing on what remained in her system of Rebecca's essence, she let her voice go raspy with fear and exertion. They were walking fast, struggling across the boggy moors. "He's a barrister. And rich. Richer than God."

"Is he now?" Pate asked, and chuckled. Robby was silent.

"He'll pay for my return. He'll pay generous," she said.

"Hard to compete with a—" Pate began, but in that instant she stumbled, breaking from his grasp. He reached for her, but she rolled onto her back and struck out with both feet. Her stout heels caught him square in the face. He staggered away with a grunt and fell. She rolled onto her knees, then lurched to her feet and ran, stumbling into the brush. Branches tore at her face, but she dared not slow down. Already she could hear footfalls thundering behind her. Finding herself through the shifting dregs of the potion, she turned her thoughts inward, creating an image of herself dashing into the water. It was firm and strong. The footfalls faltered, turned aside, and in a moment of weakness she allowed herself to glance behind. Something struck her from the side.

She went down hard with Robby atop her. He was solid and strong, despite his age. The stench of rotting fish and body odor filled her head.

She struggled against him, too panicked to think, and in that moment Pate skittered up. "Let 'er go." He was breathing hard. Anger rasped in his tone.

She glanced past Robby's shoulder at him. His nose was bleeding. Probably broken. Rage flared in his eyes.

"Let 'er up," he repeated.

Robby shuffled off her, giving her a moment to escape, but the other was already reaching for her, pulling her roughly to her feet. She was out of breath and caught off balance, but she jerked up a knee, aiming for his weakness. She struck his thigh instead. He grunted a curse and backhanded her across the face.

Pain flared like black powder in her head. She stumbled away, but he held her up.

"You're going to pay now, girlie," he growled,

and drew back his hand again. But the punch never landed. Robby held his arm in an uncompromising grasp.

"Lord Bee said not to damage 'em."

"Damn Bee."

She was trembling, but she closed her eyes, gathering her wits. Trying to concentrate.

"No commission if they're sullied," Robby said. His voice was low and dangerous, but she set the words aside, focusing.

" 'E'll never know."

"Seems to me she might tell him."

"Her word 'gainst mine." She could feel Pate's gaze rake her. "And I been dying for it ever since we nabbed the first one."

"I'll be getting me full," Robby rumbled, "little matter if you die or not."

The woods went quiet. "You threatening me?" Pate asked.

Robby stared in silence, and in that moment Madeline sent an image into the younger man's mind. It was vague. It was shaky. But it showed Pate with blood oozing from his chest. A dozen cuts had been scratched across his face. He was sprawled in the dirt, legs flung open, eyes wide and staring.

There was a moment's pause as the world held its breath, and then Pate snatched a knife from the back of his waistband. Robby did the same, thrusting her to the ground as he did so.

She fell hard and remained there, still pushing the image into the villain's mind as they leaped toward each other.

Pate swiped his blade upward. Robby ducked. More nimble than expected, he came up fast, slicing his knife across the other's arm.

Pate shrieked and stumbled backward as the other dodged in, and in that second, Madeline focused all her might on hatred, on revenge.

"What the devil is this?" rasped a voice.

It quivered with familiarity. Madeline jerked her gaze toward the underbrush. The conjured image slipped from her mind, and in that instant Lord Weatherby stepped into view.

Chapter 28

The combatants stumbled apart, vague and disoriented.

This was Lord Bee! Shock snagged Madeline, squeezing out a gasp. He glanced down, but she jerked her hand to her cheek, hiding her face as she cradled it.

"This bastard planned to gut me," Pate snarled.

"I'll have my full commission," Robby said, but Weatherby remained silent. Madeline could feel his frigid gaze on her.

She sniffled piteously.

"You'll get nothing but a shallow grave," Weatherby said finally, turning his attention to the others. "Both of you. If you don't get her inside within a minute's time."

"Listen, you high—" Pate began, but his words were interrupted by the sound of a pistol cocking.

"Get her out of sight," Weatherby ordered.

She was hoisted to her feet then, half dragged

when she stumbled. The castle loomed before her. They pulled her up stone stairs and pushed her into a room. She stumbled, tried to catch herself, and fell, ready to spring forward. But the door was already slamming shut.

Candlelight flickered in the draft, lighting on the five terrified faces that surrounded her. She stared up at them, taking in the fair hair, the wide blue eyes. Girls. All of them young, blond, pretty. She scanned their faces, skimming from one to the next until she found Marie.

She was there. Bertram's daughter. Her eyes were dull with fear, but she was alive. Madeline hustled her gaze sideways. Now was not the time to be recognized.

"She's the sixth," whispered a girl in a green frock, and began to cry, dry and quiet.

Madeline pushed herself to her feet. "Is there any way out of here?"

No one spoke. Only the hopeless sounds of weeping filled the room.

"What are your names?"

"They don't like us to talk," whispered a pale maid with timid eyes.

"I am Rebecca," Maddy said, and faced the girl. "Who are you?"

"Savina," she said, voice soft.

Madeline nodded and glanced at the others.

They were in varying stages of giving up. But that was to be expected. And acceptable. For now.

"How many guards are there?"

"Two at least." The girl who spoke had full lips and a bruise on her right cheek. Trouble brewed in her expression. Hope bloomed cautiously in Madeline's soul. "Sometimes more."

"They don't like us to talk," Savina repeated, no louder than before.

Madeline ignored her. There was no time to waste on rules that must be broken. She needed information. "What of nighttime? Where—" she began, but in that second the door burst open. Pate stepped in, lips twisted in a sneer, nose still bloody.

"You looking to cause trouble, Firebrand?" he asked.

Anger shifted uneasily in Madeline, surprising her with its rising strength, but she shook her head and forced herself to back away.

Pate chuckled and nodded, happy in the knowledge of his power. "How 'bout the rest of you?"

They seemed to shrink before him, growing smaller and more fragile in his presence. Their pale trepidation was almost more than Maddy could bear, but she let them have their weakness. For now it would act as a shield.

"Then shut your traps," he said, "or I'll sample

the lot of you." He burned her with his gaze. "Starting with you."

Madeline lowered her eyes. He chuckled with ugly glee, then retreated, slamming the door behind him.

The girl in green was crying again. Or maybe still.

"What are your names?" Maddy asked, but they shook their heads one at a time. They were trapped, overpowered. But mostly they were afraid. And it was the fear that would defeat them.

Madeline glanced around. The room was small. Five strides would cross it. There was no furniture, but flames crackled pumpkin-orange in the fireplace. Pacing to it, Maddy reached in and pulled a nearly unburned timber close to the opening. Breaking off a stubby branch, she stuck the jagged end into the fire until it had turned black. Then, using the sooty point, she wrote, *Names?*

Perhaps to another the girls' identities would seem of little importance, but they had been demoralized, beaten down, threatened, and they could not free themselves in that condition. With pride came hope. With hope came freedom.

Scanning their faces, Maddy offered the stick to the girl with the bruise.

She came forward hesitantly, but she came and scratched *Tipper* into the timber. The others were more reluctant, but finally all were accounted for in tiny charcoal letters.

Madeline nodded, then wrote, *Guard—where sleep?*

Tipper shrugged. The others shook their heads.

Maddy scowled, thinking. They were already running out of space on the log. "Do they check at night?" she asked.

A nod from the one called Milly.

"How often?"

The girl held up one finger, then two.

Twice. That would make circumstances more difficult. She glanced around the room, but there was little to work with. Not even the table Jasper had afforded her.

Taking a deep breath, she wrote again. *We escape tonight.*

They stared at her, and despite her own fear, she almost laughed at their incredulous expressions. They were too young, too untried to know their own abilities, their own worth. But they would learn.

"Sleep now," she said.

They still stared. Standing, she retrieved a blanket from the corner, doused it in water from a pitcher, then smothered the fire. They would need the wood for later, and just now she longed for darkness.

The flames sputtered out, leaving only a few wayward sparks. In the ensuing blackness, the girls shuffled toward the walls, found blankets, settled in.

But in a moment a slim body slipped close to Maddy's.

"Escape?" It was the girl named Katherine. Her face was barely visible in the darkness. But hope was in her voice.

"When the time is right. Sleep now," Maddy whispered.

"How—" asked another, but footfalls sounded outside the door, and several of the girls hissed for quiet. Silence dropped over the room like a cloud. Madeline settled her back against the wall and closed her eyes. But she did not sleep. Instead, she remembered her own life, the brief, faint years spent in her mother's care, her childhood with Ella. Les Chausettes, the sisters of her heart. And Jasper. She no longer tried to keep her thoughts from him, for she loved him. Had for many years. And it would not change. The admittance filled her with self, and when Rebecca's essence had fully dissipated, she gathered her growing consciousness and sent it through the walls and beyond.

Outside the narrow chamber two men played brag atop a battered oak barrel. Another slept on a pallet near the wall. Each was armed. But Maddy saw little else before her senses moved on, leaving her to slip into the swelling mist. The faintest of images lifted in her mind as her body floated in limbo.

Time ceased to be. Worries eased away.

"Is she dead?"

"What's amiss?"

"God help us."

The words were hissed, rising from the depths, from a thousand miles away, but they drew her back, finally, slowly. Madeline awoke to find herself surrounded. Worry shone on comely faces. Firelight gleamed in azure eyes, flickered on milky complexions. She glanced toward the fireplace. Someone had coaxed the jagged flame back to life.

"We couldn't waken you," Milly whispered, tone taut with fear. "We thought you were dead."

Madeline's struggle to regroup was simpler this time, her journey into herself almost seamless, her assimilation of discovered information quick. "I am well. Simply tired."

"Your eyes were open," Savina hissed.

"I sleep that way," she said, impatient to move on, to do, to act. The time for weakness was done.

"No one sleeps that—" Katherine began, but a gasp interrupted her words.

"I know you."

Madeline glanced to the left. Marie pushed forward, brow pinched in a scowl. "You're Lady Redcomb."

So the potion had worn off completely. "Your father worried," Maddy said simply.

"Father," Marie whispered. Tears swamped her eyes. "How—"

"Your name's not Rebecca?"

"I've little time to explain."

"Why did you lie?" Savina murmured.

"Why are you here?" asked another.

Maddy could feel their rising panic, their burgeoning doubt.

"She's going to cause trouble," Savina whispered.

"Cause trouble!" Madeline hissed, angry suddenly, and strong. More herself than she had ever dared be. "There *is* trouble whether I cause it or not."

There were nods, murmurs, but Savina spoke again.

"They'll kill us if we're troublesome. They said as much."

"They lied," Madeline said, and hoped she was right. Hoped she had the strength to be what they needed. "They want you alive. They want you . . ." she began, but telling them too much would do nothing but fuel their fear. "Whole."

"Why?"

"They'll kill us," Savina repeated, pale eyes bright with tears, tone becoming rough with terror.

"Savina," Madeline soothed, but the other continued.

"They're strong. Cruel. They've got knives and—"

"Panic will do little to help our cause."

"Nothing will help!" Her voice was rising. "No one will come. We're—"

"Savina!" Maddy said, and reaching out, grabbed hold of the girl's arms and squeezed until their gazes met. "We can help ourselves," Madeline hissed, and with that she cast an image of women rising up, expressions grim as they hoisted rough weapons in steady hands. But maybe it was her voice as much as anything that calmed the girl, that straightened her back, that lifted her chin. "We can," she said, "and we shall."

Chapter 29

It was nearly dawn. They had done what they could. The chamber pot had been wrapped in a blanket, broken as silently as possible, and placed against the wall. The rough weapons had been hidden from view. There was no more time to prepare.

Madeline glanced at the ring of faces surrounding her. They were pale, taut with worry, bright with perspiration, but their eyes were no longer the eyes of the hunted. They were the eyes of hope.

"We are strong," Madeline whispered, and glanced from face to face, holding the gaze of each girl before moving on. "We do not deserve to be mistreated. And tonight we regain ourselves."

There were nods, blind agreement that made Madeline tremble, for she knew the risk. With great bravery oft came great suffering. But they had little choice.

"Are we ready?" she whispered.

There were murmurs of agreement, excited whispers. Even Savina nodded.

"God help us," Katherine murmured.

Maddy squeezed a few more drops of blood across the wrist she had pierced, then lay down, arm outflung and limp with the shard of the porcelain chamber pot lying across her curled fingertips.

Tipper closed her eyes for a moment as if preparing herself for the stage, and shrieked. "She's dead! Dear God, she's gone!"

Madeline gave her a smile for the sheer, quaking drama in her voice, then closed her eyes.

"She's killed herself!" Milly added.

"No, she can't have. 'Tis a mortal sin." Katherine's words were little more than a whisper, adding an eerie element in the flame-shadowed chamber.

Footsteps thundered across the floor of the adjacent room, but the girls never faltered. They played their roles to the hilt, as if their very lives depended on their skills.

"God save us all."

"God has—"

"What the devil goes on here?" growled a guard, and stepped into the room. Maddy wanted to see him, to watch him come, to know when best to strike, but she could feel her comrades' fear swelling around her and concentrated on them, on fortifying them, on sending forth images of strength, of victory, of freedom. And so she lay blind, her senses locked firmly inside her.

"She's dead," Tipper wailed.

"Dead and gone," Savina whimpered. Her voice was haunting in the stillness. God bless her.

"What are you whining about?" snarled the guard. "She can't be dead."

"When we awoke we found the chamber pot broken. She's cut her wrist," Katherine said. "We didn't hear. Didn't know. 'Tis a mortal sin. We would have prevented it. But she's gone. Her breath stopped, her soul—"

"Shut up! Stand back."

They remained where they were as if shocked into immobility.

"Get the hell back!" he ordered, and they retreated, back toward the walls where their makeshift weapons lay hidden in the shadows.

Behind the first guard someone cursed. Pate perhaps. There were five men all together. All armed, all without souls. Madeline's wandering senses had discerned that much before she'd been awakened.

She waited now, motionless, silent, wanting all the guards inside. All within striking distance, but she couldn't be certain of their location, and footfalls were drawing nearer.

"Dammit!" someone cursed, guttural and low.

She heard him squat beside her, sensed him reaching for her, and in that instant, she grasped the shard and swung it upward with all her might. The guard stumbled back, breath rattling as he clawed at the glass in his throat, but she was already on her feet.

Tipper swung a log free of its blanket. The nearest guard raised his arm to ward off the blow, but Milly struck from behind and he fell. The girls had Robby trapped in a corner. His eyes gleamed feral and frightened in the lantern light.

"Shut the door!" Pate bellowed from the hallway. The portal was swinging closed. Maddy saw it in slow motion, and gathering all her powers, thrust an image of a towering wave against the guard's back. He stumbled forward, and in that instant, Maddy grabbed the latch. Marie appeared beside her, adding her strength. They ripped the portal open. The villain relinquished his hold and stumbled backward. Madeline stepped into the opening, eyes narrowed, heart pounding. Pate and another stood before her. She faced them, breathing hard, almost smiling. Her muscles felt loose, her mind dangerous. If she died, so be it.

"Come then, you bastards," she challenged, but in that moment Weatherby strode into the hall.

"Redcomb!" he rasped.

"Disappointed?" she asked, and glanced toward him. "Hoping to take defenseless girls?" She took a step forward. The men crowded back.

"I knew you were trouble," he snarled. "Knew it the moment Wendell came sniveling to you at Braxton's soiree, whining about his precious daughter. It was clear you had no *powers*," he scoffed. "But I was always aware you were looking for her, stirring up problems."

"So you sent the gunman to the cottage," she said.

"I gave them strict orders to kill you. I'm almost glad now that they failed," he drawled, and raised a pistol. But in that instant, the girls swarmed from captivity. Milly's face was streaked with blood. Savina's eyes were wild. They leaped forward, makeshift weapons swinging and stabbing.

Weatherby jerked the pistol toward Savina. Madeline launched forward, knocking the muzzle aside just as he popped off a shot, then tumbling away, but even as she rose to her feet, she saw his other weapon. He raised it at her. The black muzzle gleamed dully in the dim light. She saw him pull the trigger, saw a spark leap up from the strike of metal on powder, felt the pellet pierce her shoulder.

For a moment the world was as silent as death. Faces turned toward her in horror, in dread, and then the girls screamed in wild unison. Reaching inside for strength, they rushed forward, throwing themselves at their enemies.

For one brilliant instant, Madeline saw them rise to the occasion, saw them claim themselves, and then she was falling, dropping quietly into the beckoning darkness.

Chapter 30

There was singing. It was toneless and terrible, grating along Madeline's nerve endings like steel against steel. She scowled, winced, and cautiously opened her eyes to find Jasper Reeves sitting beside her.

He was cradling her left hand between his. His eyes were closed, his brows drawn together. A magenta bruise was healing on his unshaven cheek, and five angry scratches ran a parallel course from his throat to his chest.

"The light of my soul," he sang. The notes wobbled unsteadily. "The music of—"

"What the deuce are you doing?" she rasped.

He opened his eyes slowly. The toneless drivel ceased. His hands squeezed tight around hers, and she saw now that his eyes looked haunted and bright, his face gaunt with fatigue. "I believe I was singing," he said. His throat constricted. The corner of his mouth twitched spasmodically.

"Whatever for?" she asked, but hope was blooming gently at the sight of him. He was well, he was beautiful, and he was here with her, making her head hurt a little less, her chest . . . Wait. No, her chest still hurt like the devil.

"I am sorry," he said.

She watched him, drinking him in, reveling in his nearness, in the touch of his skin against hers. His cravat was conspicuously missing and the top two buttons of his shirt were undone, showing the furrowed course of what looked to be claw marks. She scowled and refrained momentarily from touching them.

"For what exactly?" she asked, and noticed that she was lying in her room in Lavender House. It felt . . . hopeful. Right. Without glancing away, she realized that every available surface was crowded with roses, except for those occupied by mugwort or frankincense or another rich-scented witch's remedy.

"For being a fool." Emotion twisted his face for an instant. "For underestimating you."

She smiled a little, because she loved him. Because she had always loved him. "Anything else?"

"For being cold. Unfeeling." He swallowed and clenched his teeth as if bearing some terrible pain. "For being late."

"Late?"

"I couldn't find you," he said, and his jaw ticked as if the agony was too great to hold hidden. "Didn't know where you had gone." He reached out with slow caution to cup her cheek. Against her skin, his hand trembled.

She lifted her free hand and touched the scratches on his throat. "You found me."

He swallowed and let his eyes drop closed for a moment. "Too late."

"Just in time." She trilled her fingers gently down the scratches on his chest. "How did this happen?" she asked, and raised her gaze to his.

"Even Ella couldn't sense you."

"This was not her battle."

"Neither was it—" he began, then stopped himself and tightened his fingers around hers. " 'Twas your decision to make."

She almost smiled. "Yes."

His hands tightened. "You did well."

"So the girls are safe?"

"And returned to the bosom of their families. Mr. Wendell thinks you're an angel."

"The scratches," she said, and ran her fingers gently across them. "How did you come by them?"

His mouth tightened. "You and Cur disappeared at the same time."

"So you followed him."

"With Faye's help."

Madeline nodded, happy to be back among her peers, her sisters. "Her powers are growing."

"So it would seem."

She smoothed his wounds again. "As are the boy's."

A muscle twitched in his jaw. "I realize you vowed to instruct him," he said. "But he is not . . ." His voice trailed off. "I don't know what he is."

He was lost. Alone. As each of them had been at one time or another. "I'll figure it out," she said.

"We," he countered, and drew a careful breath. "*We* will figure it out."

She did smile now, then reached up, touching the bruise on his cheek. "And this?"

He tilted his head against her palm, seeming to find peace before he spoke again. "I saw you speaking to Miss Terragon," he explained. "She had an acquaintance at Deptford you seemed to find suspicious."

She remembered the lean, hungry face of the pugilist. "You met O'Malley?"

He drew a slow breath, seeming to steady himself. "He was not what I expected."

"A street fighter who would leave an heiress for a serving girl."

"There is no serving girl," he said.

She scowled, watching him.

"As it turns out, he worried that he would ruin Miss Tarragon's future. Didn't believe he was good enough for her. The truth wasn't something he particularly cared to share with me."

"I'm sorry."

He covered her hand with his, eyes solemn. "I am not. By the time I left I was fair certain he knew nothing of the missing girls. It forced me to move on. To find Cur."

He had fought O'Malley. For her. "So Weatherby, a respected peer of the realm, was naught but evil, while a scrapper from the docks is nothing short of noble," she mused.

His brows drew together in a troubled scowl. "A fact I would have you remember when I tell you of my past."

She brushed the flats of her fingernails along the sculpted line of his jaw. "You have a past, Lord Gallo?"

He winced at the name. "One without a title."

"Oh dear," she said and scowled.

"But I am wealthy, Madeline," he said, and leaning closer, squeezed her hand. "I am accepted by the *ton*, and I am rarely ill."

She raised her brows and refrained from laughing for the sheer joy of life. "Is that all?"

"I don't imbibe," he said. "I have no excesses. And I'm tidy."

"Is *that* all?"

Silence settled into the room. Their gazes held. His hand tightened around hers once again.

"I love you," he said. His voice sounded raspy. His eyes were bright with hot intensity. "I have loved you since the moment I first saw you. From the instant you came to me, bedraggled and scared and desperate." He lifted her hand to his lips and kissed it with tender slowness, gaze locked on hers. "So small, so brave, so powerful." He drew a deep breath. "You are light and hope and goodness. You are my Esperanza." He swallowed, expression solemn. "I said I was not the sort for poems, for flowery prose, for songs. But for you I will sing, Madeline."

She smiled. A tear slipped unheeded down her cheek. "I don't think that will be necessary."

He closed his eyes and kissed the hollow of her hand with aching tenderness. "I love you," he said. "I love you now. And I shall love you forever."

"Prove it," she whispered.

"Every day of my life," he vowed, and kissed her.

Next month, don't miss these exciting new love stories only from Avon Books

Secret Life of a Vampire by Kerrelyn Sparks

No one can throw a bachelor party quite like Jack, the illegitimate son of the legendary Casanova. But when the party gets out of hand and the cops show up, Jack has some explaining to do . . . if only he wasn't struck speechless by the beauty of Officer Lara Boucher.

Sins of a Wicked Duke by Sophie Jordan

One would think the last place a beauty like Fallon O'Rourke could keep her virtue was in the mansion of London's most licentious duke. Yet Fallon is perfectly safe there . . . disguised as a footman! But how long can her deception last when she begins to desire the sinful duke himself?

Taken and Seduced by Julia Latham

Adam Hilliard, secret Earl of Keswick, lives for revenge, and Lady Florence Becket is the key. But when Adam kidnaps her, they both find far more than they ever desired . . .

Her Notorious Viscount by Jenna Petersen

Proper Jane Fenton knows the danger of associating with a notorious man like Viscount Nicholas Stoneworth, a man who could tempt any woman into certain scandal. But finding her missing brother depends on transforming Nicholas into a gentleman, so Jane must ignore the promise of sinful pleasure in his eyes . . .

At Avon Books, we know your passion for romance—once you finish one of our novels, you find yourself wanting more.

May we tempt you with . . .

- **Excerpts** from our upcoming releases.

- Entertaining **extras,** including authors' personal photo albums and book lists.

- Behind-the-scenes **scoop** on your favorite characters and series.

- **Sweepstakes** for the chance to win free books, romantic getaways, and other fun prizes.

- Writing **tips** from our authors and editors.

- **Blog** with our authors and find out why they love to write romance.

- **Exclusive content** that's not contained within the pages of our novels.

Join us at
www.avonbooks.com

AVON *An Imprint of* HarperCollins*Publishers*
www.avonromance.com

Available wherever books are sold or please call 1-800-331-3761 to order.

FTH 0708